Arlette's Story

Angela Barton

Stories that inspire emotions
www.rubyfiction.com

Published 2019 by Ruby Fiction
Penrose House, Crawley Drive, Camberley, Surrey GU15 2AB, UK
www.rubyfiction.com

A CIP catalogue record for this book is available
from the British Library

ISBN: 978-1-91255-012-8

MIX
Paper from
responsible sources
FSC
www.fsc.org
FSC® C018072

Printed and bound in Great Britain by Clays Ltd, Elcograf S.p.A.

This book is dedicated to those villagers of Oradour-sur-Glane who brutally lost their lives on June 10th 1944. May they rest in peace.

Acknowledgements

I owe an enormous debt of thanks to everyone at Choc Lit
and Ruby Fiction Publishing. Special thanks to the
Tasting Panel for believing that my book deserved to be
published, particularly those who passed the manuscript:
Jenny M, Isabelle D, Jo O, Heather P, Jo L, Barbara P,
Ruth N, Bruce E, Elena B and Katie P. For my editor
whose sharp eye and talent enabled me to polish my
book. To my designer for my book cover – I love it!

Huge thanks to all involved with Romantic
Novelists' Association and the New Writers' Scheme.
What a wonderful support for new writers. Your
guidance and feedback have been invaluable and
your readers' critiques are second to none.

Heartfelt thanks go to Nottingham Writers' Studio.
As a member I've learned so much from attending
workshops and listening to fellow writers. Special thanks
go to Frances, Andy, Gaynor and Paul, my fiction group
buddies. Your positive criticism, encouragement and
support helped to improve my manuscript each month.

I can't forget my online friends from Twitter and Facebook.
You encouraged me when I doubted my writing skills
and congratulated me each time I found some success.

Sincere thanks to the staff at the museum of the Martyred
Village at Oradour-sur-Glane. Many thanks also go to
the staff at The British War Museum in London and
the helpful teams working in Nottingham libraries.

Support your local library. They're
search engines with emotion!

Finally, to my family. I love you totally and
thank you for your love, kindness, support and
encouragement. In short, you're my world.

PS. A big furry hug to Harlyn and Brook, my Brittany
and Springer spaniels. They kept my feet warm while
I was writing in the depths of winter and show me
so much loyalty and affection. I'd never owned a dog
before we bought my hairy daughters and who knew
I'd fall hook, line and sinker for them both? Harlyn was
my inspiration for Klara the dog, in *Arlette's Story*.

All is fair in love and war.
Francis Smedley

Author's note

Millions of lives were irrevocably changed during World War 2. Loss and suffering became the norm. *Arlette's Story* tells of a young woman's experience living through France's years of occupation. It's a story about finding love in the midst of chaos and finding the strength and courage to navigate terrible obstacles in order to protect loved ones. The Blaise family live on a farm at the top of Montverre Hill. The characters in this book are fictional. Tragically, what happened to the idyllic village of Oradour-sur-Glane isn't make-believe. As it was left by the Nazis on the evening of June 10, 1944, so it remains today.

Chapter One

'Wait!'

Arlette turned to see her friend, Francine, running up Montverre Hill with her fair hair swinging from side to side and her clogs scuffing the parched ground. Arlette had been leading a cow from the barn to the field but stopped when she heard Francine shouting.

Her friend hurried across the farm entrance, scattering a cluster of chickens before stopping and leaning forwards with hands on her hips, trying to catch her breath.

'*Qu'est-ce qui se passe?*' asked Arlette.

'*C'est Pétain.*'

'*Pétain?* What about him?'

Arlette knew that when their fathers talked about the French leader, usually over a glass of *pastis*, the conversation became heated and resulted in insults being directed towards the man.

'He's abandoned Paris to the Germans.'

Arlette gave a high-pitched laugh and continued to lead the beast across the lane, its huge bulk swaying and slewing as it walked. 'Don't be silly.' Although they had both turned twenty earlier in the year, Francine was still occasionally liable to childish exaggeration.

Francine followed. 'It's true.'

'No one gives away a city as if it were a bag of apples.'

'Pétain has. Maman heard it on the wireless.'

Arlette's smile wavered. 'When?'

'Just before she'd finished cleaning the mayor's office.'

'No. I mean when was Pétain supposed to have done this?'

'This morning.'

'But why?'

Francine held out her hands, palms upturned. 'I've no idea. Papa says he's a coward.'

Arlette reached the gate to the field and unhooked the lock before slipping the cord from the cow's neck. '*Allez!*' She slapped its rump and watched it amble towards the herd. She held on to the top bar of the sun-warmed gate in a daze. Her eyes scanned the landscape, half expecting to see a line of German soldiers marching across its fields. The war – that vague, far off entity that was spoken of in hushed tones for fear of it becoming a reality – suddenly seemed so much closer.

'Stop daydreaming! Do you know what this means?' asked Francine.

'I'm not daydreaming. I'm thinking. Will they come here?'

'I hope not. Can you imagine?'

Arlette saw fear in her friend's grey eyes. 'Come on. I need to talk with Father.'

Arlette gripped Francine's hand and pulled her back towards the farm. The women hurried in the direction of the stone barn, running through the yard and dispersing the reassembled chickens, and were greeted by Klara, the farm's Brittany spaniel. Arlette opened the huge cowshed door and heard her father curse. The interior was striped with sunlight that streamed in through gaps in the eaves and the familiar smell of pungent manure stung the back of her nose. Her father, Henri, raked his hands through his thick greying hair and noticed the girls standing in the doorway.

'*Ma pêche!*' He beckoned to Arlette.

Arlette smiled. He'd called her his peach since she was a baby. She leant into his broad chest and nestled just below his shoulder, his shirt infused with laundry soap, tobacco and fresh sweat. A safe place.

'Have you heard?' asked Arlette.

'Yes. Your father was here earlier, Francine.'

'What does it mean?'

'I'm not sure how it will affect us here in the south, but Pétain's weakness won't stop us from bringing in the harvest. We're a long way from Paris and hopefully we won't be too affected by the armistice. I'm sure we'll be left alone to get on with our work.'

He tried to sound matter-of-fact but Arlette sensed a change in his voice. Despite his apparent disregard for the information, she heard a faltering that hadn't been present before.

'Where's Gilbert?' asked Francine.

It was unspoken knowledge that Francine had become sweet on Arlette's elder brother this past year.

'He went inside for bread and goats' cheese,' said Henri, loosening his embrace on his daughter. 'Go and tell him to hurry up. We won't let the Germans disrupt our lives.'

Arlette nodded. If her father wanted to pretend that everything was fine, then she would reciprocate.

Gilbert didn't move when Arlette walked into the kitchen. He was leaning back in their father's armchair with his feet resting on a stool, chewing the remnants of his sandwich. At twenty-two, he was tall, dark-haired and broad, with muscles developed through hard graft after years working on the farm.

As soon as Francine entered though, he sat up, straightened his hair and wiped crumbs from his lips. 'Hello, Francine.'

She smiled and lifted a hand in greeting, then stared at her feet.

Arlette found this unaccustomed shyness between her brother and her best friend very confusing. How was it possible that despite spending sultry summers and bitter winters together since they were children, they suddenly found it more difficult to communicate despite a growing fondness for each other?

'Father says to hurry up,' said Arlette.

She looked at her brother's dishevelled hair, scattered whiskers and large fern-green eyes, a colour they'd both inherited from their late mother. No, she couldn't tell him of their Premier's cowardice; her own bravery had escaped her for the moment. She watched him get to his feet and smile shyly at Francine before placing his mug in the stone sink and heading back to the barn.

'Do you still have the caterpillars?' asked Francine.

'Of course.' Arlette rubbed her hands together, making a shushing sound as if she were mentally washing away the anxiety that was growing inside her. She forced a smile. 'You can help me carry some more leaves upstairs. They need feeding.'

When they had aprons full of leaves from the mulberry tree that grew a short distance from the kitchen door, Arlette led her friend through the kitchen and sitting room, into the hall. The sound of their clogs echoed around the walls as they clomped upstairs and along the corridor. She opened the door facing them, pushing it with her bottom before dropping the leaves on the nearest table.

Arlette pointed. 'You spread half over those far tables and I'll do these.'

Francine wrinkled her nose. 'I'd forgotten how smelly they are.'

'You get used to it. The cows smell worse.'

They scattered the leaves and twigs over the crawling mass of caterpillars, some of which had scaled the lip of the table and fallen onto the floor. Arlette then took a small knife and cut a length of string, tightening a few corners of a wooden framework that sat on top of the tables among the writhing mass of bodies.

Francine placed a finger over the string, holding a knot in place while it was tied. 'Are you still selling the cocoons?'

'Yes. I wish I'd learnt to spin silk myself. Looking after these little creatures makes me feel as though I'm doing something to help. The more silk produced, the more parachutes are made and I also make a little money from it.'

'I need to find some work that pays, too. Helping on Papa's farm keeps me busy, but I'm an adult now. I'm getting old.'

Arlette laughed at her friend's serious expression. 'Twenty isn't old.'

For a few minutes they spread the leaves evenly between six tables without speaking, then Francine looked up. 'Do you think Gilbert will leave Montverre, like René and Albert?'

Arlette realised that Francine was as anxious as she was since hearing the latest news from Paris. 'I don't know, Ci-Ci. Your brothers are older and felt they needed to fight to keep the Germans out of France. Now Pétain has opened the door and invited the enemy inside, perhaps René and Albert will come back home.'

Francine sighed. 'We haven't heard from them in so long. I'm scared that everything is changing and that the war will swallow us all up.'

Arlette pulled her friend into a hard embrace. 'I'm sure everything will be fine,' she said, though in her heart she was just as afraid as her friend.

Chapter Two

The first Sunday of September 1940 arrived with the countryside adorned with pearls of dew and a low mist. The late summer heat and ripened fruit mingled to fill the air with a honeyed fragrance. Arlette and her brother cycled into the yard having returned from *Grande Masse* at Saint Pierre's. Their father hadn't attended a service since the death of their mother and third baby in childbirth, but had never dissuaded his children from attending.

Having leant their bikes against the barn, Arlette waved to her father who was walking towards them through the wheat field behind the farmhouse, Klara running along beside him. His eyes were shadowed beneath his hat but he smiled and strode out of the golden field, cupping his right hand in front of him.

'We're all set for tomorrow,' said Henri, rubbing the wheat heads between his palms and blowing the chaff away. He offered his children a kernel each.

'It's ready,' said Gilbert, tasting it. 'Very dry.'

Arlette bit into hers, cracking it between her teeth. She knew that if it wasn't bone dry the harvest was likely to rot.

'We start harvesting first thing tomorrow and this year is more important than ever due to the shortages,' said Henri. 'I've spoken with the neighbours. Thierry, Bruno and Monique are all willing to help. I want you to sharpen the scythes today, Gilbert. Thanks to the fuel shortages we have no choice but to harvest the old way. There'll be no tractor or conveyor belt this year.' He turned to Arlette. 'Choose two chickens for the pot today, *ma pêche*. We'll

6

eat a large dinner to prepare for the cutting and we'll make extra to feed everyone tomorrow. Let's pray for good weather.'

The following day dawned with drooping, golden heads of wheat swaying in the breeze, sounding as if they were whispering in anticipation of the harvest. Inside the kitchen a small group of neighbours huddled around the stove that Arlette had lit to take the early morning chill from the room. The logs crackled and the friends hugged their cups of coffee, discussing plans for the day. It hadn't escaped Arlette's notice that Gilbert had slowly manoeuvred his way around the kitchen so he was standing next to Francine.

Henri removed his cap and scratched his head. 'Gilbert and I will be cutting the wheat starting at the top end of the field closest to the brook. I want everyone to stay well back from the scythes. Bruno and Thierry, you'll be gathering the wheat into bundles. Ladies, your job is to tie them and stand them into stoops to dry. It looks as if it's going to be another hot day, so Arlette and Francine, please bring jugs of water and apples with you.'

Everyone nodded.

Henri shuffled and rubbed his stubbled chin. 'I just want to say, thank you. We couldn't have managed this without your help now that the tractor and binder are out of action. We have a tough couple of days ahead of us, but just think of Marshal Pétain or Hitler when you're chopping and binding, and we'll soon get it finished!'

Thierry, the pig farmer from down in the valley guffawed and Bruno and Monique, Francine's parents, exchanged a glance.

Everyone left the kitchen, crossing the farmyard. They pushed their way through the metre-high wheat field, their thighs pushing against the stalks. The sun was now above the horizon, already warming their skin and dampening their backs. The growing heat had also stirred insects, causing the friends to swipe and spit as they made their way to the far corner of the field. Refreshments were placed in the shade of a tree and covered with rectangles of muslin cloth weighted at each corner by glass beads. Arlette noticed Francine watching Gilbert as he hoisted his jacket above his head, momentarily revealing his taut stomach. Her brother glanced back at Francine, making her blush. He threw his jacket beneath the tree.

Harvesting began. Henri and Gilbert started the process, walking steadily six feet apart while swinging their scythes rhythmically from right to left. The stalks collapsed and were walked over by father and son as they continued forwards. Bruno and Thierry followed a short distance behind. They crouched to collect the fallen wheat, assemble them into piles and tie them with loose stray stalks. The girls and Francine's mother fell into step at the rear, standing bunches in groups of six and leaning them against each until they resembled miniature tepees.

This continued for over an hour until the group had walked down the length of the field and back up again, returning close to their starting point. Once there, they stopped to rest. Arlette sat beside Francine and Gilbert, all three gratefully quenching their thirst. Gilbert laid back, his chest rising and falling with each deep breath. He studied his hands.

'I've got blisters already,' he said.

'You have girl's hands,' said Thierry. He laughed while examining his own calloused palms. 'These are what you call working hands, lad.' He lifted them to show the group, causing Henri and Bruno to mock and compare areas of hardened skin.

'Can I see?' Francine asked Gilbert.

Arlette watched her friend take Gilbert's hand, running her forefinger gently over his blisters. She saw her brother swallow, his throat constricting. His gaze fell on Francine's hands holding his own. Feeling like she was intruding, Arlette reached for an apple and knife. A spiral of apple skin looped and fell like a pink ribbon onto her knees as she turned to speak to Francine's mother.

'I put a chicken casserole in the oven. The embers should cook it slowly.'

'Lovely, we'll be ready for that,' said Monique. 'I'm sure your mother is looking down from heaven and feeling very proud of you.'

After five minutes Henri stood up and batted the dust from his trousers. He spat on one palm before rubbing his hands together and reaching for his scythe. Everyone took this as an unspoken sign to resume harvesting. Arlette noted that Gilbert stood up first and offered his hand to help Francine. How wonderful it would be if her best friend were to become her sister-in-law.

By late afternoon the following day, the wheat was cut and the exhausted and dishevelled group left the field. They trudged back to the kitchen where Arlette had spent the last hour preparing a meal of rabbit, potatoes and the last of the runner beans. Dinner was to be followed by plump blackberries that she had hand picked and which had left her fingertips stained indigo.

Arlette crossed the yard to greet them, hugging her father and walking beside him towards the well.

'Food's nearly ready.'

'You're a good girl,' said Henri, kissing her forehead. 'First we need to wash the dust off our hands.'

Before answering her father, she heard her brother curse. He was looking towards the farm entrance where an open-topped truck had stopped in front of the assembled group. Two uniformed men wearing blue berets climbed out, their buttons catching the sunlight. French police. They moved to the front of their vehicle.

'Whose farm is this?' the older of the two demanded.

Henri lifted an arm.

'What's your name?'

'Henri Blaise.'

'Papers.' The policeman clicked his fingers.

'They were checked recently.'

'I'm checking them again.'

'They're inside,' said Henri.

'Fetch them. Your papers should be on you at all times.' He scanned the gathered group of neighbours.

Arlette wondered what the younger man was writing on his clipboard. She watched her father return from the kitchen with his paperwork, where it was snatched from his hands when he offered it. The man barely looked at it.

'We're taking your wheat. German soldiers in the north are short of food and we're starting a process of redistribution.'

Arlette saw her father's distraught face. This harvest would have sustained the family throughout the coming winter and also earned them a little money.

'The hell you are,' said Gilbert, taking a step forwards.

The policeman moved his hand to his belt where Arlette could see a gun.

'Who are you?' he asked her brother.

'I'm a Frenchman, like you,' said Gilbert. 'Yet only one of us is loyal to the—'

'Quiet!' The man spoke through clenched teeth and took the gun from his belt. 'We'll do this peaceably or you'll be arrested.'

Henri grabbed Gilbert's arm to calm him.

'What's your name?' the policeman demanded.

'He's my son,' said Henri. 'Gilbert Blaise. Please forgive him his impudent youth.'

'But, Father—'

Henri hissed to his son, 'Enough!'

The policeman's lips twitched in triumph. He replaced his gun. 'I would advise you to have a word with your son or you'll find yourself manning this farm alone.'

Henri nodded. 'Is it possible to keep some of our harvest for ourselves?'

His question was ignored.

'It's nearly four o'clock,' said the policeman. 'A lorry will arrive at seven. Make sure the wheat is waiting here in the yard for collection.'

'But that's impossible,' said Henri. 'We're exhausted. We've worked for two days to cut it and it'll take us at least another to shift a field of wheat.'

The policeman walked towards him. Arlette squeezed her father's hand. The man removed his glasses, leaving two shiny half-moon-shaped areas of pink skin where his glasses had been. His breath smelt of garlic.

'Then I advise you to begin now. If it's not here in three hours, there will be consequences.' He turned and addressed everyone. 'There will be consequences for everyone. Things are changing. You will share whatever you grow and whatever animals you rear. In addition, you all have until the twenty third of September to register for rationing cards in Limoges town hall. If you don't comply, you will go without altogether.'

The policeman's attention turned to Arlette. He didn't speak but studied her face. She held her breath and stared back at him, refusing to be the first to look away. She saw tiny veins patterning the whites of his eyes like rivulets of spilt red wine. He turned away and walked back to his vehicle, speaking inaudibly to the younger soldier before they both laughed. The truck's engine started and they drove away amidst a swirling cloud of dust.

Everyone spoke at once before Henri raised his hand.

'We must act quickly. Gilbert, you fetch the mare from the barn, attach the cart and take her into the field. I'm really sorry to have to ask you all to help yet again, but none of us know what these bastards are capable of.'

'Of course we'll help,' said Bruno. 'I may be asking for a favour in return if they're targeting every farm.'

'I'll hurry home and bring my horse and cart too,' said Thierry.

'Thank you. Come on, we don't have long.'

Arlette took the dinner out of the oven and placed it on their heavy mahogany table. She noticed that her hands were shaking as she reached for a muslin cloth to cover it. Before the truck had arrived, her mouth had watered at the aroma of the meat, but now she felt nauseous at the sight of it.

The next few hours passed in a daze of instructions, raised voices and tears of frustration and exhaustion, and not all from the women. Hands were cut and bloodied, clothes stained with sweat and dirt and bodies ached with pulled muscles and twisted ligaments. The sun continued to beat down. The sounds of cursing, disgruntled whinnying horses and curt orders rose from the field. A huge buzzard silently soared above them surveying the scene below.

At seven-fifteen, the last two cartloads of wheat rolled into the yard behind the horses. Arms pulled and yanked them to the ground, shortly followed by the sound of engines. Two open-topped trucks pulled into the yard and, to the surprise of everyone, six thin and dirty young men climbed out of each lorry and began to load the enormous pile of wheat. Their eyes were shadowed and not one of them looked up at the group of friends standing in front of the farmhouse.

Arlette heard Gilbert whisper at her side. 'They're prisoners. They look half starved, poor devils. If I had a gun, those policemen—'

Arlette shushed him and nudged his arm. She feared the possible consequences of her brother's impetuousness, wishing he would realise what trouble he could get in if he insisted on making his Gaullist views known.

Too exhausted to stand, everyone except Henri sat on the ground amongst the gravel, chicken excrement and stray stalks of wheat. They watched the harvest shift from the farm's yard to the backs of the trucks before being driven out of sight. No one exchanged a word as Henri walked silently into the barn and closed the door behind him.

Chapter Three

'Thank you for mending my puncture,' said Arlette, washing her breakfast bowl at the kitchen sink.

'It was a small one. Easily sealed.' Her father was looking out of the kitchen window. 'Don't forget to take the bag of vegetables I left outside the door. Give my love to your grandmother and tell her I'll ride over in the cart in two weeks' time with some more provisions. Remember what I said earlier? Don't mention that the harvest has gone. She'll only worry.'

'I won't. I'm going to call for Francine.' Arlette picked up a hessian sack full of potatoes and a plucked and gutted chicken. 'See you later.' Outside, she heaved the sack into her bike's pannier and strapped the vegetable bag behind its seat.

Oradour-sur-Glane was ten miles away, a journey that a member of the family embarked upon twice a month to ensure that her grandmother was well. Grandma Blaise was Arlette's paternal grandmother and only surviving grandparent. She was a short, plump, ebullient woman of sixty-five and was resolutely independent. On many occasions she had been invited to live at the farm with her son and grandchildren, with promises to move the silk worms into a store in order to make a bedroom for her. But she would laugh and say she would wait until she was a hundred years old and in need of a little help.

With her long conker-brown hair plaited at the nape of her neck, Arlette hoisted her smock around her knees and set off, waving to Gilbert who was tinkering with the tractor. To Arlette the tractor looked like a metal box on four wheels but she knew that it was her father's and her brother's most prized possession; not that they could use it now there were fuel shortages. She turned left out of the yard and cycled past the orchard. The copse of trees became sparser and the Lamonds' manor came into view. Its honey-coloured stone appeared to glow in the morning sunshine. Their vines would soon be ready for harvesting but the Lamonds had fled to stay with relatives in Scotland until the war was over. At least the villagers' fruit bowls and stomachs would benefit from their departure.

Arlette freewheeled down the hill towards the farm where Francine and her family lived. She stretched her legs out in front of her, the breeze whistling past her ears and momentarily masking birdsong. The lane levelled out as she passed the Giroux's higgledy-piggledy arrangement of outbuildings. She slowed and stopped at the entrance of their farm.

'Francine!' she yelled.

Three barking dogs ran towards her. Arlette had witnessed each one's birth two summers earlier and knew they were all affectionate despite their noisy welcome. She looked up from fussing the dogs to the sound of squawking chickens. Francine emerged from one of the coops with a basket in the crook of her arm.

'Hello.' Her smile was warm and wide as she walked towards Arlette. 'Where are you going?'

'To take Grandma some provisions. I was going to ask if you wanted to come, but I can see you're busy.'

'No, wait! I want to come too. Let me go and tell Maman.' Francine dashed off towards the back door of the farmhouse, clutching her basket, followed by three dogs.

A few minutes later she reappeared from behind the house wheeling her bike.

'Maman says to give you her love and she gave me some figs for your grandmother.' Francine held up a bulging brown bag.

'Here, sit them on this sack. How is Monique?' asked Arlette.

'She's nervous about strangers coming to the door begging and is fed up of Papa because he's always moaning. He's bad-tempered because there's no fuel for his machinery, but he's been even worse this past week. Ever since the police took your wheat. He worries they'll come here next.'

Arlette chewed her bottom lip. 'It's a worry, but let's try and forget for a day. We're lucky to live on farms and be able to grow our food, unlike those poor families forced from their homes with nothing.'

The girls set off along country lanes, past spired churches, through tiny hamlets and alongside stubbled fields where gangly sunflowers had grown during the summer. They waved at distant neighbours but mainly cycled in amicable silence. Occasionally one of the girls would point out a landmark of interest or draw attention to a foraging animal that had caught their eye, each trying to reassure their friend that this was just one of the many bike rides they'd shared since they were small children.

Nearing the end of their journey, Francine stopped pedalling on an arched stone bridge over the River Glane, close to Oradour. 'Can you hear that?' she said.

Arlette stopped and dismounted. She stood in front of the seat with one leg on either side of her bike. 'Is it thunder?'

Francine had stopped just ahead of her, but pushed backwards until they were next to each other in the middle of the bridge. 'It sounds like engines. What shall we do?'

'Look!' said Arlette, pointing up to the sky.

Growling aircraft appeared from behind the thick canopies of dense woodland. Aeroplanes suddenly filled the sky above. The girls watched with upturned faces, hands held to their foreheads to shield their eyes from the bright sunlight. The engines' roar reverberated in their chests as they passed overhead, drowning the sound of the river and their own shocked gasps.

'They're flying low, aren't they?' shouted Francine.

'They're German. Can you see the crosses on their wings?'

'Where are they going?'

'North. They're heading north,' shouted Arlette.

The girls watched in silence. Shadow after shadow passed overhead, their roar covering all other sound and making normal conversation impossible. Gradually the whoosh of the river returned but the friends remained silent. The resonance of the engines faded and the only evidence of their passing was a cluster of dots on the horizon resembling a flock of crows.

Arlette found her voice. 'Let's hurry to my grandma's.'

Cycling at speed, they passed a metal sign welcoming them to Oradour-sur-Glane. With her chest heaving from exertion and her skirts billowing, she was desperate to reach the tranquillity of her grandmother's house. They passed the church with its tall steeple and continued until the road opened up into a village green, bordered by neat railings. Dotted around the open space were mature chestnut trees and telegraph poles that were linked by wires looking like long empty washing lines. Arlette could see that the tram had arrived from Limoges, but its passengers held no interest for her at this moment. With a squeeze of her fingers on the brakes, she stopped her bike outside her grandmother's house and hurried through the intricate wrought iron gate that led up the steps to the front door. She ran straight inside, knowing that her grandmother never locked her doors.

Grandma Blaise was sitting in a high-backed chair wearing a white fluted bonnet while darning. Curls of grey hair escaped from beneath her bonnet around the nape of her neck. She looked up in surprise when Arlette ran into the kitchen.

'Did you hear them? Did you see them Grandma?'

Grandma Blaise hugged her granddaughter and beckoned for Francine to come in.

'I don't think they made quite as much noise as you're making now,' she said with a laugh. 'Come and sit down and I'll make you a cold drink.'

'Where do you think they're going? Do you think they're going to drop bombs?'

Grandma Blaise led the way to her front room. 'I dare say. We are at war after all, my dear. But you don't have to worry about anything. We're all quite safe. They're most likely on their way to London.'

Arlette sat at a small dining table next to her grandmother's Singer sewing machine. 'But that's terrible. All those people in England don't know that those planes are only hours away. I wish I could warn them.'

Grandma Blaise stood opposite her and touched her cheek. 'I'm sure the people in England will be well aware. I understand there's a loud siren that sounds an alarm if planes are detected. People can hide in shelters or in the underground. I'm sure they're as prepared as they can be. Just count your blessings that you don't live on the occupied side of the demarcation line. Now, tell me how Gilbert and your father are? Did they get the harvest in on time? Rain is forecast for later.'

'We cut the wheat five days ago. Francine, Thierry, Bruno and Monique helped.'

It wasn't a lie, thought Arlette. It just wasn't the whole truth.

Chapter Four

Restrictions gave way to rationing and by the following spring, the people of Montverre were experiencing shortages in the shops, regular confiscations of farm produce and the constant droning of aircraft passing overhead. Francine's mother regularly passed on the news that she'd heard on the mayor's wireless; most recently that Yugoslavia and Greece had surrendered to Germany and also that the occupiers were now allowed to use French airfields and ports. Thankfully the Germans were more of a nuisance than an enemy in Montverre and, for the most part, remained in the occupied zone of northern France. The division of France had torn apart many friendships between the inhabitants of local villages. Many distrusted the French police who worked under German orders, but there were some villagers who sympathised with Marshal Pétain's collaboration.

'If it weren't for Philippe Pétain,' the doctor had argued, 'France would be overrun by German scum. As it is, only the north is suffering.' The butcher replied by spitting on the ground and declaring that 'de Gaulle was their rightful leader, not Pétain, who was an ancient, Nazi-loving coward.'

April blustered in with gales and showers but ways of outwitting the enemy were being devised on the farm. The squally weather inadvertently aided Henri and Gilbert with one of their secret strategies for eluding large confiscations of food in the future. Having spent several days demolishing a large stone out-house that had only been used for keeping rusting bits of machinery parts, they'd transferred the stone to the back of the barn where they had piled it into several heaps.

Arlette stood just inside the barn doors watching them. She had a basket of seven fresh eggs tucked into the crook of her arm. 'How big is the room going to be?'

'As high as the hayloft and as wide as the barn,' said Gilbert. 'Its depth will only be about two metres because we don't want the size of the barn to appear noticeably smaller. You never know who will look inside.'

'You remember what to do if the police arrive, don't you, *ma pêche*?' asked her father.

'Yes, I won't forget. It's usually Fridays when they come for more provisions so we should have four days without a visit.'

Her father clapped his hands to remove dust from them. 'Bruno should be coming with more stone because we don't have enough to complete the wall. He said he'd give us notice before he brings the cart into the yard so we don't all have heart failure.' Her father laughed nervously. 'Off you go and keep watch then.'

Arlette left the barn and snapped off an apron-full of leaves from the mulberry tree before going in through the kitchen door. She shook her apron, letting the leaves fall on the kitchen table. Also on the table were a saucepan and wooden spoon, both of which were to be beaten noisily as if calling her family to eat, if a vehicle entered the farmyard. The last thing they needed was to be caught in the act of erecting a secret room.

Having fed the chickens, goats and caged rabbits, Arlette took the freshly picked leaves upstairs. It was a daily chore to look after the family's small silk production business. She had to feed the silkworms, collect cocoons and clear away any dead moths and caterpillars. She scattered the leaves over the writhing bodies and was proud to be doing her bit, however small, towards helping her country. Posters had been published by the Ministry of Agriculture and displayed in towns and villages, asking French farmers to raise silkworms with the slogan, *French parachutes woven with French silk.*

She looked repeatedly out of two small windows for any sign of the French police, but thankfully the day passed without interruption. The wall of the secret room began to grow higher and thankfully the sound of splitting stone was muffled by the growing gale and rain pounding on the roof.

The following day was much the same. The men continued to construct the wall while Arlette cooked, tended the vegetable garden and washed clothes in a stone sink. The bar of laundry soap was too small to rub directly onto the clothes now, so she had to make lather between her palms before rubbing the meagre amount of bubbles into the worst of the stains. The store in the village had run out of many things, including cleaning products.

While washing the plates from their midday meal, Arlette froze. She'd heard a noise in the yard. She grabbed the saucepan and wooden spoon. Had the police returned? How could she explain that she was calling her family to eat while clearing up after a meal? She hurried outside into the drizzle.

Francine was bent double, cleaning her clogs with a twig. Klara wagged her tail nearby, eyeing the stick.

'You frightened me. I thought you were the police,' said Arlette.

'Sorry. My shoes are too muddy to walk inside with them on. Are you expecting a visit from them?'

'Not officially, but you never know when they'll appear.'

'They visited us yesterday,' said Francine, following her friend back inside. 'They took Papa's biggest pig and six of our chickens. We only have eight good layers left now. Papa sent me to see how the wall's coming on?'

'Yesterday it was as high as their waists. I haven't been in today.'

'Is that all?' said Francine.

'They're working very hard.' Arlette frowned. 'Don't forget how wide it is.'

'I didn't mean anything by it,' said Francine, touching her friend's arm. 'It's just that I'm frightened for Gilbert. And your father, of course.'

Arlette's shoulders sank. 'I know. I didn't mean to snap. I'm just on tenterhooks at the moment.'

'Papa says I've got to let your father know that he'll bring the cart up at dusk tonight. He's spoken with Thierry and they're both going to help build the wall tomorrow.'

'That's a relief. Come on, let's tell them.'

The drizzle had eased and a weak glimmer of sunshine cast shadows across the farmyard. Birdsong could be heard amid unfurling leaves in the trees' canopies and along with the sweet scent of spring, it all seemed such an unsuitable backdrop to their clandestine plotting.

The barn door was ajar, not only to afford the men some light but also to make sure that they heard Arlette's warning sound should it be necessary. The two men were startled when the girls pulled the doors wider open and walked inside. Gilbert muttered an oath and Henri clutched his chest.

'Sorry,' said Arlette, pulling a face. It was obvious that her father and brother were a lot more frightened about deceiving the officials than they were making out.

'I'll be glad when we've finished,' said Henri. 'It's not good for my nerves.'

'Papa says he'll bring the cart up at dusk tonight and give you a hand tomorrow,' said Francine.

'That's great,' said Gilbert. He shuffled his feet amongst the grit and straw on the barn floor. 'We could do with the help.'

'Tell him we'll have a bottle of *pastis* ready for when he arrives,' said Henri. 'Now then, son, I'll make some more cement while you check on the cows in calf. Meat is precious nowadays and we can't afford to lose any beasts. Why don't you go with him, girls, but keep an ear open for vehicles?'

'I'll be able to hear much better in the kitchen,' said Arlette. 'But Francine could go with Gilbert.'

She looked at her friend whose eyes were blinking rapidly above flushed cheeks. Her brother's throat bulged as he swallowed deeply and grunted his acceptance of the idea. Arlette wandered towards the back door and smiled to herself. Francine and Gilbert rarely had any time alone and they all had to grasp at any small happiness they could. No one knew how long the war would last.

It was a mild evening and the colours in the yard were fading to hues of mauve and grey as dusk fell. Arlette sat on an old bench with her brother and father beside the vegetable garden, waiting for their neighbour. They sat in comfortable silence, smelling the earthy aromas of the garden and listening to the owls calling in the nearby wood. Bats darted silently backwards and forwards in the twilight searching for insects, and the scuffle of small mammals rustled in the hedgerows. It was at times like this that it was impossible to believe that people were being killed, towns set on fire and bombs were being dropped in Europe.

They stood up as the rattle of trap wheels and the sound of hooves came into earshot. They all greeted Bruno, who was leading his mare. The men shook hands and caught up with whispered news as they led the horse towards the barn.

The next moment, the group were silenced by shock. A car's headlights lit up the yard casting giant shadows of their silhouettes. It halted several feet from them. The same police officer that had drawn a gun on Gilbert climbed out of the driver's seat.

'What have we here?' The policeman raised his eyebrows, accentuating the question. He walked towards the cart, his footsteps crunching on the gravel. He lifted a piece of stone off the cart, throwing it up and down in his gloved palm as if guessing its weight. 'I'm returning from a meeting in the town hall and I see that you're having a meeting of your own.'

'We're going to build a pig pen,' said Henri.

Arlette breathed rapidly through her open mouth. She watched the officer sniff dismissively before throwing the stone back on the cart. He batted the dust from his gloves.

'So, you're all going to build a pen, are you? In the dark?'

'I'm just dropping off stone so we can begin tomorrow,' said Bruno.

'I see,' said the officer. 'Couldn't you have delivered it in daylight?'

'We're very busy during the day,' said Henri.

'Especially now we have to give away our produce to feed the enemy,' said Gilbert.

Arlette closed her eyes at her brother's interruption, wondering why he constantly felt the need to antagonise officials. Thankfully she saw her father step forwards before the officer focused his attention on Gilbert.

'We're all very tired after a full day's work. Perhaps it was a stupid idea to move the stone in the evening but we thought it would save time tomorrow.'

The policeman looked at Henri. 'Stupid – or necessary?'

'I don't understand,' said Henri.

'Perhaps the cover of late evening enables you to conceal something you'd rather not be discovered?'

How could he know? thought Arlette. Her heart hammered against her chest. She looked at her father, brother and then Bruno in turn. Each of them was stony-faced and impassive in the beam of the headlights.

'Perhaps you could unload them now. I wouldn't like to think that contraband was buried beneath,' said the officer.

Arlette felt a little relief. He didn't know about the construction of the secret room.

Taking this opportunity to keep the policeman's attention away from the barn, the men began to unload the pile of stone from the cart. By now dusk had deepened into night; the only light by which to see was from the headlights of the car and the kerosene lamp that Arlette was holding. Electricity might have reached Limoges and Montverre's village square, but their remote hilltop on the outskirts of the village didn't have such convenient luxuries. Arlette held up the lamp so the men could see what they were doing, its eerie glow transforming their features into mask-like copies of their faces.

The repetitive echo of stone falling on stone continued for ten minutes until the last rock clattered to the ground and rolled to a standstill. The officer surveyed the scene with hands clasped behind his back. He teetered from toe to heel and back again in rhythmical contemplation. Without a word, he walked around the cart towards Arlette. She bristled as he stood in front of her and held out his hand.

'Lamp,' he ordered.

She glanced at her father, who nodded. Arlette handed

the lamp to the policeman, his gloved fingers touching hers. Her immediate reaction was to wipe her hand on her skirt. She watched him stride around the cart, bending to shine the light beneath it. The men were silent, watching his every move. His footsteps crunched on the grit in the yard, each tread as slow and deliberate as a death knell.

Satisfied that the cart was empty, the officer strode around the yard, lifting and lowering the lamp while inspecting the area. Arlette saw his attention turn to the barn. With an unhurried gait, he moved towards it. She bit her fingernails in mute panic. He stood before its doors and she believed that the yard had never been as silent as it was at that moment. He pushed one of the huge doors letting it swing open. He flinched. The smell of the beasts' excrement must have reached his nostrils. Arlette looked at the others when the police officer lifted the lamp and shone it into the barn. Gilbert's arm twitched and her father gave a small shake of his head and grasped her brother's arm to prevent him from moving. In the lamplight Arlette could see the policeman's jaws clench. He turned and walked back towards the men.

'It seems that all is well on this occasion. I advise you not to be out after dark in future or you may find yourself under further suspicion.'

Her father nodded his head once. The lamp was placed on the ground and the policeman climbed back into his car. The car was a long way down the hill before anyone dared move or speak.

'Bloody police,' said Bruno.

'*Merde*. That was close,' Henri said, with a short laugh.

Arlette swallowed the bitter taste of fear in her mouth, noting that her father's laugh was high-pitched and forced.

'You know we're going to have to build a bloody pig

pen now, don't you?' said Bruno. 'He might come back another day to check if we were telling the truth.'

Arlette agreed. 'Bruno's right, Father. That man is horrid. I think he'll keep checking up on us.'

'What's the matter, Gilbert?' said Henri. 'You're quiet.'

'I don't trust him. Maybe he saw the wall and has gone to get more men,' said Gilbert, snatching up the lamp. 'Maybe he'll be back.' He hurried to the barn's entrance and held up the lamp. Everyone crowded behind him and stared into the interior. A white circle of light illuminated the first few feet in front of them, its glow diminishing and then disappearing a long way before reaching the back of the barn. The wall was hidden in the darkness, the lamp's light too weak to reach it.

'We can thank the stench of the cows' shit for tonight's escape,' said Bruno.

The seriousness of Bruno's delivery and the welcome release of pent up anxieties made the four of them holler with laughter while following Arlette's lamplight back into the kitchen.

Chapter Five

Arlette awoke abruptly feeling disorientated having left her dreams only seconds earlier. Klara was barking downstairs. With her eyes open wide she stared into the darkness. A deep unfamiliar voice spoke outside her window in the farmyard below. Her heart raced. She clutched the smocked yoke of her nightgown around her neck, both from the chill of the early morning and anxiety. She clambered out of bed and hurried to the window. With a swift movement she pushed open one of her shutters.

In front of the barn, uniformed men were illuminated in the amber glow of their truck's headlights. Her brother Gilbert stood in front of them. He was shouting but his words were indecipherable. How could she have slept through the sound of the vehicle's engine?

Arlette turned to grab her shawl from the bedstead. Someone cried out from below, making her jump. She rushed back to the window to see her brother clutching his head while lying on the ground in a foetal position. Her father stepped from the shadows with his hands up. He was surrendering. He was trying to placate the man with the gun. Trying to protect Gilbert. In an instant her father glanced up at her. He had fear in his eyes and gave a tiny shake of his head. His message was silent and urgent. She was to stay where she was.

Arlette took a step back and sat shaking on the edge of her bed. She held her hands to her mouth as if in prayer. Why had the police returned? There was little doubt that the war *had* reached Montverre and nothing was ever going to be the same again.

After an agonising wait, she heard the truck's engine splutter and then roar. Returning to the window, she wiped a circle in the condensation she had breathed onto the cold glass and watched the vehicle reverse out of the yard. Their cockerel crowed as if insulting the soldiers for their intrusion. Arlette pulled her shawl tightly around her shoulders, slipped on her clogs and hurried downstairs. Her father was standing over Gilbert in the kitchen, holding a compress to her brother's head.

'What happened? What did they want?'

Gilbert flinched in pain when Arlette gave him a hug.

'They wanted to check that our papers were in order,' answered her father.

Arlette looked at him. 'At this time in the morning?'

'They were probably patrolling the area and were suspicious because we were out so early. They've no idea the hours farmers put into their days.'

She turned to face her brother. 'But how did you get hurt?'

'I told them to go to hell.'

'Gilbert!'

Her brother stood up scraping the chair on the stone floor. His washed and bloodied wound gave an almost comical impression that one side of his hair was pink. 'I'm sick of all this silence and pretence!' he shouted, wiping away an errant tear that had fallen on his cheek. 'We carry on like normal as if those bastards weren't taking over our country. The people who did this,' he said, pointing to his head, 'are French, for God's sake, not Germans. Why should I obey traitors? They should stand up to Pétain and the Germans, not treat their own countrymen like rats in a sewer while they obey Hitler's orders. I didn't want to say anything to worry you, but yesterday the butcher told me he'd been to a cinema in Limoges. He watched a newsreel of Hitler leading a victory parade up the Champs Élysées. There was line upon line of German soldiers marching in our country. If that wasn't enough, the world now thinks that France is weak. He said he heard a discussion on the wireless about the occupation of France. London thinks that most Frenchmen seem to regard the collapse of their country with a resignation that has the appearance of indifference. Why aren't we fighting them with everything we have? Picks, shovels and pitchforks, if needs be? And who knows? If we let them have the north what's stopping them from moving south and coming here to Montverre? To our farm? Someone needs to stand up to them.'

His short speech was littered with pauses and his voice occasionally broke. Arlette watched her brother's chin quiver, preventing him from continuing. Her father took a step towards Gilbert and placed an arm around his son's shoulders and drew him close. He beckoned to Arlette with his free hand and she noticed that the two men were now the same height. Her little brother was tall, bursting with hatred for the Germans and the French military and full of passion for his country and Francine.

He'd become a man without her even noticing.

Chapter Six

Summer arrived and the forget-me-not blue sky was mirrored in the River Glane. It was early evening and the air pulsed to the sound of cicadas and was heavy with the scent of wild lavender and thyme. The monotonous drone of insects was occasionally punctuated with the plop of fish.

Arlette and Francine were sitting in the dappled sunlight beneath a glade of poplars by the river's far bank, having crossed a nearby bridge. In front of them was a bay of sandy soil resembling a small private beach and tied to a metal stake was a small rowing boat that was occasionally used for fishing. Beyond that, a reed bed swayed and lolled in the breeze affording them some privacy from the opposite bank. It was *their* place. A spot where they had shared secrets, fished, laughed and sulked since they were old enough to be allowed to play out alone.

Their secret place.

'When's Gilbert leaving?' Francine's voice was almost a whisper.

Arlette snapped a stalk of grass into small pieces as she watched a skimming water boatman make patterns on the surface of the Glane. 'Soon. He won't say when.'

Francine turned to her, more animatedly. 'Has he said where he's going?'

'No. He says the less we know the better. Father's tried to talk him out of it and says he's needed on the farm and that his labours benefit the people of France. But Gilbert says his work on the farm also helps to feed the filthy Boches in the north. He wants to be of more use to France's allies.'

'I think he's very courageous,' said Francine. 'Being part of the Maquis is so dangerous.'

'Shhh!' Arlette looked around. 'We can never mention the resistance. Don't ever speak of it, Francine.'

'I won't ever mention it in public. I know it's a secret and I'd never put Gilbert, René or Albert in danger.'

Arlette could see that Francine looked upset and she felt bad for raising her voice. She put her arm around her friend's shoulders. 'I'm sorry. I'm just frightened for our brothers. They've put themselves in so much danger by joining ...' She lowered her voice to a whisper. '... the Resistance. You never know who's listening or who's collaborating with the authorities.' She lay back on the grass. 'I hate this war even though we have it fairly easy at the moment.'

'What do you mean, at the moment?'

'Gilbert says he doesn't believe that Hitler will be satisfied with just the north of France. He's been talking about it for a while but more so since hearing about the leaflet drop by the Allies.'

Francine pushed a tendril of hair from her eyes. 'The news in the leaflets did help everyone's mood. It's good to know that the Allies are making progress, but Papa says that the young men leaving to fight are delusional. He says that if they think they're going to spend a few months dressed in uniform chasing the enemy back into Germany, they're mistaken. He says they're boys with no idea about the horrors they're walking into and the leaflets are propaganda in order to get even younger men to sign up and fight.'

'I know. Father thinks that reading the leaflet is what made Gilbert decide to leave.'

'How's he taking the news?' asked Francine.

'Badly. It just seems to be one thing after another

and it's getting him down. There's the requisitioning, the rationing, no fuel, not enough coupons for his tobacco and he's worried that the secret storeroom will be discovered. And, on top of all that, this year's potato harvest has failed thanks to those awful beetles. I know he also worries about Grandma in Oradour-sur-Glane, but she refuses to leave her home. And now his only son and farmhand is planning to leave. I try to tell him that we're lucky to live in the south, but he says try telling that to the shopkeepers with no stock and the mothers without food to feed their children. He still misses Mother terribly. We all do.'

Francine pulled at a clump of grass and ripped it before sprinkling the broken fronds on the ground. 'I'll miss Gilbert.'

'He'll come back to you, Ci-Ci,' said Arlette. 'We'll be sisters-in-law in a few years' time, you'll see.'

'Do you think so?' Francine's smile returned. 'I mean, I think he likes me.'

Arlette laughed. 'Silly, he adores you. It's so obvious. You *both* make it so obvious.'

'No we don't.' Francine flapped a hand in the air as if swatting a fly, but she couldn't stop herself from grinning.

'"Can I get you a drink, Gilbert?" "What are you doing, Gilbert?"' mimicked Arlette.

Francine pushed Arlette amicably and laughed. 'Fibber, I don't, I don't!' She lay down on the grass beside Arlette. 'I wish it was five years in the future,' said Francine.

'I wish it was ten years in the past,' replied Arlette, thinking about her mother.

For a few moments they lay in silence, lost in their own private thoughts. Arlette chewed her thumbnail until a grain of sand crunched between her teeth like a peppercorn. She pinched it from her tongue and looked at the sun quivering through the green canopy of leaves above her. The breeze stirred and parted the branches so that the sun flashed down with a quick and sharp light, causing her eyes to shut. It had been a long day for Arlette and she was thankful for this short time to relax with her closest friend.

Her day had started at six when she'd risen to feed the smaller animals and milk the cows. She often thought what a godsend it was living on a farm and being able to drink fresh milk every day. After milking, she'd cycled to Montverre centre while precariously balancing a basket full of cocoons on each of the handlebars. Once there, she'd taken the tram to Limoges to deliver the unprocessed silk to one of her customers. Back in Montverre, she'd called at the shops and bought bread, candles and laundry soap with her coupons. The shop had sold out of tea and coffee and while the bread she'd purchased was stale, it would be fine for dipping into a vegetable broth. Having returned to the farm, Arlette had grated two parsnips, roasted them and infused them in boiling water; parsnip tea was better than no tea. She'd taken a cup to her father and brother who were mending fences in the field, then picked some green beans, fed the goats, washed clothes, mopped the floors and prepared the vegetables for dinner. Thankfully today hadn't been interrupted by a visit from the police.

'We ought to be getting back,' said Arlette. 'It's getting late and they'll be wanting some dinner.' She groaned as she stood up, brushed the grass from her smock and slipped her feet into her clogs. She grasped Francine's outstretched hands and helped her to her feet.

'I want to ask you something,' said Francine.

'What is it?'

'You know how this is our secret place?'

'Yes.'

'Would you mind ... would it be all right if I bring Gilbert here for a picnic before he leaves?'

Arlette thought for a second or two before smiling. 'Of course it's all right, but let's agree to only invite someone special to us here. I can't imagine I'll be doing that for many years to come now.'

Arlette linked arms with her best friend and they set off along the riverbank. The distant hum of aeroplanes drew their eyes skywards, their hands cupped to their eyes against the glare of the sun.

'The sound of aeroplanes is as common as birdsong these days,' said Arlette.

The friends crossed the bridge and began the climb back up the hill and through the woods. They dawdled past the manor house, straining to see the decaying vines that had been stripped of grapes by the villagers. Finally they crossed through the Blaise family's orchard where the apples and figs looked like bulbous decorations adorning the trees in reds, greens and purples. When they reached the farmyard, Arlette noticed that Gilbert was sitting on the low wall of the well, leaning forwards and resting his elbows on his legs. Cupped in his palm was a cigarette, a plume of grey smoke spiralling into the air from its glowing tip.

'Why don't you go and speak with Gilbert before you go home?' suggested Arlette. 'I'm going inside to prepare dinner.'

Francine smiled before crossing the yard towards Gilbert. Arlette saw her brother stamp on his cigarette and shuffle sideways so Francine could sit beside him and talk of goodbyes.

I wish it were ten years ago, thought Arlette again.

Chapter Seven

Gilbert had been gone for six months and winter had been especially hard for Arlette's father. No one knew where Gilbert was staying and the thought of him living in the woods throughout the recent bad weather was unthinkable. The government in Vichy increasingly controlled the availability of food and goods and ordinary citizens responded by manipulating the system. Henri Blaise achieved this by continuing to secrete away provisions that the farm had produced or through buying goods on the black market. Earlier in the year, Marshal Pétain had claimed in a speech that *'black market traffickers are adversaries to French unity'*. He had warned that those hiding or trafficking food would be fined, have their food confiscated and would be imprisoned. The threat of the secret room being discovered tormented the family every day, but it was a necessity. The harvest, half the cows and all the farm's rabbits and goats had been taken for redistribution to feed the Germans in the north. They needed to protect as much food as possible.

The residents of Montverre frequently faced empty shelves in the local stores so Henri made the barn's room available to his friends, Bruno and Thierry. Each concealed their respective produce in the barn's covert room, sharing and dividing their yield between each other. Henri had planted winter vegetables the previous autumn and, thanks to the country having had only a moderately cold winter, broad beans, spring onions, garlic and carrots had grown successfully.

Although farming enabled Arlette and her father to eat, albeit frugally due to the season and the removal of most of their livestock, hunger brought people from further afield to their home. The starving people from outlying areas realised that eggs and chickens could be found on countryside farms and travelled long distances in search of food. It seemed that the government was turning a blind eye to such activities this time, as new roadblocks hadn't materialised. Each week, more and more strangers called at the farm, some of them begging but most willing to pay for poultry, milk and eggs. They came on foot, on horses pulling ramshackle carts or they cycled, but every person who entered the yard had the look of the haunted, their faces drawn and lined with hunger and worry.

The weekly market had continued in Montverre during the winter, with villagers emerging from front doors and nearby hamlets to buy what food they could find. They milled around, catching up on the latest war news, moaning about the lack of food and how the market lacked the pre-war atmosphere. The men had stopped buying and selling livestock, their beasts' odour no longer pervading the houses edging the square and their bellowing and bleating had long since been silenced. The farmers' wives had stopped bringing eggs, poultry, rabbits and vegetables to sell and although the gossiping continued in the regional patois, market days no longer culminated in an evening with friends and neighbours at local eating and drinking establishments. Gone was the bustle of the village square and in its place were long queues for scarce items. The war had transformed both the nature of the local markets and the convivial mix of smart city-dwellers and local peasants. Market day had ceased to be a joyous occasion even though the news of the week was that America had joined the war against Germany following a surprise attack by the Japanese on Pearl Harbor.

* * *

On this particular market day, Arlette stood beside her father's rusting cart in Montverre's square. She was displaying a meagre supply of winter carrots, spring onions and garlic for sale. Her mare, Mimi, stood patiently tied to a nearby tree with a nosebag of food tied around her neck. Arlette hadn't used her coupons on market days for weeks, ever since Madame D'Arras had vilified her in public while she had been standing in a queue waiting to buy her father's tobacco. Arlette stared sightlessly into the distance, her thoughts lost in reverie of that embarrassing day.

'I suppose you think you're the new queen of this situation,' Madame D'Arras had said.

Arlette wouldn't have turned around had it not been for a sharp jab on her shoulder blade from behind. She'd turned to see Madame D'Arras pointing a finger in her face.

'Me?' Arlette had asked.

'Yes, you. You farmers are all greedy and selfish, making the queues longer on market day. Why should you be allowed the same coupons as everyone else when you live on a productive farm? We starve while you lot fill your bellies.'

Arlette had wanted to explain about compulsory requisitioning, the long hard hours of work to produce crops and of how they gave food to hungry refugees who came begging, but an image of their secret room stocked with vegetables and the fact that several people in the queue were murmuring in sympathy with Madame D'Arras's accusations made her collect her father's tobacco in silence while her eyes stung with tears. She'd vowed never to use the family's coupons on market day again.

Taking a deep breath, she pushed the images of that day from her mind and straightened several garlic bulbs. She looked up to see a thin old lady shuffling towards her.

The woman looked as if her large coat had swallowed her, her skinny wrists and ankles protruding from its bulk and its belt wrapping around her waist twice. Arlette thought she knew everyone in the vicinity, at least by sight, but she didn't recognise this stranger and her curiosity was aroused.

'Good morning,' said Arlette.

The old lady gave a strained smile of a convalescent, pointed to the cart and spoke in a rasping voice. 'Can you spare a little of something? I have no money to give you.'

Wanting to help but aware that her father had warned her against people begging, Arlette hesitated. He'd prayed daily that his seasonal vegetables would be fit for harvest, so she was reluctant to just give them away at the market.

'Do you have a little something to exchange?' she asked, feeling dreadful for asking. 'I'm selling these vegetables for my father and he's tended them through the autumn hoping to make a little money or to trade them for something.'

When the old lady slowly raised her head, Arlette looked closer at the sallow features, colourless lips and sunken eyes. Shockingly, she vaguely recognised this woman as being a friend of her late mother. If she was right, this supposed old lady was only in her early forties.

'Camille?'

The woman squinted at her and nodded.

'I'm Arlette. Fleur Blaise's daughter.'

'I thought there was something familiar about you. You've grown very beautiful. I see your mother in you,' she said, before coughing into a closed fist.

'How are you? You look tired.' Arlette was too polite to say that she looked dreadful.

'Not so bad now, thank you. I've suffered with tuberculosis recently but I'm recovering now. How's your brother? And dear Henri?'

'Gilbert's very busy with a new job further north,' said Arlette. It wasn't exactly a lie, she thought. He *was* busy trying to sabotage German endeavours. 'And Father is always tired because he has to do twice the workload now Gilbert's left. He still misses Mother dreadfully.'

'Ah yes, Fleur was irreplaceable. I knew he'd never re-marry. We all still miss her.'

'I've brought the horse. Won't you come back with me and share some food with us?' asked Arlette. 'Father will be really pleased to see you.'

'You're very kind, but despite being a shadow of myself, sadly I still possess the vanity of my youth. Better that Henri remembers me as your mother's pretty friend than the old crone you see standing before you.'

Again Arlette lied. 'Nonsense.'

Camille untied her scarf. It was the colour of sunlight shining through a glass of rosé. 'Please take my scarf in exchange for a little food. It's too flimsy to keep me warm. I really should have worn my hat.' She bent forwards and started to cough, holding her chest and grimacing in pain as the racking cough continued.

Arlette supported Camille's arm. 'Are you sure you won't come home with me?'

Camille took a deep breath that could be heard rattling in her throat. 'I'd better be getting home to my mother, but thank you, dear Arlette.'

'Please keep your scarf. It'll keep you warmer than wearing nothing on your head. I'm sorry about earlier; I didn't recognise you otherwise I'd have gladly shared some food with you. It's what mother would have wanted.'

When Camille's hessian bag was half full and quite heavy, Arlette handed it back to her.

'Can you manage that?'

'Yes, thank you. You're a good girl. Fleur would have

been proud of you, God rest her soul.' Camille patted Arlette's hand. 'Yes, she would have been proud.'

Arlette watched her mother's friend turn and disappear into the throng and wondered what her mother would look like now. Glancing down, she saw that Camille had left the pink scarf draped over one of the wheelbarrow's handles.

An hour later Arlette had sold the remainder of her produce and had made enough money to buy some bread and carbolic soap. Shops had been forced to close for several days a week due to the shortages, so there was always a queue in whichever shop was open. She left her wheelbarrow outside the bakery and joined the line of shoppers waiting patiently. Eventually she reached the front of the column but there was little choice to be had. Since the summer of 1940, bakers had only been permitted to sell day-old bread to encourage the French to eat less of it. It looked unappetising and grey in colour, but she knew it would be filling.

On reaching the top of Montverre Hill, Arlette was met by her father who led the horse into the yard and tied the reins to a hook on the side of the barn.

'Was it busy, *ma pêche*?'

'Not really.' Arlette took hold of his outstretched hand as she climbed down from the cart. 'There wasn't much for sale and what was there looked past its best.'

They walked side by side across the yard and in through the back door. The oven filled the kitchen with a welcoming heat while Arlette unpacked the bread and lard from her bag.

'I saw Camille in the square,' said Arlette. 'She and mother used to be friends.'

Henri paused from washing his hands at the sink.

'Camille Pascal? She moved to Paris when she married. I wonder why she's returned.'

'She said she had to get back to her mother. She looked sick,' said Arlette.

'We must invite her round to share a meal with us.' Henri closed his eyes as he dried his hands, as if picturing the two young friends in his mind's eye. 'They used to turn heads wherever they went, those two. Your mother was so upset when Camille left for Paris but they still wrote to each other.'

'Oh, I forgot. She gave me this in exchange for some vegetables. I gave it back to her but when she'd gone I found it draped on the wheelbarrow.'

As Arlette held up the scarf she noticed something change in her father's expression. He crossed the kitchen as if sleep walking, cupped his hands and gently waited for her to drop the scarf into his open palms. She frowned, but placed it in her father's hands.

'What's the matter?' she asked.

'Fleur chose this for Camille as a parting gift.'

'Mother bought it?'

He smiled but his face looked pained by the memory. He held the scarf as delicately as if it were a newly hatched chick. 'I remember it clearly. See these tiny lily-of-the-valley flowers decorating the corners?' he said. 'I thought they were harebells. It was springtime so your mother went out into the orchard and brought me back a bunch of lily-of-the-valley to show me that she was right. She told me the legend of the nightingale as she wrapped it. The nightingale so loved the lily-of-the-valley that it didn't return to the woods until the flower bloomed the following May.'

'That's lovely. I'm glad you have it back.'

'No, *ma pêche*. It's for you. A gift from your mother.' He handed it back to her. 'Your mother would be happy that it found its way back to you.'

Chapter Eight

Arlette looked across at her father who was reading *L'Humanité*, a clandestine underground paper that Gilbert had brought with him during an hour-long visit the previous week. He'd asked his father about the possibility of hiding an Allied airman in the secret room until false papers could be arranged for him, but Henri had refused, saying his sister wasn't to be exposed to any additional danger. Gilbert had accepted this without argument and had immediately changed the subject and sworn them to secrecy as he regaled them about plans to target Vichy-used bailing machines. He had told them that these machines were sent to local farms to cut their crops before requisitioning their harvest, so anything that prevented the 'thieving collaborators' from feeding the Germans was on the Maquis' hit list.

'Listen to this,' said Henri, looking up from the paper.

Arlette stopped scraping potatoes at the stone sink. Her father was squinting in the dim light of a candle as he read.

'Vichy's General Secretary of the Police has said that young unemployed Jews in the unoccupied zone should be put at the disposal of rural farms.'

Arlette turned, holding a half-peeled potato in one hand and a knife in the other. 'Why Jewish men? Why not any unemployed young men?'

'Because Jews are excluded from working elsewhere thanks to the Vichy's anti-semitic legislation.' Henri shook his head. 'The north is a dangerous place for Jews at the moment so it's little wonder they're fleeing south.'

'We should look into it. Not only to help someone

who'll be feeling isolated and scared but you really do need extra help on the farm.'

Henri folded the paper. 'I'll speak with the mayor on Monday, when I pick up my tobacco rations.'

Several weeks after their conversation, the numbers living at the farmhouse had doubled. Firstly, Grandma Blaise had moved into Gilbert's bedroom. She'd brushed off any suggestion that she was finding life difficult with all the shortages and assured Henri that she was only visiting for the summer in order to lighten the workload at the farmhouse. Arlette, however, could see that her grandmother had lost weight and the old lady's usual rosy cheeks were now pallid.

'Are you sick, Grandma?' asked Arlette. 'Do you eat the meat and vegetables we bring you?'

'I'm quite well, my dear, but I've lived with the people of Oradour for nearly seventy years. They are my second family and I love many of them dearly. Do you really think that I could eat the provisions you so kindly bring me all by myself, while I watch my friends go hungry?'

'No.' Arlette paused. 'But I wonder if you ate any of it.'

'I ate sufficient. An old lady doesn't need much. I count my blessings every day that I have you two to help me.' Grandma Blaise had made the sign of the cross then hugged her granddaughter.

The second person to move into the farm was Saul Epstein. Montverre's mayor had spoken to officials and obtained a list of young Jewish men who were in need of local employment. Arlette had initially been introduced to their new farmhand the evening her father had collected him from Limoges. A mauve dusk had descended on the farmstead and she'd been locking the chickens in their coop and chasing a cockerel that refused to be fastened away. The vivid colours of the cornflowers and gerberas were fading to grey and the sun was sinking behind the orchard when Saul had dismounted from the trap with her father.

She hadn't had a chance to speak with him properly but she'd welcomed him with a smile and a bowl of mushroom soup at the kitchen table. She'd watched him devour the contents of the bowl as if he hadn't eaten properly for a week; her father later told her that he probably hadn't. His skin was pale, contrasted with dark semi-circles beneath his eyes. His hair fell in lank tendrils over his face and a ragged beard sprouted from his jaw. She liked the way he'd brush his hair from his eyes with one swift movement of his hand.

Arlette and Saul passed each other in the yard with a smile and a greeting several times a day and ate their meals together in the evenings with her father and grandmother. The new farmhand had been working with her father for ten days before the opportunity for their first proper conversation arose. Henri had cycled down the hill to speak with Thierry about sharing a market stall the following week and Grandma Blaise had taken to her bed with a headache.

Arlette was collecting a dwindling supply of mulberry leaves for the caterpillars, musing about whether to make some mint tea. Yet again the shelves in Montverre's shops had been empty that morning. On hearing Saul's urgent calls from the barn, she sat the bundle of leaves on the wall of the well and hurried across the yard. Flustered hens clucked in annoyance as her clogs crunched on the gravel and stirred swirls of dust. She broke into a run, a flurry of feathers dancing in the air behind her. Inside the barn her eyes took a little time to adjust to the dim light, but within seconds she noticed Saul kneeling in a pool of water beside a cow that was lying on the straw-strewn floor.

'What's happened?' asked Arlette, kneeling beside him.

'Her waters have broken but her calf's the wrong way round. She's struggling to give birth. I need you to help me deliver it breech otherwise we'll lose them both. I need rope.'

Arlette stood up, noticing the wide bulbous eyes of the terrified cow. Saul slid his hand inside the beast and grimaced as he tried to pull. She wondered how on earth he knew what he was doing.

'I need rope, now,' he said, with an urgency that made Arlette run out of the barn.

She hurried towards the kitchen door and grabbed a large skein of cord coiled beside some chopped logs. Scooping it up, she carried it on her wrist like an oversized bracelet back through the open barn doors. She knelt down beside him.

Saul held his bloodied hands out in front of him. 'Can you push my hair away from my eyes.'

Arlette dropped the rope onto the floor and shuffled closer to him on her knees. For a second they met each other's gaze before she reached up and pushed stray waves of coffee-coloured hair from his eyes.

'Thank you. Now tie a loop in the rope, about the size of a dish. When I ask, I need you to pass it to me.'

Arlette nodded. She twisted the twine into a loop and waited. Saul positioned himself at the rear of the groaning cow.

'Right, rope please.'

He took it from her, then inserted both his hands and the loop of rope inside the beast. The cow bellowed. Saul struggled on until he was panting with effort. Arlette noticed that his hair had fallen forwards again but

46

because he had his eyes squeezed shut anyway, she didn't think it mattered.

'Done it,' he gasped.

He wiped his bloodied hands on loose straw and stood up. 'I've tied the rope around the calf's back hooves so when she has her next contraction, I want you to help me pull.'

Arlette had seen this done many times in her lifetime but she still couldn't understand why their new farmhand appeared so calm and in control of the situation. She watched him place his hands on the beast's belly and wait.

'She's having a contraction. Pull!'

Arlette stood in front of Saul as they pulled on the rope.

'Firmly but gently,' he said, between gritted teeth.

The rope moved a few inches. Their fingers touched as they adjusted their grip.

'Wait a minute,' he panted.

Arlette was conscious of him breathing heavily behind her and felt his breath on the back of her neck. It gave her a strange sensation in the pit of her stomach.

A noise caught in the cow's throat.

'And again,' said Saul.

Arlette gripped the rope once again and took the strain. Slowly two hooves emerged, followed by a pair of bloodied legs.

'It's working,' said Saul, 'and pull.'

A glistening grey and purple mass slithered out of the cow onto the straw. Saul hurried towards it and pulled the membrane away from its body. Slowly he manipulated the calf's neck until its head was delivered with the next contraction. He grabbed a handful of straw and began to wipe the nose and mouth of the motionless animal. The calf didn't move or make a sound. Saul clutched some fresh straw and began to vigorously rub the calf's torso, mumbling to himself as he did so.

The cow had turned her thick neck and was licking her calf's face. After a few seconds the calf gave a small cough and kicked its legs. Saul sat back on his heels and exhaled noisily.

He turned to Arlette. 'Thank you.'

'That was wonderful.'

'Birth is a wondrous thing.'

'I mean, what you did. How you saved their lives.'

He winked at her. 'We both did.' He rubbed his face with the inside of his forearm. 'You were a great help. We made a good team.'

Arlette blushed. 'Would you like a cold drink?'

'I'd be grateful for a bucket of water to wash my hands and sluice away this mess, then a cold drink sounds perfect, thank you.'

Arlette returned with a pail of water from the well. 'Here you are. I'll be in the kitchen when you're ready.'

'Thank you. You're very kind.'

Inside the kitchen, Arlette felt flustered. Saul's breath on her neck and the touch of his hand on hers, however accidental, had unsettled her. She touched her neck and smiled to herself. She was glad Saul had come to work at the farm.

Arlette picked up a handful of elderflower berries from the fruit bowl and squeezed the juice through a piece of muslin. Next she added cold water causing the contents to swirl pink, as if an artist had dipped a red paint brush into the glass. Due to ongoing restrictions they didn't have any sugar, but Arlette scraped the last sticky remnants of honey from a jar to sweeten it and placed two glasses on the kitchen table. Saul appeared at the doorway.

'Come in, come in,' beckoned Arlette.

He joined her at the table, his hair wet, his hands and face clean. She noticed that after only ten days the dark circles beneath his eyes had almost gone and the sun had brought out a smattering of freckles across his now clean-shaven cheeks. She pushed the elderflower juice towards him and watched as he drank the majority of it in one go.

'How did you know what to do with a breech calf?' she asked.

'Animals are not so different from humans when it comes to giving birth. Before the war I was studying at medical school at the University of Lyon.'

Arlette's mouth gaped. 'You're a doctor?'

'Not yet.' He drew a pattern in the condensation on the glass with his finger. 'But I was in my third year and I'd spent time on the maternity ward and labour suite.'

'No wonder she was in such good hands.'

He smiled at her. 'Not that we use rope to deliver babies, you understand.'

Arlette laughed. 'Thank goodness.'

'And what about you? What do you want to do with your life?'

'Me? Oh, I don't know. No one's ever asked me that before. I always thought I'd like to teach, but my mother died when I was twelve and my schooling suffered because I had to help out here on the farm. Now we're at war and my brother has left, so you see, I'm still needed here.'

'I'm sorry to hear about your mother. I didn't like to ask Henri why I never saw Madame Blaise.'

'Fleur. Her name was Fleur.'

'A pretty name.'

Arlette nodded before finishing her drink. She liked Saul's gentle manner and the way his hair constantly fell over his left eye when he leant forwards. He'd either move it with a shake of his head or a flick of his hand. His eyes were as dark as peppercorns but with a softness about them which told of a kind man.

'Keep your hopes alive, Arlette. You can study again after the war.'

'Maybe. Where did you live before all this?' She made a gesture as if she was a waiter showing diners to their table.

'I was born in Warsaw. My father was French-Jewish and my mother is Polish. My father died fighting the Germans in 1914 but I was just a baby at the time so I don't remember him. My mother moved with me and my elder sister, Ruth, to Switzerland for a few years, but she couldn't settle. We eventually moved to Lyon where I went to school and later to university. My mother said she felt closer to my father in his homeland.'

'That's sad but romantic.'

Saul drained his glass. 'Yes, I suppose it was.'

'Is she still in Lyon?'

'No. My brother-in-law was called up so my sister and her son, Joshua, joined my mother. They left to travel to the Midi where it seemed safer.' He brushed his hair from his eyes. 'I carried on studying and training for as long as possible, but then the Nazis arrived. Soon after I left, I heard that they had taken over the airport and seized the military aircraft there. The Luftwaffe started using it as a military airfield and a radar station to detect Royal Air Force bombers that were flying over occupied France at night. Every wise Jew who was capable of doing so escaped before the Germans arrived. I don't know where my sister and mother are now. I can only pray that they're safe.'

'I can't imagine how awful it must be. It's bad enough that my brother has left to fight, but not feeling safe in your own country and having to leave your home and studies behind is dreadful. I'm so sorry. How has it come to this, Saul?'

'Ah! Now there's a question that could take forever to answer.'

'I don't know much about politics, but I do think it was madness for Marshal Pétain to let the Germans into France without a fight.'

'So the farmer's daughter is a Gaullist?'

'If that means I don't understand why or agree with it, then yes.'

Saul studied his fingernails before he spoke. 'Be careful who you share your views with, Arlette. Some say he saved the rest of France by agreeing to allow the Germans into the north; that he saved many lives because he didn't order us to defend the borders. Personally I share your views and believe him to be a weak man who handed away part of our own country through cowardice. One thing's for certain, the lives he saved at the border are vastly outweighed by the fatalities the Germans have caused since entering.'

Arlette reached across the table and touched his forearm. 'I hope this all ends soon and you find your family.'

He patted her hand. 'Thank you.'

Chapter Nine

Arlette carried a basket of washed bed sheets across the yard to the clothes line in the front garden. Some of her clearest memories were of her mother stretching high to hang her children's clothes on the line. The rope was strung from a hook underneath the red tiles of the roof to a weathered post in the far corner of the parched lawn. The sweet smell of sun on tarmac wafted in the breeze as she, like her mother before, stretched up to hang the first bed sheet. The sheet flapped like an angry bird in Arlette's hands. She pushed the pegs into place and stood back, aware of the countryside's silence. There was no bellowing of beasts in the field, no wheelbarrows squeaking under the strain of weight, no clucking chickens in the yard or banter between passing friends. She ran a palm down the damp material that she'd pegged to the line and was about to turn back to the kitchen when a sound punctured the peace. It was muffled at first, the noise gradually growing into sighs, groans and murmurs.

Arlette grasped the line and peered around the hanging sheet towards the road, her hands stretched up towards the washing line as if surrendering. Coming up the hill from the direction of Thierry's pig farm and heading towards Montverre village was a stream of people carrying suitcases, clinging to small children or pushing prams or carts stacked high with their belongings. Mattresses were strapped to carts, chairs tied to their sides, birdcages filled with clothing – their previous occupants having been set free to the mercy of the buzzards. There was no crying from the children and no talking from the adults. Everyone appeared calm; or maybe it was the eventual acceptance of their dreadful new refugee status instead of that of a working French citizen. Each insult and indignity seemed to have added to the weight they carried, both in their hearts and on their backs. The painful resignation of their situation reflected in their pale complexions and lined faces. Arlette thought they gazed like fish finally realising that struggling in the net would not free them so they may as well lie still and stare until their fate was decided for them.

'Grandma, Grandma,' called Arlette.

'What's all the noise about? You haven't been stung again, have you?' Her grandmother bustled from the side of the farmhouse, drying her hands on her pinafore. 'I've told you before—' She gaped at the bedraggled convoy of weary bodies shuffling along the lane. 'What in the Lord's name?'

'What shall we do?' asked Arlette.

'What *can* we do, my dear? There are too many of them.'

A dark-haired woman wearing her coat on this hot day looked up from the moving mass of humanity. She saw Arlette and her grandmother standing in the garden and stopped. The woman turned towards them, her eyelids blinking as if in slow motion.

'Water for my children, I beg of you.'

'Where are you from?' called Grandma Blaise.

'Just south of the demarcation line.'

'I don't understand. Why have you left if you live in the south?'

'The Germans were killing and ransacking homes a few miles away on the other side of the line. People are saying that they're going to cross over into the unoccupied zone. I couldn't take the chance that it might be true – the children, you see? We left with what we could carry and all these people from nearby villages shared the same fears.'

'But the Germans can't cross over! The armistice was signed for the north,' said Grandma Blaise.

Arlette shook her head in disbelief. 'How have you got here?'

'We travelled some of the way by train but were ordered off. They said it was needed to transfer troops. We're on our way to Limoges but hope to find provisions and rest in Montverre. Please can you help with some water to help us on our way?'

'Of course.' Grandma Blaise turned to Arlette. 'Fetch your father and Saul. Ask them to fill the buckets from the well. Hurry!'

Arlette turned and ran across the yard and past the barn calling for her father. Mimi shook her thick neck and whinnied, startled from her afternoon doze. Skirting the edge of the field, Arlette continued to call, her long dark hair falling across her face and obscuring her view. She scraped it to one side with her fingers and pushed over-grown hedgerows out of her way. Her bare brown arms were scratched by hawthorn and wild rose bushes, tiny drops of blood dotted along the weals like red beads threaded on pink cotton. Finally she saw the men working at the far corner of the field.

'Father! Father!'

To her relief, she saw them turn towards her. She beckoned to them, knowing that she couldn't explain from such a distance so waited while they ran towards her. When they drew closer, she shouted, 'We need you on the farm.'

Her father reached her first and gently grasped her upper arms. 'What's happened? Is your grandmother all right?'

'Yes, she's fine,' Arlette panted, 'but the people aren't. The people aren't fine.'

He didn't wait for an explanation but ran past her. Saul kept pace with her slower gait for a moment.

'What people are at the farm?'

'Refugees. So many hungry people. French people from close to the occupied zone fleeing the Nazis.' Arlette watched as Saul's eyes grew darker.

'I'll follow your father,' he said.

'Yes, hurry.'

Back in the yard it appeared that her grandmother had explained everything to her son and the situation was a little more organised. The men were carrying two buckets each and splashing water as they walked, leaving dark puddles on the ground. It seemed that the majority of the hundred or so fleeing families had already passed the farm continuing on their way to Montverre village, but several dozen had waited patiently holding cans, bottles and even vases in which to pour water.

When all the containers had been filled, the families began to shuffle off down the hill in the direction of Montverre village centre. A small boy remained. He walked up to Henri and tugged at his shirt.

'Monsieur, j'ai faim.'

Arlette watched her father hesitate. What could they give these people to eat? A chicken wouldn't feed many and besides, they had nothing to cook it with. Then she remembered.

'Father, the pears and apples are ripe. Yesterday I picked enough to fill six boxes to sell at the market tomorrow.'

'Of course,' said her father, 'go and fetch a couple of boxes. Saul, can you go and help her carry them?'

Minutes later, Arlette, her father, grandmother and Saul stood watching the weary group continue on their way. At the back of the convoy the small boy who had spoken about his hunger waved and grinned before biting into a large pink apple.

Grandma Blaise sighed. 'God bless the children.'

Chapter Ten

Arlette sat on the wall of the well and lowered the bucket that was fixed to a long chain. It was early evening, the time of day when the flowers' scent was more potent. The farmyard was tranquil and Klara the dog slept in the shadow of the mulberry tree. Against the wall of the farmhouse leant a fig tree, its trunk looking as if it was slouching with weariness. The wide green foliage tapped repeatedly against the sitting room window in the breeze that blew from the river. Its leaf-shadows danced on the small patch of grass in front of her. At that moment in time, Arlette felt happy. She raised her face to the sinking sun and sighed audibly.

The reason for her happiness strode out of the shadows of the barn pushing a squeaking wheelbarrow. Saul. His shirt sleeves were rolled up to his elbows and his top few buttons were undone, revealing a tanned and toned chest. Arlette now understood Francine and Gilbert's recent shyness with each other because whenever Saul was close, she became self-conscious herself. She looked away from him, not wanting to appear too forward.

Apart from the watering of the vegetable garden, her chores for the day were almost finished. Arlette could hear the bucket's hollow clang against the walls inside the darkness as she lowered it deeper, remembering that Gilbert used to tease her about the well as a child. She wondered where he was now and if he still remembered the tale he used to tell her. There had been no word from him for months. She hoped he was safe.

'Here, let me help.'

Arlette was startled and caught her breath.

'I'm sorry,' Saul said, with a smile. 'I thought you'd seen me. I didn't mean to frighten you.'

Arlette smiled back. 'I was daydreaming.'

'May I?' He indicated the wall.

She nodded.

He sat beside her and flicked his hair out of his eyes with a quick movement of his hand. His cheekbones were high and his eyes were wide and dark, his skin now golden from working in the sunshine. 'What were you daydreaming about?'

'I was remembering that my brother used to tell me that the sound of the bucket banging inside the well was a dragon knocking to tell me that it was hungry.'

He laughed. 'Did you believe him?'

'I was only young so I did for a while. Then mother told Gilbert that it was a wood nymph that would scrub little boys if they didn't go and wash themselves before bedtime. It became a sort of game then; making up funny creatures that lived down there.'

He paused. 'I'd like to have met your mother.'

Arlette didn't reply but gave a rueful smile.

'Come on then,' he said, standing up and taking the chain from her. 'Let's get this bucket up before the dragon drinks it dry!'

She took a step back and watched him with an indulgent grin. She'd pulled the bucket up more times than there were apples in the orchard, but at this moment she felt like a young lady instead of a farm girl. Arlette watched his lean arms pull the chain, hand over hand, the metal links clinking on the internal wall as the pail rose. The bucket scraped on the edge and came into view, the shimmering water flashing both gold and black as the setting sun and evening shadows were reflected on its surface.

'Thank you.'

'Do you need it taking anywhere?'

'I was going to water the vegetable garden.'

Saul unhooked the bucket from the chain and carried it in his right hand while his left arm was held out to his side for balance. Arlette followed him and Klara got up from beneath the mulberry tree and trailed behind them both. Her grandmother appeared at the kitchen door and pushed aside the curtain of beading that kept flies out. Arlette's mouth twitched and she tried not to laugh at Grandma Blaise's expression. The old lady's mouth was open like a line-caught fish as she watched the procession of three. Arlette couldn't contain her happiness any longer and grinned at her grandmother in a coquettish manner while the old lady shook her head slowly, her hands perched on her wide hips.

Saul settled the bucket on a stone. A few drops spilled over the side and marked the stone with black polka-dot stains. He emptied the water along a line of cabbages. Arlette's eyes were drawn to the muscles on his back when he bent forwards. She felt a tickle in the pit of her stomach. It was the same feeling she'd felt years earlier when she'd swung just a little too high on the garden swing: exhilaration tinged with anxiety.

'What's this you've been making?' he asked, setting down the bucket.

Arlette reached for the thick slice of cut oak that she'd painted and was now drying in the sun. 'Father gave it to me because I said I wanted to make a house sign.'

'That's a nice idea. What are you going to call the house?'

'I like the idea of our house sitting in the clouds when the weather's bad. I'm going to paint *House In The Clouds* on it.'

Saul nodded. 'I like it. Maybe I'll still be here in the autumn and I'll get to see the house in the clouds for myself.'

They exchanged a lingering look before being interrupted by her father.

'Saul!' shouted Henri, his voice emanating from inside the barn.

'Now look,' he said with a wide grin. 'You've got me into trouble.'

He winked and turned towards the barn. Arlette watched him cross the yard, a smile curling her lips because she knew that her father and Saul had become good friends over the last couple of months and knew that he was teasing her by suggesting he was in trouble. Her father enjoyed the banter and camaraderie of another man on the farm.

Arlette noticed her grandmother still standing at the kitchen door, her grey eyebrows taking on a life of their own. She met her granddaughter's glance. The old lady lifted a hand and pointed a finger at Arlette, no longer able to stop the laughter that bubbled up from her chest. 'I have eyes,' she said, still laughing as she parted the beaded curtain. 'I have eyes.'

Chapter Eleven

It was market day, but because Henri and Saul had needed Mimi that morning, Francine had come to collect Arlette on Bruno's horse and cart. Arlette looked up at her friend who was loosely holding the reins of a fidgeting mare.

'Morning, Ci-Ci.'

'Hello. Do you need a hand?'

'No, thank you. It won't take me a minute.'

Arlette lifted several boxes of apples, pears, potatoes and bunches of green beans onto the cart. She pushed them back so they sat next to a large crate containing six rabbits from the Giroux's farm. She shooed a group of chickens out of the way having freed them from their coop ten minutes earlier. They were now squawking and fluffing themselves up, causing feathers to float in the air as they shook their squat bodies and began to peck the ground for grain. The sky was clear – the colour of Sèvres blue porcelain – and even at this early hour the heat of the sun was pinching their skin.

Grandma Blaise came into the yard from the kitchen, her grey curls escaping her bonnet. She was carrying wet clothing to be hung on the washing line in the front garden.

'Bye, girls,' she called. 'Don't forget to pick me up some laundry soap, will you?'

Arlette checked her smock pocket for her ration card, and feeling it crinkle between her fingers, she waved. 'I won't forget. Bye, Grandma.'

She clambered up into the trap and sat next to Francine.

'It's going to be a hot one today,' said Arlette, pulling her straw bonnet onto her head. 'Let's hope we sell up before midday.'

'Maman's packed us some lemonade.' Francine pointed to a basket between her feet. She made a clicking noise, shook the reins and the mare began to trot out of the yard.

Francine steered the horse left towards Montverre. 'Did you see the refugees yesterday? Our dogs barked non-stop for over an hour.'

'Yes. We gave some of them water and apples, but there were so many of them.'

'I didn't like to look but there was something about the tragedy of it that kept me watching. Perhaps it's the thought that they're like you and me. They're ordinary French people who just happened to live in the north.'

'But they didn't. They came from this side of the demarcation line.'

'They couldn't have. Why would they leave their homes if they lived on this side?'

'One of the women said that the Nazis were looting and arresting people in the nearby town just inside the occupied zone. People don't think they're going to stop at the line; after all it's not a physical border that can't be crossed. Saul said that they've taken over Lyon airport to detect British planes on their way to Germany, so effectively, they're here already.'

Francine glanced at her own home as they passed it. The farmyard was quiet with just a couple of her dogs lying in the shade of a tree. 'Have you heard from Gilbert?' she asked.

Arlette shook her head. 'No, not since he came back to ask about hiding the airman. We've no idea where he's living or what the Maquis are planning.'

'I miss him.'

'I know, but Father said we must carry on and keep the farm running for when he returns.'

'What about Saul? Where will he go after the war?' asked Francine.

Arlette gave a deep sigh. 'I suppose he'll go back to Lyon and carry on with his medical studies.'

'Will you go with him?'

Arlette laughed and readjusted her bonnet. 'What do you mean?'

'Everyone can see you're sweet on each other.'

'We just ... we like each other. He makes me feel ... oh, I don't know ... special. But moving away with him? It's impossible to think like that while the war's still on. We haven't spoken about how we feel. We haven't even held hands.'

They carried on in silence for a while, the sweet smell of ripe fruit wafting in the thick air of the hot summer's morning. They greeted several distant neighbours as they passed their gardens but on reaching the outskirts of the village centre, they noticed bicycles and traps laden with produce coming in the opposite direction. A man driving his cart pulled up alongside them, his horse blowing and stamping in irritation.

'Market's cancelled,' the man shouted. 'The square's full of refugees. There's no room for the market stalls.' He shook his horse's reins and went on his way.

'What shall we do? Shall we see how bad it is?' asked Arlette.

'We don't have an option,' said Francine. 'I can't turn the trap around on this narrow lane so we'll have to go into the square to turn back anyway.'

They continued down the road, turned the corner into the square and were shocked by what they saw. Hundreds of displaced people lay or sat around the quadrangle, amongst the trees, along the roadside, in front of shops and even in the gutters. Bikes and traps containing whatever the families had left home with were parked wherever space could be found. A low hum of conversation hovered around the square with the occasional scream from a child or bark from a dog. Women fanned themselves and their children. A man was washing his face with a saucepan of water. A woman was breastfeeding a baby while her other children squabbled for space. There were far more people here than had walked past the farm yesterday. Arlette concluded that they must have arrived from different directions.

The shops surrounding the square were all closed, their doors locked and shutters fastened. Dusty refugees tried to peer through the shutters or knocked on doors, calling for the shopkeepers to open up and sell them some food. There was an odour of sweat and excrement. Someone in the throng could be heard sobbing and close by a group of men argued over space. One of the men looked up and pointed to Arlette and Francine's trap.

'They've got food,' he shouted.

Everyone within earshot turned and focused their attention on the girls and their cart of provisions. The men who were arguing began to walk towards them.

'Go, Francine. Go now.'

'I can't. Children are playing in front of us.'

The sound of scraping drew Arlette and Francine's attention to the back of the cart. Several men were pulling at the wooden boxes of fruit.

'Hey,' shouted Arlette.

The box fell to the floor causing the apples to spill and roll like marbles in different directions. More squabbling ensued as people fought over the fruit and began to climb onto the back of the trap. The caged rabbits panicked inside their crates, adding to the mayhem.

'We have to go, Francine. We have to leave now!' shouted Arlette.

'I can't! The horse will hurt the children.'

Their horse began to panic, its nostrils flaring and its eyes wide with alarm. It reared up, frightening the children away for fear of being trampled. Francine took this opportunity to move forwards. She lifted the reins and let them drop with a smack on the horse's flanks. They pulled away from the mob, leaving them to snatch and argue over the stolen produce.

Chapter Twelve

A few weeks later, the pandemonium in the square had all but been forgotten. Grandma Blaise had said that starving people have to be forgiven for acting out of character. She told Arlette that they wouldn't have hurt the two girls; it was just the food they were delirious for. She had even suggested that they both pray for the thieves, but Arlette had silently thought that she'd find that a little difficult.

Arlette was now sitting on the garden bench, podding peas. A tea towel was casually thrown across one shoulder and she occasionally slipped the odd sweet vegetable into her mouth. She liked the percussive sound they made as she dropped them into the copper saucepan by her feet. She thought of Saul and a ripple of excitement spread through her body. They had grown close over the past few weeks and she smiled to herself when she remembered the way he tucked a stray tendril of her hair behind her ear the day before. She shivered with pleasure at the memory and craned her neck to see if she could catch a glimpse of him across the road in the orchard. With the fruit trees still in leaf, their thick canopies hid the orchard floor. Her father had asked Saul to collect the latest harvest of apples and plums while he helped Thierry with some digging. She was hurrying to pod the peas so she could join him and help.

A cry made her look up and frown. 'Saul,' she called. 'Was that you?'

No reply. She stood up, knocking the saucepan of peas over. They scattered on the grass like beads from a broken necklace. 'Are you all right, Saul?'

She heard a mumbled response. Rushing out of the

yard she crossed the lane. Saul was leaning against a trunk holding one of his hands. By his feet lay a knife and a basket of fruit.

'What happened?' asked Arlette.

'Cut myself.'

'Let me see.'

Saul released his grasp on his hand. Instantly blood poured from a deep cut. It began to drip on to his trousers where each drop spread out into large red circles. Arlette pulled the tea towel from her shoulder and wrapped it around his hand. She squeezed it tightly.

'Raise your hand,' she instructed.

Arlette took one look at Saul's colourless face and knew that he was about to faint. 'Sit down.'

Saul's legs buckled when she exerted pressure on his shoulders. At first they both knelt on the floor but then he collapsed onto Arlette's shoulder. His weight pushed her abruptly on to the taupe-coloured grass. She let go of his wounded hand and, after a struggle, carefully laid him flat on the orchard floor. With his hand still bleeding, she applied pressure and raised his forearm to rest against her body.

Colour slowly returned to his face and a hint of pink was restored to his lips, but his eyes remained closed. Her own hands began to ache with the pressure she was exerting on his cut, but she knew she needed to continue. Her knees were pressed against him and she could feel the heat of his body as she held his hand upright, inches from her lips. His fingers were long and scratched, his nails short and dirty from hard work. She breathed faster at the thought of kissing his hand, but quickly shook her head dispelling the image.

Saul's eyes flickered and opened.

'You fainted.'

'Sorry.'

'Don't be silly.'

He propped himself up on his elbow, his injured hand still in Arlette's grasp. 'This is embarrassing.'

'What is?'

'Doctors shouldn't do this.'

'Aren't doctors allowed to faint?'

'Yes, but surely not over the sight of blood.'

'You were wonderful when the heifer had a breech calf.'

'I'm fine with other people or animals. It's the sight of my own blood that I have a problem with.'

She laughed shyly before moving the tea towel away from his hand and inspecting his wound. It oozed but no longer bled profusely. Their faces were inches apart. He smelt of fresh air, his breath tinged with the scent of the sweet apples he'd been eating while harvesting. She could feel his breath on her hands and wished that she wasn't so naïve and inexperienced. She yearned to kiss him but knew it was unseemly for a girl to make the first move. Besides, how do you kiss a man? She knew it was different from the kiss on the cheek she gave her father each evening.

Saul looked at her with a lopsided smile. 'You saved my life.'

Arlette laughed more loudly than was necessary. She needed to distract herself because he stirred emotions in her that were new. They made her feel out of control and more than ever she needed her wits about her nowadays. Wasn't Grandma Blaise always telling her so?

She squeezed his hand again, despite the blood flow having slowed. 'The cut's fairly small but quite deep. I could take you to the doctor in Limoges. The cart's in the barn.'

'I'll be fine. It just needs wrapping tightly.'

Arlette looked at his earnest face. She forced herself to kneel back and distance herself. 'Come on. I'm sure you'll be more comfortable sitting down inside.' She stood up first and helped Saul to his feet. He was still a bit wobbly as she led him across the lane, through the yard and into a corner of the kitchen. She pulled a chair out for him and he sat down holding on to his own hand. Blood had soaked through the tea towel.

'Squeeze tightly,' she said, before leaving him and pouring some water from a jug into a glass. 'Sip this. The colour's coming back to your cheeks now.'

The light shone through the window and onto Saul's face, making his eyes narrow against the glare. While he took a mouthful of water, she noticed the small round bone that protruded from the back of his wrist and the soft hairs on his forearm. Arlette knew why her heart quickened in her chest when he was near.

She had fallen in love with Saul Epstein.

Chapter Thirteen

Several weeks passed and life on the farm grew into a tolerable routine. Crops were harvested, the remaining animals were fed and cared for, vegetables were secreted in the barn and the police continued to visit and confiscate hessian bags full of produce. Throughout France, nature's blossoms were losing their lustre as summer faded into autumn, but Arlette hardly noticed the changing season; her thoughts were elsewhere.

On a mild October evening, as a purple dusk descended, Arlette leant against the mulberry tree beside the well, talking to Francine.

'Grandma's losing her patience with me. I can't concentrate; he's on my mind all day.'

'Now you understand how I feel about Gilbert,' said Francine. 'He never leaves my thoughts. He's always there, mentally if not physically.'

Arlette laughed. 'Actually, I can't understand anyone feeling like this over my irritating brother!'

'I bet Saul's sister thinks the same about anyone who's fond of him,' said Francine. 'Anyway, Gilbert's not irritating.'

'Of course I miss him, but you have to agree that he can be ... well, he can be a bit impulsive and speak before thinking and that can be really annoying as well as dangerous these days.'

'He's passionate about what he believes in, that's all.' Francine leant back onto a bank of grass and sighed dramatically. 'Maybe he'll grow passionate about me when he returns. They say absence makes the heart grow fonder.'

Arlette picked a buttercup and twisted its stem between her thumb and finger. 'Saul's resting in the hayloft just over there,' she said, pointing across the farmyard, 'but I can't imagine feeling any more in love with him than I am now. I have a physical ache to be next to him. It's as if he's become my focus, my one stable thought in this chaotic world.'

'Go and speak with him. I need to get back before dark so I'm leaving in five minutes.'

'No! It wouldn't be seemly. What would Father or Grandma say if they saw me climbing into the hayloft? Besides, I don't want to be like a puppy dog following him around everywhere. Grandma says that men like to pursue a lady.'

Francine rolled onto her stomach and looked up at her friend. 'Grandma Blaise said such a thing?'

'Yes. She was telling me about when Father met Mother.'

'It's strange when old people talk about those sorts of things.' Francine rolled onto her back once again and looked into the sky, her finger tracing the movement of a cloud. 'Can you believe that we've both fallen in love? We thought it would never happen and now it's almost all we speak about. Whatever did we talk about before?'

'I think it was about the latest litter of piglets or the latest calf to be born.'

'And now we talk of *love*.' Francine spoke the word with an exaggerated sigh.

They lay quietly for a short while, each lost in their own thoughts before Arlette broke the silence.

'I'd like to meet Saul's mother and sister. I wonder if they're dark like him. His sister has a little boy called Joshua.'

'Yes, I know. You've told me ... several times.'

'I wonder where they are? I hope they're safe.'

'Me too. It's bad enough not knowing where René and Albert are, but I can't imagine if it were Maman who was missing.'

Arlette looked over towards the barn and hayloft. 'I can see the light from Saul's lamp. I wonder if he's reading? I wish we could have more than a couple of snatched conversations a day.'

Francine sat up. 'Has he kissed you yet?'

'Francine!'

'Well, has he?'

'How is he ever going to kiss me with Father and Grandma always around the farm?'

Francine opened her mouth to speak, before closing her lips tightly together.

'What?' asked Arlette.

'Nothing.'

'You were going to say something.'

Francine sat up. 'Can you keep a secret?'

'What secret?' asked Arlette, leaning forwards.

'No, you've got to promise.'

'I promise.'

Francine lowered her voice. 'I've had a proper kiss.'

'When? Who?'

'Shh!'

'Who?'

'John Hepstone.'

'The baker's son?'

'Yes. Do you remember the small gathering we had at the Mairie's office in July?'

'On Bastille Day?'

'Yes. Father asked him to walk me home while he and Maman helped to clear up after the party. John kissed me when we reached our gate.' She lowered her voice conspiratorially. 'And he touched me.' Francine pointed to her breasts.

'What was it like?'

'It was good. Monsieur Péricaud played the accordion while—'

'Ci-Ci! I meant the kiss!'

Francine spluttered with laughter causing Arlette to shush her again.

'It was wet ... and tasted of tobacco.'

'Did you like it?'

Francine considered this for a moment. 'It was all right. I'm glad he kissed me because it made me feel like a woman instead of just the farmer's daughter. I imagine it would be wonderful if someone you loved kissed you.'

Arlette sighed. 'I can only imagine.'

'I have an idea. You could go for a walk and show him our special place by the river.'

Arlette sat forwards, looking at her friend with wide, excited eyes.

The following week, Arlette glanced back at the farmhouse, where a golden glow emanated from the kitchen's open shutters. The moon was high and the residual warmth of the mild autumn day lingered in the evening air. The sound of an owl's ghostly call came from the nearby orchard. She inhaled the decaying sweetness of autumn and imagined that the aroma of windfalls smelt like apple pie.

Turning towards Saul, she smiled. He held out his hand and she slipped her fingers inside his. His warm hand enclosed hers and she felt as if the war was a million miles away as they walked hand in hand beneath the fruit trees. The star-studded sky was splintered through the half skeletal branches as their lamp and the glow from a full moon guided their way through the pathways towards the river. The air was perfumed with sweet chestnuts, moss and pine needles as they walked through the copse of trees bordering the deserted manor house.

'I wonder when the Lamonds will return. It's such a beautiful house to be so neglected,' said Arlette.

Saul looked past her to the silhouetted building, its turrets highlighted in the moonlight. 'I can imagine one of Honoré de Balzac's characters living there.'

'Who?'

'He was a French writer I studied at school. He was one of the founders of realism in European literature.'

Arlette gave a deep audible sigh.

'What was that for?' asked Saul.

'I know so little. What local schooling I had didn't cover such things. I don't think I'll ever become a teacher.'

He took out a crumpled packet of cigarettes from his pocket, lit one and drew deeply on it. 'After the war, there won't be anything stopping you from studying again. Maybe you could come back to Lyon with me.'

Arlette's eyes widened. 'I've never been further than Oradour-sur-Glane in all my life.'

'Then I'll show you around and maybe even take you to Paris. One day the war will end, the Lamonds will return and, before we set off on our adventures, we'll share a bottle of their finest wine together.'

Saul pulled Arlette closer, his arm remaining around her as they walked. She leant her head against his shoulder, feeling an unfamiliar exhilaration when she sensed the warmth of his skin through the thin material of his shirt. Excitement and anticipation quickened her breath because she knew for certain that before she returned home, Saul would have kissed her.

'I wish you could have seen the grape harvest before the war,' said Arlette. 'The Lamonds used to invite the village to the *fête des vendages*. There'd be celebrations late into the night after the grape pickers had harvested the fruit. I used to love watching them with wicker baskets strapped to their backs cutting the vines with short thick knives. They'd throw bunches of grapes over their shoulders to land in the baskets as they walked up and down the vineyards.'

He turned towards her and kissed her forehead. 'You can show me after the war when the Lamonds have returned home.'

Arlette closed her eyes for a moment, the sensation of his lips on her skin still lingering. Her arm was draped around Saul's waist and as they walked through the orchard, her fingers could feel the movement of his muscles beneath her touch and she wondered how she could ever be happier than she was at that moment.

A little further on, Saul asked, 'Are you going to tell me where you're taking me?'

'We're nearly there.' She nudged him with her hip. 'Be patient.'

Soon they were crossing the bridge that traversed the River Glane. The water spat and hissed as it bubbled over rocks and licked at the riverbanks. Saul threw his cigarette over the wall. They walked a little further, keeping to the path that skirted the water's edge. Soon they came to the small bay that she and Francine called their secret place. She sat her lamp on the ground, illuminating the small sandy river beach, the clumps of reeds, the semicircle of grass beneath the trees and the rowing boat that bobbed and swayed.

'I wanted to show you this place because it's very special to me. Francine and I have spent countless hours sitting beneath these trees together talking, planning and dreaming about the future. We agreed that we weren't allowed to bring anyone else here unless they were someone very special to us.' She turned to look at him. 'So I've brought you.'

Saul raised his hands and cupped her face in his palms. She could see the outline of his features in the dim light, the shadow of his cheekbones, the strands of dark hair having fallen over one eye. Standing beside the river, there was a slight chill in the air hinting at the coming winter, but as Saul leaned forwards and his lips touched hers, they were soft and warm. He smelt of hay and sweet tobacco. He pulled her closer, his tongue exploring her mouth, the moment burning itself into Arlette's memory.

Chapter Fourteen

For the next fortnight, Arlette spent every day with a smile on her lips and a skip in her step. It didn't matter to her that an easterly wind was blowing and the temperature had plummeted. She collected eggs, fed the chickens, caged rabbits and the last two remaining cows and dug up autumn tubers for the pot. Throughout the day she and Saul would exchange snatched kisses and whispered endearments, her collection of love tokens growing by the day: twisted hay fashioned into a bracelet, a heart-shaped stone, late flowering stems. For Arlette, the war was a distant nuisance.

One evening in November, she waved to Saul before he walked through the barn door towards the hayloft. She waited until the glow of his lamp rose up the ladder before she turned towards the farmhouse. She crossed her arms and hugged her body, her skin damp from lying on the dewy grass by the river. She was in love and nothing else mattered.

As she neared the kitchen door something made her stop. She listened. Her father wasn't alone. She could distinctly hear two voices and feared that one was a member of the French police. But why would they come at this time? She crept towards the door trying not to disturb the gravel beneath her tread. Turning her head, she pressed her ear against the door and listened.

Her joy at hearing Gilbert's familiar voice almost led her to crash through the door and into her brother's arms, but there was something about the urgent hushed tone of his voice that made her stay and listen.

'He's a Jew. That revokes his citizenship,' she heard Gilbert say.

'But he has all the correct papers,' her father replied.

'No Jew is safe now. I wouldn't have put myself in such danger by coming here if I didn't believe the threat to be real. The filthy Boches crossed the demarcation line yesterday.'

'They've crossed into the south? God help us.'

'They're spreading into every town and village. It won't be long before they reach Montverre, maybe a few days. I can't stress strongly enough how much danger Saul's in. How much danger you're all in if he's found here. Make no mistake, Father, he will be found if he stays. The Germans will find his name on a list of Jews allocated to farmsteads in the area.'

Her father sounded agitated. 'But I thought Pétain was protecting the Jews in the south. They've been given employment on farms and they don't even have to wear the Star of David on their clothing here.'

'Father, I need you to listen and understand. That was then. It's different now.'

Arlette felt sick. She glanced over towards the barn that was now in darkness. Saul must have settled down to sleep already. She listened at the door again having missed her father's response. It was Gilbert who was speaking.

'Things are getting worse. Jews and even their children are being tortured, thrown into camps or executed. But it's not only the Jews. People who shelter them are being arrested too. Saul must leave.'

Arlette opened the kitchen door but didn't move. Both her father and her brother looked over to her. Gilbert looked thin and dishevelled, his dark auburn hair and beard grown long. His shoulders sank and he bowed his head. He was shaking it as he crossed the room towards her and took her in his arms.

'Arlette, I never meant you to hear such things.'

Arlette hugged him tightly before pulling back. 'Is it true?'

He nodded. 'I can't stay any longer but I had to let you know.'

'You say the Germans are in the south now?'

He nodded again. 'It's bad. I'm sorry. Saul must leave.'

Arlette held her head, feeling dizzy and confused having spent a perfect evening with Saul. Now, moments later, she was standing in the middle of a nightmare. 'Where are you staying? Can he go with you? You look so thin. You could look after each other.'

'That's impossible. We have forged papers but our supplier was arrested last week. Besides, being a Jew – it's unfeasible. As things are at the moment, we might stand a chance if our identity documents were examined.'

'But where are you living?'

'In woods, caves, empty barns. We need to continue our fight against the Nazis and the pathetic Vichy government.' His eyes sparkled with passion despite his drawn features. 'I must leave. Others are waiting for me. I said I'd only be ten minutes.' He embraced his father and turned to Arlette.

'How is Francine?' he asked.

'She's well and often asks after you. She'll be so cross to have missed you.'

'Will you give her something for me?' asked Gilbert, searching in a pocket inside his coat.

Arlette waited and he brought out a red rose that was intricately cut out of felt with tiny bugle beads set at its heart.

'It's beautiful. She'll treasure it,' she said.

'It's not much, but I came across it and – you know.' His smile seemed sad for a moment but then he straightened his back and took a deep breath. 'Please let her know that I've met up with René and Albert. They're well and wanted Monique and Bruno to know they're fine.' He hugged her and turned to walk towards the kitchen door.

'Wait,' cried Arlette. She hurried to the cupboard and pulled out some stale bread, two apples and the remaining piece of a fish that Henri had caught the day before. 'You look hungry. We don't have much but take this.' She stuffed the pockets of his stained oversized coat with the food.

'Thank you.' He hugged Henri, kissed Arlette's cheek, then left without looking back.

Arlette turned and ran to her father, wrapping her arms around his waist. 'What shall we do? Saul *can't* leave!'

'It sounds as if things are going to get much worse, *ma pêche*. We need to talk to him and find out if he has any relatives who can hide him.'

Arlette began to cry. 'But I love him.'

'I've seen enough of you two making eyes at each other to understand you've both grown fond of each other. He's a fine man who I'd be happy to welcome into the family – under normal circumstances.'

Arlette pulled back and looked pleadingly into his eyes.

'It's my job to protect you and your grandmother,' he said. 'It's a blessing she's visiting friends tonight. Saul's a Jew. You know what that means. What good is love if we're all killed?'

Arlette was shaking her head. 'There must be a way to keep him close.'

'You heard Gilbert. It's too dangerous for him to stay.'

'Maybe we could hide him in the roof space,' she urged.

Henri shook his head. 'It's the first place the Germans would look if he wasn't found in the house or outbuildings.'

Arlette lifted her head from Henri's shoulder and looked

at him. 'It's ridiculous! We manage to hide provisions from under the officials' noses, so why not—' Arlette stopped crying and wiped her tear-stained face. 'The secret room!' She grabbed hold of her father's rough hands. 'Please say he can hide in the barn, Father. Remember the officer who looked in there and didn't find anything?'

'Woah! Slow down. It was dark that night and the policeman only had a dim lamp. What if they searched the barn in daylight?'

'But the wall looks old since you and Gilbert rubbed it with mud and milk. Moss and mould have grown on it and the cows are penned in that corner so the partition to the room is hidden. It's perfect, Father.'

He rubbed his stubbled chin with his palm. 'I need to think about it.'

Chapter Fifteen

Dawn. That indistinct time in the morning that resembles an artist's first colour wash on his canvas; edges smudged and contours softened by the absence of perceptible hues. It was the Sunday before Christmas and Henri had taken Grandma Blaise to the early *Grande Masse* at Montverre Church. He never stayed for the service but instead called at Bruno's farm for unpalatable coffee and equally bitter conversation about the occupation of France.

Meanwhile, Arlette sat on the edge of her bed. Her head was bowed. She was focusing on her clenched fists resting on her lap. It had now been three mornings in a row that she'd been sick and couldn't face breakfast and she was ten days late with her monthlies. She could feel the steady pounding of her heart in her chest at the enormity of what this meant. She couldn't put it down to an upset stomach or a mistake in her calculations.

She was carrying Saul's baby.

Arlette lay down on her rose-patterned eiderdown and closed her eyes. Sleep wasn't even a consideration due to the myriad of thoughts rushing through her mind. Firstly, there was Saul. Three weeks earlier he'd moved from the hayloft into the windowless secret room at the back of the barn. The dwindling hidden provisions had been moved to one end of the room and a straw mattress and bedding had been placed at the other. In addition there was a bucket of water and towel for washing and another bucket to be used as a toilet during daylight hours. It was far from ideal but he was close by, and for the most part, safe

An additional worry was that the Germans were due to arrive in Montverre any day. It had taken longer than expected for them to reach their small village but news had reached the locals that they were already evicting people from their homes in nearby Limoges. They wanted the accommodation for themselves. Despite living on the outskirts of Montverre, German motorcycles and occasionally a large black car prowled up and down the hill like night shadows in a child's imagination.

Arlette laid her palms on her flat stomach and spoke aloud. 'What sort of world have we created you in?'

An overwhelming need to speak with Saul made her sit up again. She had taken him his breakfast earlier and he had assured her that the straw mattress was comfortable and that he was warm enough. Arlette slipped her clogs on and clumped down the stone stairs, through the sitting room and into the kitchen. Klara was sprawled out on a thin rug in front of a meagre open fire. She picked up her shawl that was draped over a dining chair, wrapped it around her shoulders and went outside.

All was quiet in the yard. The chickens were keeping warm and dry in their coops and the cows were penned in the barn, unwittingly hiding the small opening to the secret room. Arlette's eyes adjusted to the dim light. The smell of dung and ammonia was familiar yet always potent. Saul had already been warned not to make a sound if he heard anyone, just in case the Germans had decided to search the farm. Lifting a hessian sack from a pile draped over the bonnet of their abandoned tractor, she climbed into the cattle pen. She walked along the edge of the muddy straw, keeping the cows to her left. Arlette ushered a cow away from the corner of the barn and laid the sacking down at the entrance of a three foot boarded entrance. Sliding the muddied metal partition to one side, she knelt down on the clean sacking before crawling inside the room.

Saul helped her stand up and held her in his arms. The room was dark with fragments of light shining through cracks in the cement. It made Saul's smell and touch all the more intoxicating.

'No change?' he asked. His breath was warm against her hair.

'No. Just the occasional motorcycle passing by.' She stood up straight and held his hands, a small shaft of sunshine highlighting his features. 'How was your omelette?'

'Perfect, thank you. Look, I knocked out a small stone here for some light.'

Arlette walked over to a small gap in the wall and stooped to look through it. It wasn't even big enough to fit her hand through, but it enabled Saul to look across to the orchard and see a small section of the lane.

'Is it safe?' she asked.

'It's small and feels less like a cell if I can see some trees and know when it's daylight.'

Arlette bit her lip. She wasn't sure how to tell him her news.

'Try not to worry,' said Saul, cupping her cheeks. 'I'm happier being locked in here close to you than I would be if I were safe and free without you.'

His loving words made her cry. How can a kind word from a loved-one create tears when a sharp word from a stranger made her more resolute? She felt his arms wrap around her shoulders.

'Darling, please don't cry. We'll get through this. Remember what I said? We're going to sit at your favourite place by the river when this is all over, and share a bottle of the Lamonds' best wine and raise a glass to our future. Just the two of us.'

Arlette sniffed. 'There won't be just two of us though.'

'I know,' he said, with a smile. 'Henri will be here and Gilbert will be home and your grandma might stay on at the farm instead of returning to Oradour.'

'I'm pregnant, Saul.'

Silence filled the room. Snatches of sound filtered into the dim interior. A dog barked far off down the valley, heard through the new gap in the wall. The cows shuffled in the straw on the other side of the small entrance and a fly buzzed in the darkness above them. Saul let her go and sank onto the mattress in the corner. Her eyes had adjusted to the dim interior and she could see him sitting with his head in his hands, gripping his hair tightly while shaking his head.

'Saul?'

He looked up and reached for her hand, gently pulling her down to sit beside him.

It was now her turn to reassure him. 'Saul, it will be all right.'

'I'm so sorry ... so very sorry. How could I have been so stupid?' he said.

'Please don't say it was stupid. It was so special.'

He grabbed her hands and held them to his chest. 'The few times we've visited the riverbank are the most wonderful evenings of my life and if I die tonight, I die a happy man.'

'Please, don't say—'

'No, please listen. The three times we've lain together has moulded my heart to yours as if sculptured by Auguste Rodin. It is not that which I believe to be stupid. It was my passion that obscured this possible outcome. I should have thought. I should have stopped. But this,' he said, laying his palm against her stomach, 'this is wonderful but also terrifying. How can we have brought a baby into this war? How can I protect my child?'

Her guilt weighed heavy. Hadn't she tingled with anticipation each time they'd walked through the orchard towards the secret place? Hadn't she hoped that they'd be in each other's arms before the night was over? 'Remember I played a part in making this baby. You mustn't just blame yourself. Besides, the war might not last much longer. No one knows.'

'You're right,' said Saul. 'And one thing I shall eternally thank the Germans for is showing me the way to you.'

Chapter Sixteen

'They're coming. I can see them.' Arlette pointed to the far corner of the square.

It was 2nd January, two months after Gilbert had come out of hiding to alert them to the danger Saul was in from the invading Germans. Arlette noticed Francine touch the felt rose pinned to her coat, perhaps for comfort. She had given Gilbert's gift to her friend the day following his visit.

They watched the Nazis march in to Montverre. Despite being frightened, Arlette had needed to know what they looked like; these vile monsters who'd wanted to rid the world of her beloved Saul and all Jews. With Saul safely secreted in the barn and their child hidden in her womb, she held on to her best friend's arm as the rain glistened on the cobbles and darkened everyone's clothing.

Soldiers marched in rows of six. They were dressed in green field uniforms and wearing metal hats that reminded Arlette of Grandma Blaise's mixing bowl. They almost looked comical. Hardly how she'd expected murderers to look. Their faces were stern and impenetrable, but as they strutted past her position outside the shoemakers', she noticed a few of the soldiers glance furtively to one side. They snatched glances at the gathered villagers and the damp grey buildings that were to become their new homes. Like a drumbeat, the Germans stomped in rhythm, followed by soldiers on horseback. Horses shook their thick shiny necks, their eyes bulging. They proceeded at a slow pace behind the marching infantry. To the rear of the horses a sleek black Daimler slipped by, flanked by motorcycles. At the back of the procession came several more cars and half a dozen trucks, their green canvas sides quivering in the wind as if trembling. A few villagers mumbled in disbelief at the audacity of a driver who waved at them from a lorry.

'The cheek of that bastard,' said Maurice, the shoemaker's teenage son.

Francine shook Arlette. She pointed to the front lines of soldiers. The Germans were trudging out of the village centre.

'Why are they going that way?' she asked.

Arlette looked to the front of the convoy. 'No!' she said, looking aghast at her friend. 'They're taking the road to Montverre Hill.'

The last truck passed in front of them and the villagers spread out into the road muttering their disapproval and wrinkling their noses at the piles of steaming manure left behind.

'Quickly, get your bike. We need to follow them,' said Arlette, wheeling her bike onto the road and climbing onto it.

'Why?' Francine caught hold of Arlette's sleeve. 'It's okay. Saul's left. You told me he escaped before the Germans reached Montverre.'

Arlette swallowed. She hated lying to her dearest friend, but the fewer people who knew he was hiding in the barn, or that she was pregnant, the safer it would be for all of them. 'I still need to warn Father and Grandma. They'll panic.'

Francine appeared to appreciate her fears and the two friends pedalled after the last truck. They dodged people who were wandering aimlessly as if in a trance. Turning out of the square, they continued past a terrace of houses and towards open countryside.

'They might turn right towards the church hall,' called Francine.

Arlette doubted that so many men, with vehicles to park and horses to shelter, would be heading towards such a small hall. Sure enough, the procession continued past Saint-Pierre's and then up Montverre Hill and towards their farm.

Arlette was panting now, not through exercise but fear. 'What shall we do? I can't get in front to warn Father.'

'Perhaps they'll keep going until they reach Lorient,' suggested Francine.

Arlette wiped the rain from her eyes and shouted to be heard over the sound of the vehicles' engines. 'That's six miles away. There's no way those men will keep marching that far. They'd have transported them some other way.'

Ten minutes later, the road narrowed into a lane. The Giroux's higgledy-piggledy farm buildings began a short distance from this point. Monique and Bruno were leaning against their wide farm gate, watching the spectacle pass by. They were shocked to see the girls cycling at the back of the convoy.

'What are you two doing following that lot?' demanded Monique. 'Are you begging to be questioned and searched?'

'I need to see where they're going. Do you think they're going to our house?' asked Arlette. Tears pricked her eyes.

'Don't worry,' Monique assured her. 'You may get a visit soon but it should only be a couple of them checking papers.'

'We thought they'd stay in the village or maybe in the church hall,' said Francine.

'That lot won't be sleeping on mattresses in any church hall,' said Bruno. He flicked a thumb towards the disappearing convoy. The soldiers at the front were lost from view in the low cloud that hung over the summit. 'I heard rumours this morning they're taking over the manor and it certainly looks like that's the case. Bloody bad news that they'll be living so close to us. It's a good job your father's farmhand left when he did.'

Arlette bit her thumbnail.

'Try not to worry and get along home,' said Monique. 'You look done in and wet through. And you, madam,' she said to Francine, 'get in and heat some water on the fire. It's the tub for you before you catch your death.'

Arlette hugged her friend goodbye and began to push the bike up the hill. Her clothes were wet and sticking to her and she felt an overwhelming tiredness she had not experienced before. Maybe it had something to do with her pregnancy, maybe it was the pressure of the secret that Saul was still at the farm, but Arlette had a feeling of dread that was intensifying with every step.

Chapter Seventeen

January continued with bitter winds and snowdrifts that cast a wintry pallor over Montverre. Ice in the cattle troughs needed to be broken each morning in order for their remaining cows to drink. Unfortunately the weather was so cold that the cows weren't producing much milk, added to which, the corn that had been secreted in the barn had run out. The remaining handful of chickens now poked and jabbed amongst the earth and gravel in the yard for food. To add to their worries, it wasn't only the hungry livestock that caused sleepless nights. Since the coal dust *boulets* had run out, fruit trees in the orchard had to be cut down and used for fuel. As fruit supplied a source of food and income in summer and autumn on market days, this was bad news.

Grandma Blaise and Saul were sick and everyone was worried about Gilbert in this freezing weather. The Nazis had taken over Montverre and the manor and the only blessing about the harsh weather conditions was that the Germans hadn't ventured onto the farm.

Arlette's grandmother had coughed until the whites of her eyes had become patterned with tiny red veins and she'd lost her voice. She was tucked up in bed with extra blankets, every now and then gratefully receiving a drink of warm milk or weak chicken broth. Each time she drank with her granddaughter's help, clouds of white breath escaped from her wrinkled mouth into the icy bedroom. She had lost more weight, her once plump cheeks now sagging around her jowls like folds of pastry.

Each time her grandmother settled, Arlette would turn her attention to Saul. Before he'd become sick, Saul's night-time routine was to escape the cramped secret room to stretch his legs by the vegetable garden at the back of the farm. He'd spend an anxious thirty minutes in the kitchen, eating a late dinner that had been kept warm in the residual heat of the oven. After his meal he would change into clean clothes that Arlette and her grandmother had laundered. After a few minutes of further conversation while warming himself in front of the fire, he would take the lantern into the outdoor washroom and earth toilet to continue with more private ablutions. Arlette would then check that the lane was safe and signal for him to cross the yard and return to the cold barn. She would hurry after him, where they would share a lingering kiss until he crawled through the sliding partition and into the safety of the secret room.

However, since Saul had been ill, these regular late visits into the kitchen had stopped. Arlette lifted the warming stone out of the stove and wrapped it in a clean towel. She poured watery chicken soup into a mug, left the kitchen and made her way across the farmyard.

Outside was bitter and grey. Her boots broke the silence by crunching and squeaking in the snow. January's bitter blast pinched her uncovered face and flakes swirled around her like a child's snow globe. She crossed to the barn. Its doors were closed to keep out the biting wind. She felt the heat of the warming stone against her chest and nudged one door open with her knee. With the stone held in the crook of her arm and the mug in one hand, she picked up a hessian sack. It was covered in dry mud but protected her clothing to some degree when crawling through the small opening. Thankfully the last two cows were huddled together puffing and blowing at the far corner of their enclosure. Arlette sat the mug and stone on a clean area of straw and slid the partition open. Having climbed through, she turned and retrieved the items.

There had been no arms to help her stand up or hold her tightly for the past week. Thin streaks of light shone in through gaps in the stone, giving a meagre amount of daylight to see by. Arlette could make out the outline of Saul's body curled up beneath blankets on the straw mattress. His body began to shake as his cough racked through the small room, bubbling in his chest and wheezing from his lungs.

Arlette knelt beside the mattress, her teeth chattering with cold. Startled, he turned quickly. His sloe berry black eyes searched for the intruder. He relaxed on seeing her.

'It's only me, my love,' she said. 'Can you sit up? I've brought you some soup.'

Saul groaned and coughed into a corner of the blanket. He struggled to sit up.

'Here.' She handed him the mug.

He took it from her and cradled its warmth between his hands. He drained the mug and held its residual heat to his cheek.

'That feels good,' he croaked.

'I've brought you a fresh warming stone. Do you have the one I brought earlier?'

Saul reached for the cold smooth stone and handed it to her.

'Thank you. I'm sorry for being such a nuisance.' He took the warm stone from her and hugged it.

'You're not a nuisance at all. I'm just so sorry you're not able to sleep by the fire inside.'

'I'm glad you have a fire again. We'll plant more apple trees after the war. Go back inside and sit in the warmth. I need you both to stay well.'

Arlette automatically laid her palm against her stomach at the thought of their baby. She waited until he'd finished another bout of coughing.

'I'm sorry to ask but I need the jar again,' said Saul.

Arlette no longer blushed as Saul relieved himself into a large jar that had once stored olives. For six days now he'd been too sick and weak to leave his bed, so emptying the jar into a bucket several times a day had become a routine that had ceased to embarrass either of them.

An engine. Their eyes widened with fear. They both stopped dead. Each held their breath. They strained to hear through the small opening that Saul had made in the wall the previous month. Only Germans drove these days.

'Quick,' whispered Saul. 'Go.'

Arlette dropped the mug and cold stone. She hurried back through the opening. She slid the partition back into place then rubbed some dirt over the fingerprints she'd left. Grabbing the sack from the ground, she climbed back through the cattle pen. As she neared the front of the barn, she shooed the cows to the back half of their enclosure helping to conceal the partition. A car door slammed in the yard. She took a deep breath.

Arlette watched from the hidden safety of the barn. A German dressed in a grey uniform climbed out of the back of the car. He removed his peak cap and scratched his head. His hair was so severely cropped it must have been cut recently. He replaced his hat, brushed imaginary dust from his tunic and lit a cigarette. Arlette was breathing quickly. Her mind was racing with nerves. A sharp pain stung her thumb. She'd bitten her nail until it had bled.

The German surveyed the farmhouse and yard before ordering the driver to wait for him. Arlette knew she had to stop him before he knocked on the door and disturbed her grandmother – although Klara's wild barking from inside the kitchen had probably done that already, she thought.

She purposely banged the barn door shut to alert the

German to her presence, feigning surprise at seeing him. The weak sunshine glinted on his boot buckles and the gun on his belt. He was tall and broad with hollow cheeks and thin lips. His eyebrows were so fair it appeared from a distance that he didn't have any. They walked towards each other and met in the centre of the yard. Arlette could see the driver's face pressed against the car window, watching.

'Good morning. I'm Kommandant Hans Steiner. May I ask who you are?'

Arlette noticed his French was precise and unrushed although his German accent remained strong.

'Mademoiselle Blaise.'

'Do you have a first name Mademoiselle Blaise?'

'Arlette.'

He nodded slowly. His gaze was so intense she wondered if he could read her thoughts. Angry with herself because she could feel guilt burning her face, she reasoned that there was no way he could know where she had just been.

'Are you busy?' he asked, nodding towards the barn.

'I was checking the cows. This weather is not good for them.' As luck would have it, one of the cows bellowed from inside the barn.

'Who else lives here?' he asked.

'My father and grandmother.'

'And where are they?'

Arlette made a show of rubbing the mud off her hands to hide the fact that she needed to swallow hard to regain her composure. She looked up into the Kommandant's face, hoping he couldn't see her fear. 'My father is in town and my grandmother is sick in bed.'

'I'm sorry to hear that.'

He paused and Arlette was sure his eyes glanced at the

curve of her breasts that were now swelling in pregnancy. She wrapped her shawl tighter around her shoulders and shivered.

He raised his chin and continued. 'We are neighbours now. The High Command has taken over the manor for the time being and I need to speak with your father. Please inform him I shall return this evening.'

Arlette's bitten nail made her thumb ache. She nodded.

Kommandant Steiner clicked his heels together, nodded once and returned to the car. She watched it turn and drive right out of the yard in the direction of Thierry's pig farm. She sucked her sore thumb, tasting metallic blood. The imprints of the tyres and the Kommandant's footprints remained like an intrusive insult.

Chapter Eighteen

By four o'clock it was too dark to decipher colour outside. Arlette sat at her bedroom window watching for her father's return. She was weary from caring for her grandmother and Saul all day, and her own throat was now sore. She absentmindedly pulled long strips of ice from the inside edges of the wooden window frame where it had formed on the glass. Small fragments became stuck beneath her fingernails before melting. A knot of worry tightened in her stomach at the thought of Kommandant Steiner returning before her father came back from Limoges. Her father was trying to buy grain to feed the chickens because they'd run out. Since all wheat had been requisitioned it was forbidden to feed grain to poultry, but as villagers had learnt, using a little discretion and having some money made most things possible. His absence at this late hour must mean that he was finding it difficult to locate a new supply of grain. He hadn't been hopeful before leaving and told her that everyone was in the same boat, but that he would try his best.

Arlette snapped the lengths of ice in half, worrying about her father's health. He had been looking tired and thin recently and she knew he was missing Saul's manual help and camaraderie. Realising that her feet and fingers were growing numb with cold, she decided to go back downstairs and sit by the fire to wait for her father.

In the kitchen she threw some kindling and two logs on the dying embers of the fire and sat in an armchair. The fire crackled and sparked into life and she wiggled her toes in front of the orange flames. The perfumed smell of wood filled the kitchen like sweet baking and the licking flames bathed the room with a cosy glow. Glancing up at the clock on the mantelpiece, Arlette saw that it was four-thirty. Slowly the feeling in her toes returned and her eyes grew heavy. Maybe she would have a five-minute nap before checking on her grandmother again.

A loud hammering interrupted her dreams. She jumped in shock. She felt nauseous and her throat was burning but fear was her overriding emotion. Her father still wasn't back. It was probably Kommandant Steiner at the kitchen door. She noticed that the fire was mostly silver with burned ash. How had she slept for so long? She looked up at the hands of the clock. It was nearly six. Hammering disturbed the peace of the house for a second time and Klara growled.

'Stay,' said Arlette, pointing at her dog.

Arlette slipped her feet into her clogs and went to open the door, dreading another conversation with the German. He made her feel vulnerable. She unlocked the door and pulled it open. A bitter snow-scented gust of wind took her breath away and billowed at her skirt pressing it tightly to her legs. Kommandant Steiner stood at the door, now wearing a long grey coat with a high collar and a swastika on the upper arm of his sleeve. He frowned against the winter blast as a light sprinkling of snow fell about him.

He clicked his heels sharply and gave a small bow. 'Good evening, Mademoiselle Blaise.'

'Kommandant Steiner.'

'I wish to speak with your father.'

'I'm sorry, but he hasn't returned from Limoges yet.'

The German looked sceptical and pursed his lips. Arlette prayed he'd leave now because the warm kitchen air was escaping and her teeth were beginning to chatter.

'May I step inside?' he asked.

Arlette hesitated. *Please God, don't let him come in and wait with me until Father returns*, she thought.

'Mademoiselle Blaise?' His frown deepened.

Arlette stepped backwards and held the door wider for him to step inside, then closed it behind him.

'Thank you,' he said, removing his cap and tapping the snowflakes from it with his black leather gloves. They fell to the floor like wet feathers before dissolving. 'I'm sorry to disturb you at this hour but in the absence of your father, I need to inform you of some new rules. I'd be grateful if you would notify your father and grandmother of them.'

Arlette didn't reply. She wasn't going to make this easy for the German. He was in their country, intruding in their home and yet it was he who was setting the rules. She refused to have a friendly conversation, offer him refreshment or ask him to take a seat. They stood just inside the doorway and he continued, undeterred.

'We are imposing a curfew at night. Here are the rules.' He handed her a sheet of paper. 'No one must leave their property after the time stated or there will be consequences. I will overlook your father's late hour this once as he's unaware he's breaking the rules. Many of the lower ranks will be staying in empty properties in the village centre. The higher command will be living at the manor on the other side of the wood. We will need supplies, so I came to give your father notice that we are requisitioning your remaining livestock. We've also spoken to other farmers in the area and just to be clear, livestock includes everyone's horses, chickens, pigs – everything.'

He spoke of restricting their freedom and stealing from them as if he was reciting a shopping list, direct and without intonation. Arlette smelt coffee on his breath. It felt like an additional abuse because they hadn't been able to buy coffee in the shops for over a year. He looked down at her and she was aware of how tall he was. Physically powerful as well as verbally demanding. The silence seemed to stretch between them. She hated this man with his thin lips, pale eyebrows and hair so closely cropped that the contours of his skull could be clearly seen.

Arlette's mouth had turned dry and she found it difficult to speak. She repeated incredulously, 'You wish to take our remaining animals and confine us to our homes at night?'

Kommandant Steiner nodded as if Arlette had been affirming his instructions rather than repeating his instructions in disbelief.

'Good,' he said. 'Thank you for co-operating. We will be expecting your father and the animals in the morning. Please ask him to deliver them to the barn behind the manor house.' He turned and took a step towards the door before stopping. He looked over his shoulder at her. 'One more thing. I wish you to accompany your father. While he's settling the animals into the manor's barn, you will knock at the front door and ask for me.' His eyes met hers. 'I have a proposition for you.'

Chapter Nineteen

Arlette trudged after her father who was leading a convoy of two bony cows, one goat and their mare, Mimi, out of the farmyard. In the grey light and snowfall, Mimi appeared to be striped due to her protruding ribs. The family had shed tears that she'd been requisitioned to fight for the Germans in the north and wondered how their weak hungry horse could pull ammunition for hours on end. She was barely fit to trot into the village these days.

Arlette looked ahead and noticed how her father's shoulders stooped inside his thick coat. He was already covered in a layer of snowflakes. His hat was pulled low over his brow but Arlette knew that beneath the wool, deep creases of worry lined his skin. These pitiful animals were the last of their remaining livestock and they had to be delivered to the Gestapo with only a small monetary remuneration that certainly wouldn't cover their worth. She supposed the derisible amount of money they were to be given assuaged the Germans' guilt to some degree. All their provisions stored in the secret room had been eaten although Henri had killed three chickens and hidden them in snow before packing the rest into large baskets for transporting across to the manor.

Arlette wore her mother's scarf wrapped tightly around her head and neck, its brightly-coloured embroidery contemptuous of the land's bland blanket of white. She was carrying two baskets with their lids closed, but the recognisable squawking and scratching of chickens could be heard from inside the wicker containers. She followed her father through the orchard and along the edge of the woodland surrounding the manor, every now and again stopping to lay down the baskets and cough into her hands. There was a sudden rustling. She stopped walking, startled. The iridescent plumage of a pheasant ran in front of her and across the decaying plants. It squawked as it flapped into a low-level flustered flight. She held her hand to her throat, realising that she was more anxious than she'd thought.

A short while later, she stood in front of the elegant building, having left the chickens with her father near the barn. The snow underfoot was grey and grooved from tyre tracks and boot prints. Someone had cleared a path in the snow, its uneven edges appearing like ripped paper. She straightened her scarf and brushed snow from her skirt, noticing several feathers and a mustard-coloured smear near the hem. She wafted away the feathers and wiped the chicken excrement from her clothing with a handful of frosted leaves. No German was going to see her as anything but strong and dignified.

She looked up at the apricot stone of the building, which, when the sun shone, radiated a depth of colour that could be seen across the river valley. Today, however, it seemed insipid beige. Many of the numerous windows had their shutters open now that the rooms were occupied by the Gestapo and she wondered what the Lamonds would say if they knew that their beautiful home had been forced open and overrun by the enemy.

Arlette walked up the main drive through an avenue of plane trees, their branches seeming to shiver in the cold as violently as she was. She climbed six broad stone steps and faced the front door, her hand cupped against her raw throat. She felt dreadful and knew she'd caught whatever illness Saul and her grandmother were suffering from. A brass lion's head stared back at her. She lifted the metal bar beneath it and rapped on the door.

A middle-aged man opened it. He was wearing a grey

uniform but his top button was open and his hat and jacket were noticeably absent. It could almost have been Monsieur Lamond opening the door for her, except this man wore a gun at his waist.

He frowned, his French grammar poor. 'Why do you want?'

'Kommandant Steiner has given orders that he wishes to speak with me,' said Arlette.

The man hesitated before standing back and letting her walk inside. He'd obviously heard Kommandant Steiner's name even if he hadn't understood the rest of her sentence.

The vastness of the hall surprised her. She'd visited the grounds many times during grape harvesting and annual summer parties, but had never stepped inside the manor. At the back of the entrance hall curved a wide carpeted staircase that rose to the first floor. Its camber seemed to embrace a glass chandelier that hung from the ceiling. Ornate gilt-framed mirrors and oil paintings decorated the walls and a parquet floor amplified the sound of passing soldiers' footsteps. Her stomach growled at the aroma of food that wafted through the hallway. Was that bacon she could smell?

'Pleased to be following me,' ordered the soldier.

Arlette followed him across the wooden flooring. Her eyes scanned the interior and she noticed personal items strewn around the place. A red flag bearing the image of a swastika was draped over a set of antlers fixed to the wall. Boots, jackets and helmets were strewn over chair-backs and left on surfaces, along with packets of cigarettes and wine bottles, no doubt from the Lamonds' cellar. A line of family portraits curved along the wall of the staircase and, unbelievably, Arlette saw that a picture of Adolf Hitler had been nailed to one of the paintings, looking as if he was one of the family's ancestors.

She trailed after the man and passed an open doorway. Glancing inside she saw several uniformed men lounging on sofas in front of a blazing fire. They were laughing and eating in a fog of cigarette smoke. The smell of bacon was strongest at this doorway. She felt her anger rising. They had not only requisitioned some of Thierry's pigs but they had the gall to ask her neighbour to butcher the animals as well.

At the next doorway, the man stopped. 'Who is your name?'

'Mademoiselle Blaise.'

He knocked, pressed his ear closer to the door and waited. After a muffled response, he opened the door and leant forwards, only his hips and legs remaining visible to her. She waited. A soldier walked past her and blew a kiss in her direction. Arlette gave him a look of disdain, determined to remain defiant despite feeling the need to lie down and sleep. She coughed into her scarf making her chest ache.

The man stood to one side. 'Kommandant Steiner say to go in now.'

Arlette stepped inside the sizeable room that was immediately recognisable as the library. Heaving bookshelves lined two walls and lamps had been lit despite it being morning. Their golden arcs spread a warm luminosity across a bureau, a piano and swathes of maroon curtaining to either side of a large window. It seemed strange to see electricity so close to her candlelit farmhouse. A fire was crackling in the hearth, in front of which were two sofas positioned adjacent to the huge stone fire surround.

'Come in, Mademoielle Blaise.'

Arlette couldn't see Kommandant Steiner, but as she walked further inside the room, his highly-polished boots and a silver swirl of cigarette smoke became visible. He was sitting in a wide winged *bergère* chair, one leg draped over the chair's arm. He was posing arrogantly, almost as if he believed he truly was the lord of the manor. The closer she walked, the more of him was revealed. His trousers, the creases in the legs ironed knife-sharp. The buckle on his belt. The swell of his belly beneath his shirt. Badges on his chest. Finally, his thin-lipped hard features. He smiled with such self-importance it resembled a sneer.

'Very fetching,' he said.

'Sorry?'

He removed his leg from the arm of the chair and stood up, flicking the cigarette butt into the fire. 'Your scarf. It's a welcome touch of colour in this drab countryside.'

Arlette bit her tongue. Suggesting that he returned to his own countryside if he didn't like the colours of France wouldn't be the most helpful way to start this unwanted conversation.

'It's my mother's.'

He frowned. 'You didn't mention your mother when I called at the farm yesterday.'

'She's dead.' Arlette wasn't going to make this conversation easy for him.

He seemed wrong-footed and stretched his neck to one side and rubbed it. 'I'm sorry to hear that. Please, take a seat.'

'I'd prefer to stand. My father's waiting outside. We've brought our remaining livestock, so now you have it all and we have nothing.'

Kommandant Steiner bit his lip and stared at her. 'I am trying to be polite, Mademoiselle Blaise. I sense your bitterness but advise you to accept your new situation. I'm in charge of the village's requisitioning and also the placing of my men in local accommodation. It's also my responsibility to ensure that all the rules are obeyed. I presume you've spoken to your father about the curfew.'

'Yes.'

'Good. You see, we're progressing.'

Arlette wasn't sure how much longer she could put on this bold front. The heat from the fire was causing her to feel unsteady and her head ached. Kommandant Steiner didn't appear to be in clear focus and she was afraid that her nausea could make her run from the room at any minute to find the nearest bathroom. That would certainly puncture her bravado.

She coughed into her mother's scarf.

'You seem unwell, Mademoiselle Blaise.'

'I have a cold. I'm fine.'

'May I arrange a glass of water for you?'

Despite wanting to remain strong, Arlette was desperate for cold water to quench her thirst and ease her throat. 'Thank you.'

Kommandant Steiner nodded curtly and walked towards the door. He shouted something in German, a harsh language that sounded to Arlette as if it were spoken solely in consonants. While his back was turned, Arlette seated herself on a sofa at the furthest end from the fire. She told herself she made the decision to sit by herself; she hadn't handed him a small victory.

He returned and sat on the opposite sofa, leaning forwards while resting his forearms on his knees. 'I have a proposition for you. How would you like a job?'

She tried to hide her surprise. 'I have a job. I look after my father, my grandmother and the animals.'

'A sore point I know, but you no longer have animals to worry about and your father has a son's duty towards his mother. Yes, I see your next question in your eyes. I know she is your paternal grandmother because I have access to all the villagers' records.'

'Spring will soon be here and I have vegetables to grow and nurture. I cook for my family and I have a silk business which, despite its small size, demands much of my time.' Arlette wasn't going to admit to him that she had ceased working on the family silk business until the war was over, simply because there wasn't anyone prepared to buy her cocoons. If people had money nowadays, it was spent on food or fuel.

There was a knock at the door and the same man who had shown Arlette to the library brought in a glass of water. Arlette took it gratefully and drank half of the cool water at once. She cradled the glass in her cupped palms.

'If you were to accept my offer, it would provide yourself and your family with extra food,' he said.

'We have sufficient and, as I said, we'll soon be growing vegetables again.'

Hans Steiner stood up and rubbed his hands over his shaven head that made a rasping sound. He raised his voice. 'You are a stubborn woman, Mademoiselle Blaise. I am offering you employment and food.'

Arlette felt satisfied. She'd won the first small victory of the battle. He had lost his temper and shown emotion.

'We have your cows so you no longer have milk, butter, cheese or meat.' He marched around the sofa like it was a parade ground, clapping one hand into the other to stress each point he made. 'We have your chickens so you no longer have eggs or white meat. It is January. The soil is like rock so there won't be any vegetables for a long time.'

Arlette closed her eyes. The second victory had been won by Kommandant Steiner. She drank the remaining water.

'Now, will you listen to my proposition?'

Arlette squeezed the glass and nodded.

His thin lips stretched into a satisfied smile. 'There are sixteen soldiers of the High Command living here, each delegated with different responsibilities ranging from requisitioning, to law enforcement, to administration or seeking black marketeers, thieves, Jews and such like.'

Arlette felt her anger burning as hot as her fever. He'd disparagingly linked the words Jew and thieves together, even though he'd just ordered the removal of their animals – their livelihood. Did wearing a uniform make it any less than thievery?

'You're right,' said Arlette, her throat hot and dry but determined not to ask him for more water. 'Thieves should be arrested. It's morally wrong to take that which doesn't belong to you.'

She held his gaze. He looked away.

He continued. 'We need a cook and a housekeeper. You will work here from eight in the morning until six in the evening. For your service, your family will be allowed extra coupons for rations.'

Her fever was preventing her from thinking clearly. She spoke with vitriol without giving much thought to the consequences. 'Extra coupons? Do you seriously think I'll spend my days preparing meals for Germans, for extra coupons? Do you have any idea what coupons buy nowadays? Stale bread, rusty tins of food and meat that makes people sick; and that's if they're lucky enough to find a store that has anything left on its shelves. Do you think that a few extra loaves of hard bread would entice me to work here?'

'Enough!' Kommandant Steiner stood up. 'I have given you more time and civility than you deserve. I was asking for your services politely, but I can see now that I was wrong to afford you such courtesy. You *will* work here. It's an order.'

Arlette stood up and wobbled slightly, feeling disorientated. She brushed imaginary droplets of water from her skirt to disguise the fact she felt dizzy. 'I think

I'd better leave now. My father is waiting and it's still snowing outside.'

Kommandant Steiner took a step forwards, towering above her. She could see an infected boil on his neck where his starched shirt collar had rubbed against his skin. She turned to leave but he grasped her wrist.

'I will make this as clear as I can.' He appeared to be hissing through his teeth. 'I have great authority here and can arrest anyone for any misdemeanour. Perhaps your father has sold something on the black market? Maybe not, but I certainly know that he was out after curfew last night. That is against the rules and punishable.'

'But ... but you know he wasn't aware of the new curfew rules then,' Arlette stammered.

'Do I?' He smiled, insincerely. 'Also, as I mentioned earlier, I have access to documents and every household's inhabitants. Where is your brother, Gilbert Blaise? A mystery, don't you think? Maybe he is hiding in your attic? Perhaps we should search your farm, Mademoiselle Blaise. I don't think cowardice would go down too well in this small village if the villagers should be made aware of this fact. Or perhaps he's joined a pathetic band of men who believe they're saving France?' He held up his hand, palm facing her face to halt her response. 'Then again, if you agree to work here, maybe your father's rule-breaking and your brother's disappearance will be placed at the bottom of my list of infractions.'

His voice had begun to echo in Arlette's head and the colours in the room appeared to swirl into each other. Her head and chest ached and she realised she had to sit down again. She reached for the arm of the sofa but all pain and dread disappeared in an instant.

She was unaware that the Kommandant had caught her as she fell.

Chapter Twenty

Arlette opened her eyes a fraction, her mind still in that indistinct moment where dreams and reality overlap. An insipid ray of sunlight shone through the gap in the curtains, highlighting dust that floated in the room. She lay in bed feeling so much warmer and more comfortable than she usually felt on waking, added to which the reassuring sound of Montverre's church bells chimed in the distance across the river valley. She closed her eyes again, her thoughts finding clarity as she remembered she must get up and make Saul and her grandmother some breakfast. Her hand reached instinctively to her sore throat and she swallowed painfully. Then, her whole body stiffened where she lay.

Curtains!

The farmhouse didn't have curtains upstairs in the bedrooms. It had shutters. She was instantly wide awake and staring up at an unfamiliar ceiling rose from where an ornate light fitting hung. She sat up causing her head to throb. Another sound flooded the room. Rhythmical pounding was coming from outside the window. Dragging her aching body out of bed, she groped her way to the curtains. Her white knuckles grasped the sill to prevent her weakened body from falling. She pulled aside a handful of material, taking a few seconds to focus on the scene below.

Line upon line of soldiers dressed in grey-green uniforms marched up and down the wide expanse of land between the manor's barn and the house itself. She could see Kommandant Steiner standing at the front. He was dressed in full uniform and shouting orders while clutching a baton. The snow in the grounds was crushed and bruised from the stamping of feet, causing one of the men to slip on the grey slush beneath his boots. She was horrified that she had fallen asleep at the German occupied manor, but couldn't think clearly enough to remember what had happened.

Arlette sat on the bed shaking from shock and cold. She remembered meeting Kommandant Steiner in the library, but couldn't recall leaving the room after he'd threatened her family with severe repercussions if she didn't agree to work for him. She must have fainted or fallen asleep a few hours ago, after all, it was still daylight so she couldn't have slept for too long. Her main concern now was to get out of the building before the soldiers had finished their drill.

She looked around the wide floorboards for her boots, but couldn't see them. Then something dawned on her that made her gasp in shame. She was still wearing one of her mother's sheer petticoats, but the rest of her clothing was gone. Her hands flew to her gaping mouth at the appalling thought that Kommandant Steiner may have undressed her. Surely her father wouldn't have allowed such a thing to happen. He wouldn't have left her here to the mercy of the Gestapo.

She began to hyperventilate. What if he had been arrested like Kommandant Steiner had threatened yesterday? How could he possibly survive those awful prison conditions? And who would have taken food to Saul and her grandmother?

Arlette dragged her aching limbs around the bedroom. She searched in drawers. She pulled open wardrobe doors and lifted the lid to a blanket box. Her clothes weren't there. The frantic search set off a bout of coughing that left her weak and clutching her sore chest. Stumbling back to the window, she saw the soldiers dispersing from ranks to the sound of boot-spurs clanking. At that moment, Kommandant Steiner looked up. Their eyes met. Arlette gasped and took a step back from the window. He was bound to come upstairs and speak with her now. She sat on the edge of the wrought iron bed and pulled a blanket around her shoulders for warmth and modesty. And waited.

She was under no illusion that he might not come. She knew that at that moment he would be making his way towards her bedroom. The silence filled the room while she waited. The manor occasionally groaned like the timbers of a wooden ship lost at sea. A sudden gust of wind rattled the sash windows. Then it came. A distant tap-tapping of footsteps that grew louder and closer until they stopped. A man cleared his throat preceding a knock on the door.

'Where's my father?' she called.

The handle turned and Kommandant Steiner stepped inside the room. He was dressed in a thick grey coat, leather gloves, highly polished jackboots and a peaked cap. In one hand he still held a baton and in the other a half smoked cigarette.

'I'm pleased to see you have recovered somewhat.'

'Where is my father and why am I here? I need my clothes.'

'I can see that you're still angry but you'll learn that it won't help matters. I don't expect gratitude, but you were too sick to go home yesterday, so we—'

'Yesterday!'

He pulled back the cuff of his coat and looked at his watch. 'You have been asleep for twenty hours.'

'That's impossible. I don't believe you. My father would never have let me stay here for that long.' She thought of Saul and wondered who had looked after him for the past day.

Her panic caused her to suffer another bout of coughing, so fierce that she retched. Embarrassed that the German was watching, she struggled to regain her composure.

'Your father is a sensible man. He listened to the doctor's advice and could see you had a bad fever. He understood that you were too sick to be moved from here. It was snowing and he would have been foolish to try.'

'I need my clothes.'

'Your clothes are being washed and your boots are being dried.'

'You had no right—' Arlette protested, but at that moment a younger man with a thin moustache appeared in the doorway behind Kommandant Steiner.

After a few seconds of whispered discussion, the German turned back to her.

'Before manoeuvres this morning, I arranged for someone to help you to freshen up. They've arrived so I'll send them in.' He clicked his heels and nodded once before leaving.

The door was left ajar and Arlette listened as the two soldiers walked back down the corridor. She was horrified that a stranger had been ordered to help wash her, but without clothing or footwear, she was helpless. Eventually, a quieter tread was heard walking towards her room. Arlette's bravado finally dissolved when she saw her best friend standing in the doorway. Francine closed the door behind her and hurried into Arlette's open arms. They sat side by side on the edge of the bed and hugged each other.

'I'm so glad it's you. I can't believe I've been here for a whole day,' said Arlette.

'You were very poorly. Kommandant Steiner brought your father inside until the doctor arrived. He gave you a sedative and left some medicine to reduce your fever. He gave strict instructions that you couldn't be moved back home until you were stronger.'

'But who—' Arlette pointed at her flimsy under garment.

'When the doctor had left, your father came to our farm to ask for mother's help, but she'd gone into the village to help Mrs Bouvier deliver her baby. So I came and got you out of your wet clothes and tucked you into bed. I stayed with you all day too.'

Arlette hugged her friend. 'Thank you very much. I can't tell you what a relief it is to know it was you.'

'I took your clothes home to wash and your boots needed drying by the fire.'

'Did you bring them with you?'

'The doctor said it would be at least forty-eight hours before you could set foot outside,' said Francine.

'No, I can't stay Ci-Ci. Not with *them*.'

'Kommandant Steiner was really worried about you. He paid the doctor and has been kind.'

'Francine! Germans aren't kind. They're cruel. They're murderers. They're anything but kind.'

'I meant with you. He seemed to genuinely care.'

'If I was a Jew he would have shot me, so don't try and persuade me that he has a conscience. Yesterday he blackmailed me into accepting a job here to cook for the High Command and threatened to send Father to prison and to hunt Gilbert down if I didn't. How's that for kindness?'

Francine pinched her lips and touched her felt rose, now a permanent feature on whatever she wore. 'How do they know about Gilbert?'

'His name's on paperwork at the Mairie's office. The Kommandant suggested he might be in hiding or working against Germans and threatened to search the farm. That's why I have no choice but to work here. I can't gamble with Father and Grandma's freedom.'

'Of course not. Gilbert would be devastated if he knew he'd compromised you in this way.'

Arlette sneezed three times and held her head. 'I hate this war. It could be years before he's home and I'm not sure what's more dangerous, doing what he's doing now or working on the farm.'

Francine whispered. 'I overheard Papa telling Maman that two members of the Resistance were hanged in public when they were caught last week.'

'Remember that when you try to tell me that Kommandant Steiner is kind.' Arlette sighed. 'Oh, I can't believe I have to stay here another day.'

Francine paused before looking directly at Arlette. 'I know your secret.'

Arlette met her gaze. 'You do?'

Francine nodded. 'Why didn't you mention it? I'm your best friend.'

Arlette laid her hand over Francine's and whispered, 'It's not that I don't trust you. But the fewer people who know that we're hiding Saul in the secret room, the safer it will be for everyone.'

'Saul's in the barn?' she exclaimed.

'Shhh!' hissed Arlette. 'I thought you said you knew.'

'Not that,' whispered Francine. 'He never left then? Where is he?'

Arlette shook her head. 'In the secret room.' She had another attack of coughing.

Francine patted her back until she'd finished. 'Do you have any idea how dangerous that is? Especially now the Gestapo live here.'

'Of course I do,' snapped Arlette. 'But not as dangerous as letting him roam the countryside at the mercy of Germans or the elements. I love him. What were we supposed to do, wave goodbye and forget we knew him?

Only Grandma, Father and I know where he is. Except now you do.' Arlette grasped Francine's hands. 'Please promise you won't tell anyone. Not even your parents.'

'I promise. My head's spinning with all this new information,' said Francine. 'The secret I meant was that you're pregnant.'

Arlette's jaw fell open. 'I don't understand! Only Saul knows.'

'I got you undressed yesterday and having helped Maman with pregnant women over the years, I've seen enough swollen breasts to recognise the early stages of pregnancy. Then I remembered that bout of sickness you had and how you've suddenly gone off eggs.'

'That's just as well, isn't it? We've had our entire livestock requisitioned.'

'Don't change the subject. You can't keep it a secret for long and how are you going to explain your pregnancy when all the young men have left the village?'

'Maybe I won't grow too big and I can wear smocks. Maybe the baby can live with Saul in the secret room.'

'You know that's not realistic. Your baby will only have to cry once when the Germans are visiting and Saul will be discovered and arrested. And your family too.'

Arlette sighed. 'I've no idea what I'm going to do. I'm trying not to think that far ahead. At the moment it's difficult to believe that in seven months' time I'll have a baby.' She pressed the tips of her fingers against her temples. 'My head aches and I feel like a tractor tyre is sitting on my chest. I might just lie down again for ten minutes. I'm scared, Ci-Ci.'

Francine settled her friend under the blankets and stroked her hair. 'I know. Try not to worry too much,' she said, lying down next to her. 'Lots of people love you and we're all here to help. You're not on your own.'

Chapter Twenty-One

The new year continued as the old one had ended, with little food and an abundance of suspicion. Neighbours peered from behind shutters, out of attic windows and through gaps in doorways. Everyone was keeping watch on the comings and goings of the Gestapo. Selling and buying on the black market had reduced drastically due to the enemy's proximity and the curfew restricted such activity anyway.

Everyone's health had improved at the farmhouse, although Saul's cough had lingered due to the fact that he was still living in the damp barn. Hot weak broth, warming stones and mountains of blankets could only help so much. Since Arlette had begun sharing her medicine with him, his fever appeared to have eased.

In order to delay working at the manor, Arlette used her wiles to negotiate not commencing work until the following Monday. Arlette had cited hers and her grandmother's ill health and reasoned that starting work too soon could slow her recovery. The Kommandant had seemed pleased that she'd spoken to him with more openness and he had willingly acquiesced to her suggestion. Although she'd maintained sufficient reserve to appear proper, she felt ashamed for smiling half-heartedly at Kommandant Steiner during this conversation. However, she also felt pleased that she had won another small victory by manipulating him.

And so it was on Saturday 16th January 1943, two days before she was due to become cook and housekeeper for the Gestapo, that she and Francine had walked into Montverre village. They were taking a small bunch of snowdrops to Arlette's mother at *cimetière* Saint-Pierre and then meeting Francine's mother at the mayor's office where she'd been cleaning – albeit for the Germans now as they'd commandeered the building. But as Monique Giroux had said, 'Cleaning is cleaning and money is money during hard times. One man's dirty toilet is much the same as another's.'

Clutching the delicate bunch of flowers between her fingers, Arlette left the farmyard and turned towards Francine's home at the bottom of the hill. Although the snow had melted and the temperature had risen above freezing, the sky was gunmetal-grey and clouds hung low and heavy over the river valley. The summit of the hill looked like an island in a white sea – truly a house in the clouds.

Arlette walked through the mist, the moisture dampening her face and clothes. She watched her boots while she walked, enabling her to keep to the road and prevent her from falling into a ditch. By the time she had reached the Giroux's farm, she had passed through the cloud and the air was now clear, the rooftops glistening like fish scales due to the recent rain. Bruno was wandering around his farmyard. He looked despondent.

'Morning,' he mumbled, opening the gate for her. 'How are you? I've heard that you and Henri's mother have been poorly.'

Arlette stepped through, avoiding the worst of the mud and puddles. 'I'm much better thank you, Monsieur Giroux. Grandma's stronger too.'

He walked with her towards the kitchen door, sucking deeply on a cigarette but not attempting to continue the conversation until he muttered, 'They have our animals, our crops and our village. Our dignity, no less. Now they want an hour. They want our bloody time. Where will it end?'

Arlette looked at Bruno but he didn't seem to be directly addressing her or waiting for a response. He walked past the kitchen door shaking his head. He continued on towards the barn without saying goodbye to her. She'd known him all her life and the change in this once handsome, optimistic and humorous man was almost tangible. His mood also seemed to echo that of her father. The Germans appeared to have stolen the men's spirits as well as their livelihoods.

She knocked on the door and stepped inside without waiting for an answer, the custom in Montverre. Inside the kitchen a log fire burned in the grate. The air was damp with condensation due to laundry being draped and drying over every piece of available furniture.

'Is that you, Papa?' Francine called.

Arlette could hear her running downstairs. 'No, it's me.'

Her friend came into the kitchen. 'Hello.'

'I spoke with your father outside. He seems upset about something.'

Francine nodded. 'He can't bear the fact that the Germans have made us all turn our clocks back one hour in line with German time. He refuses to change his watch or the house clocks. He's also had a row with Maman about her cleaning for the enemy. She says that what small amount she earns helps to buy essentials now that he's not farming. I think his pride is hurt because she is the one earning at the moment. But at least we have our fathers at home. There are rumours that older men are being enlisted to work in German factories.'

'I'd heard that farmers may be exempt because they need to work the land. Besides, our fathers are too old. Grandma said she heard that it was men up to the age of thirty.'

Francine draped a shawl around her shoulders. 'I don't know how farmers can work the land if their machinery, produce and livestock have been taken.'

'Surely the Germans will want the farmers to continue

growing wheat and vegetables, if only to steal everything for themselves?'

'Maybe.'

Arlette stamped her feet in a childlike manner. 'I can't bear the thought that I'll be working for them on Monday.'

Francine pulled on her boots. 'Try not to worry. Remember that you're agreeing to work at the manor to protect your loved ones from any consequences.' Francine shook her head. 'How has it come to this? Men can't protect or provide for their families the way they have done in the past.'

Arlette shrugged. 'Have you heard from your brothers recently?' she asked.

They left the kitchen and closed the door behind them.

'We had a letter from René mid-December. Someone left it in the chicken coop. He said that he and Hubert were both tired but well. He obviously couldn't say what they were doing or where they were.'

'Still, it must have been a huge relief for your mother to have received a letter.'

'It was. She was delighted to have heard they were safe before Christmas. She said the news was a special gift.'

'I wonder when Gilbert will be in touch next,' said Arlette.

'Soon, I hope.'

Before long they arrived at the ornate metal gates to *cimetière* Saint-Pierre. To one side of the lychgate an arch had been carved into the wall where a crucifix of Christ stood as a shrine. Shrivelled leaves lay in front of Christ's weathered metal body. Withered fronds obscured a rusty stain that ran down the wooden cross onto the stone. Arlette slid the stem of a single white flower behind one of Christ's shoulder blades and made the sign of the cross. The gate squeaked when they pushed it open and walked the well-trodden path towards Fleur Blaise's grave.

Moving forwards, the friends passed stone angels and crosses that stood alongside more modest plaques and stones. Arlette looked at the familiar simple arched headstone beneath which her mother lay. She brushed a twig from its rough surface and paused for a moment in prayer before bending to remove dried leaves and berries that she'd placed there before she'd become ill. The snowdrops had already grown limp in her hands but she laid them at the base of the stone. She smiled at Francine. There was no need to speak because they'd shared this experience too many times over the years to feel the need for words. They left the cemetery and walked the short distance into Montverre village.

Turning the corner into the square, they collided with a gangly boy running in the opposite direction. Something dropped to the floor. Arlette recognised the shoemaker's teenage son, Maurice.

'Oh, Maurice. Sorry.'

'I didn't steal it, honest. I found it on the floor.'

Arlette saw a seed potato lying in the dirt. Roots were growing from its eyes and it looked inedible. 'Don't worry. I wasn't accusing you. But it might be helpful not to run so fast next time you find something. It'll draw less attention from the Germans.'

'You mean the filthy Boches,' he said, before lowering his head. 'Sorry.'

Arlette picked up the seed potato and handed it to him. 'You don't need to say sorry, Maurice. I know you have good reason to be angry, but try to make it less obvious in future or you might find yourself in big trouble. Haven't you noticed how everyone moves slowly and quietly, trying not to be noticed?'

Maurice shrugged. 'Can I go now?'

Arlette smiled. 'Of course you can. Next time you're

passing our farm, pop inside and I'll find you something to eat. Even though it's watery, we've usually got some sort of broth bubbling on the stove.'

'Thank you, miss.'

She watched the skeletal youth run towards the church and disappear into an alleyway. She pulled a face at Francine. It was dreadful to see a once chubby lad turn into a gangly petty thief. She remembered seeing him sitting with his father in the summertime, painting flowers onto wooden clogs that the family business produced. The shoemaker had died fighting for his country and everyone knew that Maurice's mother had all but lost her mind following the news. The poor lad was starving, freezing and neglected.

They walked arm in arm towards the building where the Mairie used to work before he fled the invading troops. They used to wait for Francine's mother inside, sitting on chairs in the waiting room but since the Nazis had taken over the offices, they hadn't stepped inside.

Arlette stamped her feet and hugged her upper arms in an effort to keep warm. Montverre village centre was as quiet as usual since being occupied. The displaced families had left, either being arrested or moved on. A couple of locals scampered like frightened mice to the store clutching coupons. They would emerge from the shop and hurry back home again, heads bowed while carrying a dark loaf. No longer did friends call a greeting from one open window to another. There were no gatherings of men outside cafés playing cards in the sunshine. Germans would saunter across the square, hands thrust into warm coat pockets, seemingly oblivious to the suffering around them. They occasionally stopped to talk and share a cigarette with fellow soldiers. A large red flag emblazoned with a spidery swastika billowed from the flagpole in the centre of the village square, leaving no one in any doubt as to who was in charge now.

Monique Giroux bustled out of the door rummaging in her handbag and muttering under her breath. She walked straight past the girls.

'Maman,' called Francine.

Monique looked up and turned, surprised to see them. 'Oh, girls. What are you doing here?'

'We were fed up so we decided to take some flowers to Fleur's grave and then meet you.'

Monique kissed them both but seemed agitated. 'That's kind of you but I wasn't going straight home today.'

'Never mind. We'll come to the store with you.'

'I wasn't going to the store either.' Monique pointed across the square but didn't elaborate.

'What's the matter?' asked Francine.

Monique tutted. 'I suppose you can keep a secret. I was going to old Monsieur Péricaud's house to ...' She looked around to make sure no one was listening. '... to listen to his wireless.'

Francine gasped. 'You can't! What if you're caught? You know it's illegal to listen to the wireless now.'

'Who would suspect an old man of eighty-two to defy orders? How else do we find out what's happening in the world?'

'Your mother's right, Ci-Ci,' said Arlette. 'It's important to know what's happening outside Montverre. How do you think villagers hide things in time, stay away from certain areas and find out how the Allies are doing? We need to know what the Germans have up their sleeves.' She looked at Monique Giroux. 'I want to come too.'

Francine was shocked. 'Don't be ridiculous.'

'It's important.' Arlette opened her eyes wide to convey

the message she couldn't speak. She needed to know the latest situation regarding Jewish citizens.

'I think you're both mad,' said Francine. 'I'll wait outside and keep watch. I'll knock on the window if any soldiers come close to the house.'

Ten minutes later, Arlette, Monique and half a dozen villagers crowded around a wooden-cased wireless in a small musty sitting room. A bare bulb swung from a wire in the middle of the ceiling and cast eerie shadows. Monsieur Péricaud's gnarled fingers twiddled the Bakelite dials, causing the speaker to hiss with high-pitched squeaks as he searched for reception. Then, a clear voice spoke to them all through the wireless.

'*Ici Londres, demain à ...*'

The group listened in silence. They were informed of the Allies' progress and disappointments, of battles that had been fought on the ground and in the skies and of Hitler's latest speech. They heard how the US Marine Corps and US Army aircraft attacked ten Japanese destroyer ships and of the attacks on Tripoli by the British. The wireless crackled, momentarily distorting news about a terrific attack involving well over a thousand sorties by bombers and fighters. Enemy airfields, including lines of communication and encampments of guns and troops, were all bombed. British submarines in the Mediterranean successfully damaged and sunk enemy ships and their air forces were swept from the skies. It was all heartening news to relay back to others.

Arlette didn't realise just how on edge she was until Francine rapped on the glass pane making her jump. Monique scrambled towards the window and peered through a gap in the tobacco-stained curtains

'Grey uniforms! It's the High Command from the manor. We've got to go but not all at once, mind.'

Chapter Twenty-Two

One by one they left Monsieur Péricaud's house. Each person walked in different directions. Arlette linked arms with Francine and crossed the road with Monique. No one had stepped out of the sleek black car since it had parked five minutes earlier.

'Keep your heads down,' said Monique.

'It is Kommandant Steiner's car,' said Arlette. 'It's the same one he used when he came to look for Father.'

They were almost at the corner of the square when a deep rumbling filled the air, becoming louder with each second. Shortly the crunch of boots added to the engine's noise, causing everyone in the vicinity to stop and look.

'It's a tank,' said Francine, pointing in disbelief.

From the opposite corner of the marketplace moved a surprisingly fast tank. A squat tower sat on the top of the vehicle, inside which stood a soldier visible to the waist. Behind the tank marched columns of men dressed in heavy grey coats and boots laced to their ankles. Following the men came a motorcycle with a sidecar. The parade halted in the centre of the square beneath the swastika flag.

'What's going on?'

Arlette turned to see Maurice standing beside them, a speck of raw potato nestled in the corner of his mouth. He shivered with cold.

'We don't know yet, Maurice, but no doubt someone will tell us.'

'Look,' hissed Francine. 'It *is* Kommandant Steiner. He's getting out of the car.'

Arlette turned to speak to Maurice. 'Keep away from—' But the skinny youth had vanished.

More villagers emerged from their houses like hermit

crabs from their shells. The motorcyclist dismounted and removed his gloves, throwing them on the seat of the sidecar. He walked towards Kommandant Steiner and both men could be seen with heads bowed towards each other in conversation.

'I don't like the look of this,' said Monique. 'I'm going a little closer to see what's happening.'

'Maman, stay here,' hissed Francine. 'Arlette! Not you as well.'

Arlette walked in step with Monique towards the men. They stopped a short distance away. The motorcyclist returned to his bike and reached inside the sidecar, retrieving a cone-shaped megaphone. He strode to the flagpole and stood beside the soldiers who were standing in line looking straight ahead. His shoulders rose when he inhaled and raised the megaphone to his mouth.

'All Jews are to assemble here now. Anyone knowing the whereabouts of a Jew must inform Kommandant Steiner.' The man pointed him out. 'Anyone found to be aiding or hiding a Jew will be arrested and face a firing squad. All Jewish materials such as books by Jewish authors, symbols, religious objects or clothing must be collected together now and brought into the square for burning. You have a short amount of time to accomplish this before these troops will search your properties to ensure you have complied.'

Monique steadied Arlette who had wobbled. 'What's the matter? Are you feeling unwell?'

'I feel a little light-headed. I think I'd better get home.' For what felt like the hundredth time since the war had found their village, she silently thanked the Lord that they lived away from its centre.

Francine joined them and spoke to Arlette with wide eyes, understanding what this announcement meant to the Blaise family. 'You need to go home. We all need to leave now.'

Arlette swallowed. 'Yes.'

The women turned to leave but stopped when Kommandant Steiner shouted, 'Halt!'

All three swung round terrified. They mistakenly believed they were being ordered to stay. Just at that moment a thin figure darted towards the shoemaker's shop. They watched Kommandant Steiner hurry towards the person while pushing the front of his coat to one side. Arlette gasped. The Kommandant pulled a gun from his belt and aimed. A shot resonated around the marketplace. At first there was silence. Everyone looked towards Maurice who was leaning against the shoemaker's door. He turned towards Kommandant Steiner while clutching a red patch of blood on his stomach. He coughed and spat blood towards the German.

'You filthy Boche. You murdering Hun. You—'

Kommandant Steiner raised his gun and a second shot echoed around the village. Maurice's head was thrown back several inches cracking against the shop door before he fell lifeless to the floor. A red starburst was sprayed across the door's paintwork.

The village was silent.

Kommandant Steiner replaced his gun and straightened his coat before walking towards the soldier holding the megaphone. He took it from him and raised it.

'I shot a thief. Anyone caught stealing will meet the same fate. Continue with the ejection of Jews and Jewish materials immediately. You have ten minutes before your houses are searched. Under no circumstances are you to remove the body until the investigation is concluded. It will remain as a warning to you all.'

Arlette looked down at Maurice's twisted body, a circle of blood at his stomach and a bullet hole above his left eye. In his hands were clutched the motorcyclist's black leather gloves.

Chapter Twenty-Three

Arlette burst through the kitchen door, surprising both her father and grandmother who were sitting by the open fire. Grandma Blaise put down her darning and Henri stood up.

'Whatever's the matter, *ma pêche*?' he said, curling an arm around her shoulders.

He led her towards the fire and coaxed her into his still-warm chair. Klara jumped up to greet her but was ordered down by Grandma Blaise. Arlette was almost hysterical and finding it difficult to catch her breath.

'What's happened? Are you all right?'

'Maurice. His hands. He was cold. He took some gloves. Kommandant Steiner shot him.'

'Calm down. You're not making any sense, my dear,' said Grandma Blaise. 'Henri,' she said, turning to her son. 'Fetch a swallow of *pastis* with a little water for the poor girl.'

Henri returned holding a tiny glass between his thumb and forefinger and encouraged his daughter to take a sip. Arlette gulped a mouthful and coughed as the alcohol stung the back of her throat.

'Now try again,' said Henri.

Arlette wiped her wet cheeks on her sleeve and sniffed. 'A tank came into the square with lots of Germans. Everyone was ordered to reveal where Jews were hidden and told to throw out everything Jewish in their homes. But—'

'What?' her father urged.

'We'd been talking to Maurice. You know, the shoemaker's son?'

Henri nodded.

'He was starving. He was so thin and cold. Kommandant Steiner killed him for taking some gloves to keep his hands warm. He was right in front of me.' Arlette sobbed into her hands. Grandma Blaise put another log on the fire and wrapped a blanket around her granddaughter's shoulders. Henri knelt in front of her and took hold of her hands.

'I'm sorry you've seen such a terrible thing, *ma pêche*, but I need you to tell me what was said about the Jews in the village.'

'They're sending soldiers to search houses for Jews and Jewish materials. Anyone found hiding a Jew will be shot.'

Henri nodded. 'Well, we knew the time would come, didn't we? There's still time to move Saul before they arrive if anyone wants to change their mind about him staying.'

'Of course he stays,' said Grandma Blaise.

'I haven't changed my mind,' Arlette cried.

'That's three of us in agreement then. We need to warn him that it'll be dangerous for us to visit him as often as we do.'

'I'll go and speak with him,' said Arlette.

'Be very careful,' said Grandma Blaise.

Saul helped Arlette to stand up after she'd crawled through the opening into the secret room. They clung to each other for a few moments. His stubble had grown into a full beard, his hair had grown long and he was wrapped in a blanket spiked with pieces of straw. His face was pale and he no longer flicked his head to move his hair from his eyes. It was now long enough to tuck behind his ears.

'I've brought you some water to wash with and a little food,' said Arlette.

She bent to retrieve a few things that she'd left at the entrance before handing Saul a saucepan of hot water, a cloth and some cooked fish that Henri had caught in the river. Saul laid the items down and beckoned to her, the blanket resembling wings as it draped from his outstretched arms.

'Come here,' said Saul. 'I need to hold you again.'

Arlette sank against him, the blanket engulfing her body as he embraced her. She felt his chest rising and falling while she laid her cheek against him.

'How are you feeling?' he asked.

Arlette could feel the warmth of his breath on her hair as he spoke. She looked up at him and smiled. 'I'm fine, but I need to speak with you. It's important. Let's sit down.'

They moved to Saul's straw mattress where they settled themselves facing each other, holding hands.

'Things have escalated, my love. It's become even more dangerous,' said Arlette. 'Francine and I went into the village this morning and the Germans were actively searching houses for Jewish people.'

'Don't look so frightened. We knew it would happen,' said Saul. 'It's only the bad weather that has delayed the searches.'

'It means I can't visit as often for a while. I'll bring you food and water late at night and stay for as long as I can, but I won't be able to come in daylight while things are so tense.'

She didn't mention Maurice's execution. Why add to the horror of Saul's imprisonment?

'I understand. Please don't worry about me. I have books to read by the gap in the wall and I'm blessed to have this hiding place. I get to see the woman I love every day. So many of my people don't have such luxuries.' He kissed her forehead.

'Will you promise me to stay quiet all the time?' asked Arlette. 'Not a sneeze or a cough unless it's deep into your blanket.'

'I'll be so quiet that I'll make a mouse sound as if it's wearing clogs.'

Arlette wrapped her arms around his shoulders. 'This will end one day. Remember you said we'd share a bottle of the Lamonds' wine by the river? Maybe it'll be this summer.'

They froze. The barn doors had creaked open. Footfall could be heard scuffing the floor now that the cows were gone. A voice called in a loud whisper.

'Arlette.'

Arlette pulled a confused face at Saul. She stood up and hurried towards the small entrance, crouching down to answer. 'Gilbert! What are you doing here in daylight?'

'Who are you talking to?'

It suddenly dawned on her that her brother didn't know that Saul was still here. She turned to Saul who had joined her at the small opening. 'I'll be back later tonight. Remember, not a sound,' she whispered.

She turned to leave but Gilbert's head had already appeared through the opening. He looked dishevelled and his hair had grown even longer.

'Bloody fools,' he said, crawling all the way through. He stood up and faced his sister without embracing her. 'What the hell is he doing here?' He held his head in his hands before holding them out in front of him as if he was about to catch a ball. 'Do you know what they do with people who shelter Jews? I can't believe Father would allow this.'

She grabbed her brother's forearm. 'It's safe here. It'll be all right.'

'I've waited for an hour in the orchard just to be able to

move without being seen, and how the hell do you think I knew you were here? I heard voices through the wall.'

They all looked at the small gap Saul had made in the solid wall that faced the lane.

Gilbert turned to face Saul, pushing his shoulder roughly. 'How dare you put my family in danger? Why did you agree to stay?'

Arlette stepped between them before Saul could answer. She faced her brother. 'We love each other. I'm pregnant.'

Gilbert's mouth fell open. 'I hope you're not expecting me to say congratulations. You certainly know how to complicate matters, don't you? You're having a bastard with a Jew.'

Saul grasped Gilbert's shirt and pulled him forward. Their faces were close enough to feel each other's breath on their skin. 'How dare you judge us? This baby will be loved.'

Gilbert knocked his arm away and threw a punch. Saul sidestepped it.

'Stop it, both of you. There's enough fighting without family doing it too.'

The men appeared to listen and stepped apart. They composed themselves.

'I have nothing against Jews,' said Gilbert. 'The fact is that your baby will be half Jewish and those bastards will have a big problem with that. You don't know what you've done. You'll all be hunted like vermin by those German dogs and you won't stand a chance. You can't even close the partition behind you when you come into this supposedly safe room. It's got fingerprints all over it. You may as well leave Hitler's henchmen a trail leading here. For God's sake, Arlette, the Gestapo have their headquarters at the manor. Five minutes' walk away.'

Arlette felt sick despite her anger. How could she

have left the partition open or forgotten to rub off her fingerprints? She'd been careless. They'd both been careless by not whispering. It could easily have been Kommandant Steiner standing here with them now. She didn't dare contemplate what Gilbert would say if he found out that she was going to work at the manor.

'It won't happen again. We were both saying that we have to be more careful,' said Arlette. 'I've never forgotten to close the partition before and the cows used to be in the barn hiding it up until recently.'

'Where are the beasts?' asked Gilbert.

'The Gestapo requisitioned them,' said Arlette.

'Greedy, thieving Boches,' spat Gilbert. 'I'm going inside to speak with Father.'

They watched Gilbert crawl back through the opening and close the partition behind him.

Saul shook his head. 'He's right. What was I thinking? I've been so selfish.'

'No,' said Arlette. She rubbed his upper arms comfortingly and faced him. 'I begged you to stay, remember? Then I found out I was pregnant and you've only just recovered from being very sick. And where would you go? You'd have been found immediately and sent off to a camp. Or worse. I couldn't bear it, Saul. We need you,' she said, touching her stomach.

He leaned his forehead against hers. 'Don't climb through every night. Just slide in some provisions, wipe your fingerprints and prop something up against the door to conceal it. We'll be fine for several days at a time without seeing each other. It's safer for everyone.'

They clung to each other before Arlette crawled back through the opening and rubbed dirt over her fingerprints. Next she leant a wooden ladder and box of tools against the metal sheet. How was she was going to manage without holding Saul for days on end? Added to which, she was dreading starting work at the manor.

Back inside the house, Gilbert, her father and grandmother stopped their conversation and looked at her. She closed the kitchen door behind her.

'You're pregnant?' asked Henri.

Gilbert looked contrite. 'I didn't know you hadn't told them.'

Arlette didn't move from the doormat. 'Yes, I am.'

'How far on?' asked Grandma Blaise.

'Ten weeks! It was an accident. We didn't mean it to happen.'

'How many times in history have those words been spoken?' said Henri.

'It is what it is,' said Grandma Blaise. She bustled towards Arlette and pulled her to her bosom. 'Words and blame are useless now. Looking back never helped anyone and besides, a new life to distract us may be just what's needed.'

Arlette hugged her grandmother. 'Thank you,' she whispered.

Chapter Twenty-Four

The Germans' search of the farmhouse appeared to be a noisy rather than a thorough affair. Half a dozen young soldiers strode around the house and yard, each strutting like a cockerel in a hen house. The new recruits appeared fresh-faced and seemed to like making themselves noticed in their brand new uniforms instead of doing a comprehensive job. They upturned boxes, opened doors and searched through cupboards. Unbeknown to Arlette, she was helping with the pitiable search because the young men seemed even keener on catching her eye than on catching a Jew.

From Arlette's perspective, she read the Germans' glances as hostile. She thought they were watching for her reactions to give them a clue to their search. She lingered at the doorway of the barn biting her thumbnail while they searched its interior. Could they see her trembling? *Please don't make a sound, Saul.*

Piles of wood were knocked over, machinery was moved aside, crates upturned and tools strewn across the floor. After a fairly perfunctory inspection they left the barn. Arlette let out a long silent breath she hadn't realised she'd been holding in. She watched them search the washroom, chicken coop and the pigpen. Although Henri had never kept pigs, Arlette remembered the night the French policeman had inspected their cart full of stone. Her father had lied that they were building a pigpen, so one had to be built just in case.

The soldiers left a short time later, conversing in German and occasionally laughing as they repeatedly turned for one last glance at the pretty farm girl.

* * *

It was now February and Arlette had been working at the manor for several weeks. She had risen at seven that morning and breakfasted on watery porridge oats before taking a weak cup of grilled-barley coffee to her father, grandmother and Saul. The barley was old and gave the drink a slightly bitter taste, but it was hot and better than plain water. She'd been informed that she was to take orders from a German called Siegfried, who was also in charge of local requisitioning. Despite trying to remain aloof and get on with the cleaning and cooking with her head bowed and eyes lowered, she couldn't help but like Siegfried. He was short and muscular with pale blue eyes and cropped brown hair. Although he was an officer in the Gestapo, Siegfried was the only German who had shown a natural kindness. He'd smile at her and talk passionately about fishing in the deep lakes of his homeland while she cooked. He spoke of his passion for opera, his love of long walks and of his longing for his family. It was as if he had an urgent need to say, *look at me – I am an ordinary man being forced into living a life of oppression against my will*. He would reassure her that she was in no danger working at the manor and would often lift a heavy saucepan from her and take instructions as to where it needed placing. Arlette didn't like to think of it as taking advantage of this affable man, but she would furtively steal provisions from the larder. She appeased her conscience by telling herself that it was probably food that had been forcibly requisitioned from her own family some months earlier. Because she knew that chickens laid eggs infrequently during winter, she had managed to hide several eggs in her coat pocket. She had then informed Siegfried that the egg-layers weren't producing due to the cold and limited daylight. The previous week she had scraped breakfast leftovers of bacon and fried potatoes into some waxed paper and hidden it in her apron. Although it had been cold when the family ate it later that evening, they'd all agreed that it was delicious.

Arlette stood washing the breakfast crockery, looking out of the manor's kitchen window. The landscape still looked bleak but the snow had gone and the wind had abated. Between the skeletal branches of the Lamonds' mature trees, she could see the river winding its way through the pale mist of the valley.

Siegfried entered the kitchen carrying an empty cup. 'The beauty of the land slows many a worker's hands.'

Arlette turned and stretched her lips into a half-smile. It was the sincerest greeting she'd afforded any of the Germans living there.

'I live in Frankfurt close to the Odenwald Forest and the hills of the Taunus,' he said. 'The hills are perfect for growing grapes and making delicious Rieslings. It's a wonderful place to visit. At least, it was before the war.'

Arlette leaned to one side, giving him space to rinse his cup in the soapy water. 'I was just thinking that there'll be no grape harvest again this year at the manor,' she said.

Siegfried nodded and pursed his lips. 'Yes, you're right, I'm afraid. But let's stay cheerful and say maybe next year.'

Arlette liked him despite his being German. She handed him a cloth to wipe his cup and smiled. At that moment Kommandant Steiner walked into the kitchen. His features set hard when he saw her smiling and touching Siegfried as the cloth exchanged hands.

'Are you still cleaning the kitchen?' His words were clipped. 'It's almost eight o'clock and the other rooms are a mess. I want the ground floor rooms in order before we've finished manoeuvres outside. I have a meeting in the library later this morning.' He looked at Siegfried.

'Drill is in ten minutes' time and you don't look ready. I suggest you leave and attend to your uniform.'

Siegfried clicked his heels together and stood to attention. 'Yes, Herr Kommandant.'

Arlette watched him leave the kitchen wishing she could follow him out of the room, but she was left alone with Kommandant Steiner. He walked towards her, his boots resonating on the faded red-tiled flooring.

'When you leave this evening, I wish you to take this letter to your father,' he said, holding out an envelope.

She went to take it from his hands, ensuring not to touch his fingers, but at first he refused to let go. For a few seconds she was in the exact same position as she'd been in when handing the cloth to Siegfried. She wondered if he'd engineered it that way. Not exactly the same, thought Arlette. She wasn't smiling. She would never smile at the man who shot Maurice.

He let go and she slipped the envelope into the pocket of her apron.

'I'd better hurry if you have a meeting and need the library cleaned,' said Arlette.

She turned from the Kommandant and bent to collect some cleaning materials from a cupboard, sensing his gaze upon her while she searched for the necessary supplies. She was careful not to meet his eye and hurried from the kitchen leaving him where he stood. Once inside the library, Arlette closed the door behind her and leant against it taking a deep breath. The musty smell of books and fading aroma of tobacco lingered in the cool air. It was a shame that Kommandant Steiner had chosen this room as his office because she would have loved to escape here more often and explore the collection of books.

Ten minutes later when the remnants of the previous fire in the hearth had been emptied and the fire re-laid,

Arlette could hear the sound of noisy footfall marching to and fro. Every morning the lower ranking soldiers would arrive from their accommodation in the village, and then practise drills, before being given orders for the day. Knowing that she had half an hour in which she wouldn't be disturbed, Arlette put down her dustpan and brush and wandered towards a bookshelf. She ran her fingers along the spines of several volumes before choosing Lewis Carroll's *The Hunting of the Snark* translated by Louis Aragon. She flicked through the illustrations of the surreal characters in the poem and read a few verses. She smiled at the nonsense before sliding the book back into the gap left on the shelf. How wonderful it would be to sit with the luxury of time and decent coffee to read more of the silly rhyme. She stretched, her arms spread wide above her as a small squeak escaped her throat. Kommandant Steiner's desk caught her attention and although she had been ordered not to open or read any documents, she moved towards it. Her eyes scanned its surface. A crumpled blue packet of Gauloises lay next to a full ashtray. Pens, files and notepads were scattered on top of the desk with a large blotting pad positioned in front of his seat. A hardback book lay open on his desk and curiosity about his choice of reading material made Arlette look at the front cover. She half closed the book to read the title when the pages slipped from her grasp. The book fell shut with a thud. *Mein Kampf* by Adolf Hitler. She hurriedly picked up the book and let the pages fall open of their own accord, praying that she could find the correct place it had been left open at. But the pages just fanned out evenly. She opened it randomly, sat it on the desk and rubbed her hands together trying to erase the fact that she had disturbed something of his.

Arlette reached for the ashtray intending to empty it

but her hand stopped midway across the desk. Something was written in a corner of the blotting paper that confused her. With her heart pounding against her ribs, she moved round to the front of the desk and looked closer. Written beside doodled swastikas and abstract patterns, the word couldn't be misconstrued as anything else.

Arlette

She bit her lip and lowered herself onto the edge of the Kommandant's desk chair. She had obviously been on his mind. It was a thought that made her shiver. He either had some future plan that involved her or, more worryingly, and as Francine had alluded to, he had become attracted to her. Either scenario unnerved her. She had to think quickly. Arlette didn't know why she felt the need to conceal the fact that she had seen her name. There was just a niggling belief that he would be more menacing if he knew she'd seen a weakness in him. He may or may not notice that his book was lying open on the wrong page, but if she emptied his ashtray, it would be obvious that she had seen what he'd written. She walked away from the desk leaving it untouched.

Later that evening, back at the farmhouse, Arlette was freshening up in the outdoor washroom when the letter fell out of her work apron. She had forgotten all about it. Hurrying to finish her ablutions in the cold air and dim lamp light, she returned to the warmth and safety of the kitchen where her grandmother was serving winter potatoes and some unknown grey meat bought with coupons. Klara fussed around Arlette's legs looking for attention by nudging her mistress with her muzzle.

'Good dog,' said Arlette, bending to stroke the soft fur behind Klara's ears. 'Now go and lie down by the fire while I eat dinner.' She looked up at her father. 'Has Saul eaten yet?'

'Yes, *ma pêche*. I took him fresh water, food and a warming stone just before you came in. He says you mustn't take the risk and visit him. He says he's fine.'

Arlette sat down at the kitchen table. 'Oh I must, only for five minutes. I haven't seen him for two days.'

'I don't need to tell you that every time any of us enter the secret room we're putting the whole family at risk. We were lucky last month when the patrol found nothing here, but we must remain vigilant. A lamp at night will attract the attention of patrolling Germans.'

'I hate this war,' snapped Arlette, knowing that she sounded childish. 'It seems to be going on forever.'

'We must thank the Lord for our blessings, my dear,' said Grandma Blaise, placing an earthenware bowl in the centre of the table. 'We have food and warmth which many can only dream of.'

Arlette felt chastened. 'I know, Grandma, and I do appreciate it. Really I do. It just sometimes helps to moan. Siegfried says a good grumble helps to release tension.'

'Does he now?' Grandma Blaise raised her eyebrows. 'Don't you be letting him get too close to you, young lady.'

'Grandma, it's nothing like that. He just likes to talk about his homeland. He's not trying to be fresh with me.'

'He's a man far from home and probably lonely. Heed my warning.'

Henri sat down having stoked the fire. He said grace and began to serve the evening meal.

'Sorry I couldn't bring any food back from the manor today,' said Arlette. 'But Kommandant Steiner had an important meeting and there seemed to be more soldiers than usual there today.'

'I'd rather you didn't take any provisions from there,'

said Henri. 'It's far too dangerous and besides, we can manage without their help.'

'Oh, I keep forgetting. Kommandant Steiner gave me a letter to give to you.' Arlette pulled it from her pocket and slid it across the table.

'Why do I think no good will come from its contents?' said Grandma Blaise.

'There's nothing left they can confiscate,' said Henri. He ripped open the envelope.

Arlette watched her father read the letter's contents, his mouth moving while he silently mouthed the words. She saw his jaw clench and his face turn as grey as wood ash.

'What is it?'

Henri lifted his hand to silence her and continued reading. She and her grandmother exchanged worried glances. Her father laid the letter on the table and pushed his dinner away.

'I'm being ordered to leave.'

'What do you mean?' asked Arlette.

'Leave to go where?' said Grandma Blaise.

'The letter says that Frenchmen are being sent to work in Germany to compensate for its loss of German manpower. Many of their citizens are fighting the war and I'm being sent with others to work in a munitions factory under the *Service de Travail Obligatoire.*'

'No, they've got it wrong. I overheard them talking about the STO last week and I wasn't worried because they were ordering young men aged between twenty-one and thirty to work in Germany.'

Henri pushed the letter towards her. 'See for yourself. It's addressed to Monsieur Henri Blaise.'

Arlette pushed her dinner aside and read the letter. It was indeed ordering her father to be ready to leave in a week's time to be transported to Germany.

'I will speak with Kommandant Steiner tomorrow. I will see what I can do,' said Arlette.

She folded the letter, a sense of dread slithering down her back and making her shudder. This letter had been handwritten personally by Kommandant Steiner. For some reason he wanted her father out of the way.

Chapter Twenty-Five

'*Herein!*'

Arlette had knocked on Kommandant Steiner's office enough times to understand his instruction for her to enter. Still clutching a duster, she pushed the door open and walked towards his desk despite the fact that he hadn't looked up yet. She waited in a haze of tobacco smoke until he finally put his pen down, placed his cigarette on the edge of the ashtray and raised his head. His words were punctuated with wisps of smoke.

'Ah! Mademoiselle Blaise. Good morning. I didn't realise it was you who'd knocked.'

Arlette swallowed, unsure of how to question him without disrespecting his seniority. He might be the enemy, but there was little doubt that he held the power. She glanced at his blotting paper and noticed that the one with her name doodled on it had been replaced.

'Good morning, Herr Steiner.'

The Kommandant swung his chair sideways and paid her his full attention. He wore spectacles with thin wire frames that accentuated his aquiline nose and narrow lips. His eyes were blue, but cold like frozen ponds. She noticed them flicker momentarily to her breasts before looking back at her face.

'You can call me Hans when we're alone if you like. How can I be of help, Arlette?'

Arlette blinked, unaccustomed to him using her Christian name and taken aback at his informal manner. She twisted the duster between her hands. 'I think there may have been a misunderstanding.'

The Kommandant looked amused, one eyebrow

rising slightly as he cocked his head to one side. 'A misunderstanding?'

'It's about the letter you wrote to my father. I believe it was written in error.'

Kommandant Steiner folded his arms and leant back in his chair. 'How so?'

'My father's in his forties and I understand that the *Service de Travail Obligatoire* is for men between the ages of twenty-one and thirty years.'

'That is correct for the most part,' he said, looking directly at her, 'but I feel the younger men may need direction and support from someone more experienced.'

'But Father's never worked in a munitions factory before, so he won't be able to offer any knowledge.'

'Maybe not about the workings of the factory, but I'm sure he'll be a calming influence. Shall we say a father figure?'

'But, Herr Steiner, we need my father at the farm. My grandmother is growing frail and I work here all day. It's difficult to get to market because you've taken Mimi and if my father were to leave, Grandma would be unable to tend the farm or buy provisions from the village.' Or look after Saul, she thought.

'Who is this Mimi we are supposed to have taken?'

'Our mare. She pulls the cart and helps us move heavy objects around the yard. We'll need her for market days when the crops start growing.'

He laughed loudly. 'We all have to make sacrifices, Arlette. Your father is needed for the German war effort and your grandmother will have to manage. With your animals re-homed, I believe her workload will be greatly diminished.'

Arlette felt a mixture of anger and hopelessness churning inside her. He sat before her with a pungent arrogance oozing from his pores like sweat. He spoke of everyone making sacrifices, yet he sat here with the fire crackling in the hearth, a steaming coffee on his desk and the distinct smell of garlic on his breath. His stomach was rounded from a good diet and from a near endless supply of wine that had been raided from the Lamonds' cellar. And as for re-homing the farm's animals, every last one of them had been forcibly requisitioned by the Nazis. The last thing Arlette wanted to do was beg, but maybe she could benefit from the fact that she knew he liked her. After all, her father meant more to her than her dignity.

'I would be so grateful, Hans.' She shuddered inwardly for using his first name. It felt like a betrayal to Saul, Maurice and everyone the Germans had persecuted. 'If there was some way you could let my father stay, I'd be grateful. I could work longer hours or help you with filing or run errands.'

She held her breath. Herr Steiner stood up and walked the two steps that separated them. He towered above her, a faint smell of body odour reaching her nostrils. He lifted his hands and placed them on her shoulders, his fingertips moving slightly against her clothing.

'Look at me, Arlette.' His voice was quiet, almost tender.

Arlette raised her eyes to meet his but could only hold their impenetrable gaze for a couple of seconds before focusing on a badge of an eagle on his lapel instead.

'You know that you have nothing to worry about, don't you?'

Arlette nodded, wishing he'd remove his hands from her shoulders. Instead, his hands slid from her shoulders and lightly grasped her upper arms. She looked up at his face once again, his features intense, almost adoring.

'I will look after you when your father has gone.'

She blinked, realisation dawning like a slap. Kommandant Steiner wanted her father out of the way for personal reasons; reasons that had nothing to do with the German war effort. The letter had been handwritten by him because it hadn't been an official order at all. He didn't want her father getting in the way. But in the way of what?

He turned back to his desk, pulled the Bakelite telephone towards him and dialled. After a short pause he spoke into the receiver. 'Do we still have the Blaise's horse? Good. I want you to ensure that it's returned immediately.' He replaced the receiver, then his fingers probed an empty packet of Gauloises before he screwed it up and threw it in the waste paper basket.

'Thank you, Herr Kommandant.'

He smiled, his thin lips disappearing altogether. 'You see, we are not all as bad as they say we are. Remember when you were sick before Christmas? Didn't I ensure you were attended to by a doctor, settled the debt for your medicine and arranged for you to recover here where it's warm?'

'Yes, but—'

'Aren't you treated well and now I've returned your horse at your request?'

'Yes, but—'

'I have an idea. Why don't you consider moving to a room here in the manor?'

'Here?'

'I know, I know,' said Kommandant Steiner, holding up a hand. 'Your grandmother needs you, but maybe we could find her a nice place to stay where she will be looked after and have her meals cooked for her.'

Arlette was horrified. She'd come here to negotiate her father's freedom and now the Kommandant was talking about removing her grandmother too.

'No, please don't make my grandmother move away. She's old and I'm afraid it may be too much for her.'

Kommandant Steiner reached inside his desk drawer and brought out another packet of cigarettes. He tapped the packet onto the palm of his hand before sliding a cigarette out.

'Maybe we could come to an arrangement.'

Arlette frowned. 'I don't understand.'

He placed the slim cigarette between his lips and lit it, squinting as the grey smoke swirled into his eyes. He blew a long trail towards the ceiling. 'We're adults. We're both alone in difficult times. Perhaps one favour could be repaid by another.' He stared at her, once again drawing deeply on his cigarette but this time opening his mouth to let the cloud of silver smoke linger around his lips. Before it had time to escape into the room, he sucked it back over his tongue, inhaling it deep into his lungs. A muscle twitched beneath his right eye.

Having been innocent of such matters until a few months earlier when she had slept with Saul, she gasped in repulsion. 'That's impossible, Herr Steiner. '

He nodded and spoke kindly. 'I know what you're going to say. I am a German and supposedly your enemy, but do you believe in fate, Arlette? Do you believe that when two people are destined to be together, nothing will stop their meeting each other whatever the circumstances, even war?' He stubbed his cigarette out.

'No. That's not what I meant,' said Arlette.

Before she could continue, he'd leant forwards and grasped each side of her face with his large hands. She could see a red patch of broken blood vessels in one eye, like an intricate pattern of lace. His mouth was slightly open, his tongue flicking across his lips before pulling her towards him.

'No,' she cried, pushing him backwards with all her strength.

The Kommandant stopped and blinked. He appeared to be genuinely shocked that she had rejected his advance. He stood before her, a frown furrowing his brow. 'No?'

She shook her head, eyes wide with horror.

'But you agreed to come and work here for me. You stay late to bring me a brandy at my desk each evening. You came to my office on the pretext of cancelling my order to send your father away and you called me Hans. Is it because someone might walk in the room? I could lock the door.'

Arlette took a step backwards, disgust etched on her face and fear giving her the voice to answer despite visibly shaking. 'You've got this all wrong. Coming to speak with you was a sincere request to ask if my father could stay. As for working here and bringing you brandy before I leave, I'm obeying orders. You threatened my family if I didn't work here and told me to bring you brandy before I left each evening. The only reason I come to the manor is for my family.' She swallowed audibly. 'Do you think I could think fondly of a man who killed a boy for being cold?'

'Tread carefully, Mademoiselle Blaise. That youth was shot for theft of German property.'

'A pair of gloves?'

'Don't involve yourself with matters that don't concern you. A firm hand must be taken when dealing with these people. I'm trying to show you kindness.'

'I don't want your kindness, Herr Steiner. These people are my people. Maurice was one of my people. And I'm in love with one of them.'

The Kommandant's mouth fell open in surprise but he quickly composed himself.

'Who?'

'He's gone away. I don't know where.'

The Kommandant's eyes grew narrow and his mouth twisted into a snarl. 'Who?'

'A man from the village.'

He loomed over her. 'His name?'

The sound of material ripping made her blink. They both looked down at her hands where she'd torn a large hole in the duster with her white-knuckled fists. She gasped when he took hold of her throat with one hand and pulled her chin up to look at him.

'Has he touched you?' He closed his eyes as if to block out the image.

'You have no right to ask.'

'No right? Are you aware of the seniority of my position? Don't you understand that I have the right to do anything I please? Even this.'

He pressed his hard lips roughly against hers. His stubble scratched her chin. She grasped at his collar trying to push him away from her, but her fingers lost their purchase on the material. She kicked out at his calves but nothing seemed to stop him. His panting garlic breath covered her face. He ripped her apron from her shoulders. Arlette pummelled him with her fists and attempted to grasp his hair. She wanted to pull his head away from her face, but his hair was so short there was nothing to grip. He grunted as his hands brushed over her breast, ripping at the buttons of her blouse. Pushing her backwards over his desk and with one hand holding her down by the neck, he ripped her blouse open.

He froze.

Arlette was lying on her back focusing on her breathing. His grip was so tight on her neck that she felt her eyes bulging and her windpipe painfully restricted. Just as she thought she would pass out, he loosened his grip. She took a few deep breaths, the buzzing noise in her ears fading.

The Kommandant, now breathless and pale, was staring at her body. Arlette followed his stare to her midriff, her own gaze falling on her swollen belly.

Chapter Twenty-Six

The morning following Kommandant Steiner's shocking attack, Arlette felt immense relief on hearing that he had been unexpectedly summoned to Paris in order to attend a series of meetings with the German High Command. She hadn't slept much that night. She was tormented by the thought that both her father and grandmother would be sent away and was also worried about how the Kommandant would treat her now that he had discovered her secret.

She had fled his office the previous day and stumbled home having left him standing ashen-faced at his desk. Back at the farmhouse, her father had met her in the yard and pointed to the barn where their horse had been returned.

'I don't know what you said to that man, but thank you, *ma pêche*.'

Arlette hadn't wanted to burden her family with the knowledge of the German's actions. They had enough to worry about and, besides, if her father knew about the assault she was in no doubt that he'd go marching down to the manor and find himself arrested for hitting a high ranking German. She couldn't risk it, so she'd smiled and kept her anguish to herself.

Midges danced in the last rays of sunshine that shone through the small opening in the secret room's stonework. Beneath the flurry of insects Arlette stood clinging to Saul, weeping. It had been a week since the Kommandant had left for Paris and thankfully he hadn't yet returned, but neither had he cancelled his order to send her father away.

'Father's gone,' she cried. 'A truck full of men has just left.'

Saul stroked her hair and kissed her forehead. 'I watched through the gap in the wall. I'm so sorry. I feel wretched that you have to face so much on your own.'

'I don't care about me,' she sniffed. 'What if they're cruel to him? I've heard such wicked stories about prison camps and poor Maurice was shot in front of everyone.'

She felt him squeeze her tighter. 'He's a strong man and he'll be treated well. Remember that forced labourers aren't prisoners but a precious commodity working for the German war effort. He'll probably work in a clean, warm factory. They'll be well looked after.'

Arlette wiped her eyes. 'I hope so. Thank you.'

'What for?'

'For reassuring me. For loving me.'

Saul placed two fingers beneath her chin, raised her face and kissed her lips. His mouth felt soft and warm, so unlike the rough pressure she'd felt from the Kommandant's. She shivered at the memory.

'You're cold, darling,' said Saul.

'Just a little, but I'm fine. I'll take the bowl of water away now you've finished with it. I need to make a drink for Grandma. She's very upset.'

'I wish I could come in and look after you both. I feel so useless. Such a burden.'

She stood on her toes and kissed him repeatedly on his eyes, cheeks and lips with light touches of her lips. His cheeks were clean-shaven from his recent ablutions and he smelt of citrus having washed with her homemade soap of fat, lemon juice and caustic soda. 'You're not a burden. So many women are without their loved ones, so it's wonderful to have the man I love so close.' She hesitated for a second and touched her stomach.

'I felt a kick.' She placed his hand beneath hers.

He grinned. 'It must be a boy.'

'If it is, we'll call him Saul Henri Epstein.'

'Perfect.' He stroked her hair. 'We will be married as soon as this war is over, my love.'

She nodded. 'And at the wedding we'll drink a bottle of the—'

'—Lamonds' finest wine,' finished Saul.

Arlette pressed her cheek against his shoulder. He had washed and changed his clothes earlier that afternoon when she'd brought him fresh water and laundry. Now his outfit smelt of line dried linen and fresh hay. With Kommandant Steiner away, she'd taken to hurrying home at lunchtime to check on the household and pay an extra visit to Saul. She had even felt brave enough to smuggle the occasional reading book from the manor's library to stave off Saul's boredom and had continued to take food out of the Germans' larder. She had been able to hide it beneath her coat without the close scrutiny she usually suffered from the Kommandant.

'I'll bring your supper later. If you've read the latest book I'll exchange it tomorrow.'

'It's bad enough you having to work over there, but I don't like you taking such chances by removing things. I worry for you.'

'I'm only borrowing the books and remember they belong to the Lamonds, not the Germans. Besides, it makes me feel as if I've taken a tiny piece of power back when I leave the house with something I shouldn't have.' She planted a perfunctory kiss on his nose before picking up the bowl of dirty water. 'See you soon. I love you.'

Back outside in the yard, the sun had dipped below the orchard's canopy causing the warmth in the air to cool. Perfumed scents drifted in the breeze which made her skirt billow, pressing its material tight against the outline of her legs. The corrugated mauve and peach clouds of early sunset decorated the sky with lines of colour. Arlette emptied the dirty water on to one corner of the vegetable garden. She shooed away a lazy fly while wondering if the prisoners in the camps could also see the beauty of the setting sun.

Remembering that there was a scraping of coffee left over from their rations, she decided to comfort her grandmother with a hot drink of weak coffee, and maybe she would read her some poems from one of the borrowed books. Arlette lowered the bucket into the well, listening as it clanked against the well's murky sides. When she heard a hollow splash she began to pull the bucket back to the surface. Her thoughts wandered to the time she and Saul had sat there and spoken of ethereal creatures. The earthy smell from the depth of the well and sweet wood smoke from the kitchen fire hung in the air like a childhood memory, both comforting and familiar. At first she was so deep in thought that she wasn't aware of any sound, but soon a noise dragged her from her daydreams and back to an uncertain present.

Footsteps.

Arlette recognised the purposeful rhythm of the footfall without having to turn to be proved right, like knowing that a bruise will hurt if you press it but without the proof of a finger's touch. With a feeling of dread she lifted the half-filled bucket and sat it on the wall. *Please don't stir from your nap, Grandma. Please don't make a sound, Saul*, she silently prayed.

'Mademoiselle Blaise.'

Reluctantly, she turned to face Kommandant Steiner. Anxiety quickened her breath. The silence stretched between them. She noticed afresh how tall and heavy set he was.

He cleared his throat and gave a quick bow of his head. 'I trust I find you well.'

Arlette raised her chin, feigning bravado. 'Very well thank you, Herr Steiner.'

She saw the detail on his face: the scars, a healing shaving cut, a sprinkling of open pores and his thin hard lips. She met his stare with hers, determined to protect her unborn child with her life if necessary.

'I've been informed that you've worked well in my absence.'

'It's what I've been ordered to do.'

She noticed his right hand splay open wide and close into a fist several times. His lips creased into a crooked smile. He reached into his coat pocket, retrieving something silver. 'I've brought you some chocolate. It's Swiss.' He held it out towards her.

Arlette was so shocked her mouth fell open. The last time they had been together, he had abused her before discovering she was pregnant. Was this his idea of an apology?

'Please,' he said, jerking the bar an inch closer. Its wrapping crackled in his grip.

Her imagination could almost taste the chocolate. She envisaged snapping off one corner before placing it on her tongue. Somewhere in her distant memory she could feel its luxurious texture. She visualised it melting in her mouth, its smooth sweetness making her eyes close in order to savour it with a grateful moan.

She remained silent and shook her head.

He looked disappointed and his smile vanished. 'But you like chocolate.' He nudged the bar closer to her once again.

It was so close that she could smell it. Her mouth watered and she instinctively swallowed, knowing that he had noticed the movement of her throat. Knowing it was a sign of weakness. 'It's not appropriate,' she said.

Kommandant Steiner took a step closer making her flinch, but he merely placed the bar on the wall of the well. 'Maybe for your grandmother then?'

Arlette remembered his earlier threat to send her grandmother away. She must keep him appeased, so she nodded her head once. 'Thank you.'

His throat made a noise like a satisfied grunt. He rubbed his hands together and pinched his nose, his feet rocking from toe to heel several times. 'I've had time to think and I understand that you've had, shall we say, a dreadful experience.'

She inclined her head almost imperceptibly towards him, not quite believing that he was about to speak of regret for his actions.

'You have quite obviously been taken advantage of.' He pinched his nose again.

Arlette listened.

'If you would give me the name of the man who abused your good nature and made you with child, I assure you that he will be arrested and dealt with severely. Having been away I've had time to think and I realise that you're not the kind of girl who would act in such a loose manner. I applaud your bravery in pretending that you were in love with this man before he left. It's admirable that you have found such strength from such misfortune.'

Arlette opened her mouth to speak.

He held up a hand to silence her and stepped closer. She froze as he lifted a hand and touched one side of her face so delicately that she could barely feel it. The smell of stale tobacco on his fingers made her feel nauseous. She closed her eyes to block out his features, aware that to anger him would put her baby, her grandmother and

Saul in jeopardy. If she were to scream or cause a fuss, surely Saul would reveal himself to protect her. He leant forwards. She held her breath. He kissed her forehead.

'I will ensure that you have everything you need when the child is born. You have no need to worry.'

Chapter Twenty-Seven

Arlette walked past the cemetery and made a hurried sign of the cross. She had been entrusted with an envelope and asked to deliver it to the Mairie's office, now being used as offices by the Germans. She always welcomed these excursions because it was a chance to escape the Kommandant's scrutiny.

Walking into Montverre's empty market place, she noticed a handful of villagers shuffling back and forth across the square. Their clothes were loose, covering shrunken bodies and withered skin. Empty bellies were to blame for the excess material, thought Arlette. As if to underline the disparity of the situation the townspeople were living in, a rotund German officer walked out of the Mairie's office. He belched into his closed fist, no doubt still digesting a hearty meal. Arlette clenched her jaws at the injustice and stepped inside the hallway of the building. The reception desk was unmanned. Glancing down at the name on the envelope, she bumped shoulders with someone. The letter fell to the floor.

'Sorry,' she said, bending to retrieve it.

'Oh hello, my dear. I was searching for a handkerchief in my bag and not watching where I was walking.'

Arlette looked up to see Monique. She smiled at Francine's mother. 'Nor was I.'

'What are you doing here?'

'I've been asked to deliver this letter to Sergeant Strauss before going home.' She flapped the envelope in front of her as if fanning herself.

'Do you know where to take it?'

'Not really. I usually leave messages here at reception,

but I was specifically asked to give the letter to the sergeant.'

Monique scratched her head absentmindedly. 'Take it upstairs to the second floor. That's where the administration offices are. If you ask there, I'm sure they'll let you know where to find him.'

'Thank you.'

'Don't be long, will you? It'll be curfew in an hour or two. I've finished my cleaning for the day so I'm off home to prepare my daily magic trick.'

Arlette looked perplexed.

Monique laughed and rubbed Arlette's upper arm. 'I'm going to try and make a meal out of the scraps we can find. I feel like a conjurer every mealtime.'

Arlette smiled.

'Right,' said Monique, 'hurry upstairs and then get yourself home. I'll see you soon.'

'Bye.'

Arlette watched her bustle out of the hallway, down the steps and sidestep a black cat. The cat arched its back and stretched like a length of elastic, its tail pointing skyward. Its movements were unhurried and casual. It knew nothing of war.

The stairway smelt of disinfectant with an overlying layer of a recently cooked meal. Dust and fluff could be seen nestling in the corners of each tread. She climbed to the second floor and stood on a landing only to be greeted by several closed doors. Not having been on this level before, Arlette didn't know which one to knock on. While she was debating which room to choose, the furthest door opened. A soldier wearing a black uniform with lightning flashes on his jacket collar marched out, head bowed while placing a peaked cap on his head. His cap in place, he stopped abruptly when he saw her. He was short, had a bulbous red nose and was older than the majority of Germans she'd seen. A too-tight shirt collar puckered the loose skin on his neck.

'What are you doing upstairs?' he barked.

'I've come to deliver a letter.'

'You shouldn't be here. It's private.'

Arlette bit back a retort. This building was French. The Mairie who had worked here previously had been ousted from his office by the enemy. And now this man was claiming that it was *she* who was trespassing. Germans appeared to have double standards, she thought.

'Well?' urged the man. His eyes were shadowed by the peak of his cap, causing his nose to appear enormous. His impatience was clear to see by the way he squeezed his black leather gloves between his fingers.

Arlette raised her chin and looked levelly at him. 'I've known this building all my life and have been inside it too many times to remember. I've been asked to deliver this letter to Sergeant Strauss.'

'Give me the letter and leave.' He held out his hand.

Arlette swallowed. He was speaking to her as if she was worthless. She hated him. She imagined striking him. Her hand twitched as she slapped his pasty jowls in her imagination.

He clicked his fingers with impatience. 'The letter.'

'I've been asked to give the letter specifically to Sergeant Strauss.'

'Do you know who I am?' A spray of spittle landed on her face and made her blink. His large nose appeared to grow darker, almost purple.

'No.'

'I'm Lieutenant Fleischer. I'm in charge here. Everyone answers to me.'

'I'm only obeying Kommandant Steiner's orders.'

'You impertinent ...'

Arlette saw him lurch forwards. She blinked in surprise. He grasped her by her upper arm and pulled her towards a door. His gloves fell to the floor when he turned the handle. He pushed her inside and closed the door again. She heard a key turn and a fumbling on the floor as he retrieved his gloves before leaving.

Arlette rubbed the arm that had been pinched by his tight grip, and looked around. She was standing in a small office. There was a desk with a chair pushed up against it and a picture of Adolf Hitler on the wall. It tilted to one side. A filing cabinet and standard lamp were positioned adjacent to the desk. The room smelt bitter, like spilt ink. She walked to a window that overlooked the square. Dusk was falling. The black cat was playing with a dry leaf that was cartwheeling in the gutter, occasionally striking it with a paw. Arlette sighed. Why had he irritated her so much? Why hadn't she just handed him the envelope and left? She would be walking up Montverre Hill by now. Hopefully he had gone to fetch the sergeant.

Five minutes turned into what seemed like an hour. Then two. She tried the door numerous times but it remained locked. Fortunately the building had been supplied with electricity several years earlier, so she had switched on the lamp half an hour earlier. She had no idea of the time but surely it must be curfew by now. She knocked on the door and listened. Silence. She sat on the hard wooden chair once again.

Eventually she heard footsteps and sat bolt upright. A key turned in the lock but the footsteps walked away again. Arlette frowned. That was odd, she thought. She stood up and moved tentatively towards the door, the envelope still in her hand. By now she was cold, tired and hungry and decided that she would push the letter under any door and hurry back home. More footsteps. She stumbled backwards and waited.

A tall, bald man stepped inside the door. 'I'm Sergeant Strauss. I understand you have a letter for me?'

'Yes.' She held it out to him.

'You've brought it at a late hour? Curfew is in ten minutes.' He took the letter from her.

'I've been here some time.'

'I apologise for your wait. Lieutenant Fleischer has just this minute informed me of your presence.'

She pointed to the letter, now in his hands. 'It's from Kommandant Steiner.'

'Thank you. Yes. I've been expecting it.' He looked at his watch. 'Do you live far away?'

'At the top of Montverre Hill.'

'You had better hurry.'

Arlette nodded and left the room, wishing that more Germans were as affable as Sergeant Strauss. She ran down the two flights of stairs and out into the street. She knew that Lieutenant Fleischer had purposefully locked her in the room as punishment for daring to answer him back. It must have been him who had unlocked the door just before the sergeant had come to find her. She clenched her fists, hating the vindictive little man.

It was dark outside and lamps could be seen shining inside front windows. She started to run, holding her shawl tight against the increasing wind. Tiring easily due to her condition, she slowed to a quick walk. Her breath was loud and fast and she could hear her heartbeat in her ears. Turning the corner she hurried past a row of terraced houses towards the church. The clock chimed. Curfew.

Should she stay overnight at Francine's house? It was only a few minutes away. No, her grandmother would not sleep for worrying, and the old lady was also too frail to climb in to the cattle pen and deliver Saul's supper. Even if her grandmother could manage the task, Saul would ask where she was. She had no choice but to continue up Montverre Hill.

Electricity hadn't reached the lanes on the outskirts of Montverre and the country road was in complete darkness. Arlette walked slowly, her clogs feeling for the edge of the road and the beginning of the grass verge. Huge trees creaked in the wind, their boughs rocking to and fro. She was scared. Her eyes were wide, searching for any silhouette to give her some bearing. Eventually she felt the incline of the hill underfoot and walked a little faster. Instinct made her walk with one arm holding her shawl to her body, but her other one held out in front of her in the black night. She swung it left and right, feeling for anything but hoping for nothing. Small animals could be heard scurrying and scratching in the undergrowth. An owl hooted, its ghostly call causing Arlette to catch her breath. 'Nearly there, nearly there.' Her whispered voice sounded loud in the silence.

Clouds swept across the sky, occasionally revealing a scattering of stars. Then, much to her relief, a larger section of clear sky exposed a three-quarter moon. Its luminescence highlighted the contours of the lane with a pale silver glow. She hurried forwards. Nearing the summit of the hill, she passed the twitchel that led to the wooded area close to the manor. The wind lulled for a moment. She heard a twig snap. Was it an animal? Fear made her stop and look into the blackness. For a second she thought she saw a tiny orange dot glowing several metres away. Once again she wrapped the shawl tighter around her body and began to move on. She sniffed the air. Was that tobacco smoke?

The sound of a car engine could be heard. Where could

she hide? Hedgerows were thick and prickly on both sides of the lane. She began to panic, turning this way and that hoping for somewhere to conceal herself. It was too late. The headlights blinded her. She raised her arms to her eyes. The car stopped.

She was hyperventilating, her chest heaving while she waited. A figure climbed out of the car and came towards her. He walked out of the shadows and stood in the beam of the headlights.

'What have we here? Do you know it's after curfew?'

It was Lieutenant Fleischer. Arlette didn't answer.

'Nothing to say for yourself?'

'I was delayed because you locked me in a room.'

'Still an impudent whore! I'll teach you some manners.'

Arlette cowered as he strode towards her. She raised her arms to protect her head.

'Stop!'

Another voice. She dared to glance up. Lieutenant Fleischer had stopped a stride in front of her, his arm raised. He was looking towards the woods. Rustling could be heard. Someone else was moving towards them.

The familiar aroma of Gauloises cigarettes reached her nostrils. She only knew one person who smoked them. Kommandant Steiner moved from the darkness into the yellow glare of the headlights. He sucked on his cigarette, its tip glowing orange. He addressed Lieutenant Fleischer.

'What seems to be the problem here?' Smoke punctuated each word as he spoke.

The lieutenant clicked his heels together and saluted the senior officer. 'Herr Steiner. This woman is out after curfew.'

The Kommandant nodded slowly. 'I will deal with this.'

The soldier pointed at Arlette. 'But, sir …'

The Kommandant raised his voice. 'Don't be insubordinate. I said I will deal with this.'

Arlette could see the lieutenant's lips twitch but he didn't argue. He clicked the heels of his boots together once again and nodded. 'As you say.' He turned, walked back to his car and slammed the door. Neither Arlette nor the Kommandant said a word until he had driven away.

Unnervingly, they were both in near darkness once again. The moon was still out, illuminating his silhouette and casting shadows across his features. She had to admit, if only to herself, she was relieved he had intervened.

'Why are you out after curfew, Arlette?'

'He locked me in a room until ten minutes before curfew began.'

'Why would he do that?'

'I told him the letter was for Sergeant Strauss when he asked for it. He didn't like it.'

She heard the Kommandant make a sound. Could it possibly have been a chuckle?

'I will deal with him in my own way. Go home.'

She paused. 'I can go?'

'Yes. Go home before I change my mind.'

He sounded like an indulgent uncle, but she turned and hurried to the summit of the hill where she walked into the farmyard and safety.

Chapter Twenty-Eight

Swathes of bluebells bowed their heads at the sides of the lane into Montverre. Arlette sat on the trap and steered Mimi towards the village. It was a warm evening in May and Arlette had finished her day's work at the manor. She had become used to the monotonous repetition of cooking and cleaning at the big house but still never felt comfortable in the presence of the Kommandant or any of the other Germans living there. Siegfried, the soldier who'd befriended her, had been stationed elsewhere two months earlier and Arlette was left in no doubt as to who had sent him away. Her thoughts on Herr Steiner were confusing. She was unnerved by him, disliked him and felt relieved when he was away on business. But paradoxically, she also felt a degree of protection from him.

As she was free to clean where and when she pleased, except for the Kommandant's desk, she had become quite skilled at avoiding the household for much of the day. When the soldiers were eating in the dining room, she'd clean the bedrooms and bathrooms upstairs. When the men were outside practising a strange stiff-legged march in front of the barn, she would take that opportunity to prepare vegetables and clean the kitchen. Thankfully, Kommandant Steiner seemed to get busier as the months went by and he was frequently called to Limoges or occasionally Paris. Arlette took these opportunities to clean his office in the library although there was no avoiding him altogether. Whenever she turned to find he had unexpectedly entered the same room she was in, his eyes would bore into hers with such depth of pain for her condition that she would have to leave at the earliest opportunity. She was certain that the baby growing inside her was, for the time being, protecting her from any further physical advances on his part.

Arlette reached the bottom of Montverre Hill and pulled into the verge close to the Giroux's Farm.

'Ci-Ci,' she called.

Francine appeared from behind the family's well and hurried towards her carrying a bunch of wild flowers. She climbed up beside Arlette and kissed her on both cheeks.

'How are you feeling? It must be two weeks since I last saw you. You look a bit tired,' said Francine.

Arlette shook the reins and Mimi started to trot. 'I've had backache all night and couldn't get comfortable so I didn't sleep well. I suppose I'll have to put up with aches and pains for the next couple of months.'

'How are you managing to work at the manor?'

'Fine. I'm just taking things a little slower.'

'Have you heard from Gilbert recently?'

Arlette batted a fly away from her face. 'No. Not since he got angry with Saul in the barn.'

'He was only worried about his family. You can't blame your brother for that, can you?'

'Of course not, but neither is it Saul's fault that the Germans hate him and would sooner kill him than speak to him. Oh, listen to us! Let's try and forget everything and enjoy this beautiful evening. We've only got an hour and a half before curfew.'

The two friends rode towards the *cimetière* Saint-Pierre, their conversation more cheerful. They spoke of the food they would eat when the war was over. They imagined new dresses they would buy and the places they would visit when Arlette's baby was a little older. When the war was just a bad memory.

'What would your dream day be when this awful mess is over?' asked Francine.

Arlette's face relaxed, a smile playing on her lips. 'It would be a summer's afternoon. Our field would be golden with corn and vegetables would be bursting from their plot. Saul and I would be holding our son's hand as we walked along the riverbank to show our little boy the fish and frogs in the water. We might take a small picnic tea. No, a huge one because there wouldn't be any rationing. We'd eat it on the rowing boat and stay out as late as we wished because there wouldn't be a curfew either.' Arlette let out a long sigh.

'That sounds wonderful,' said Francine. 'My perfect evening would be sitting in that same boat with you, Saul and your son, but I'd be at the other end of the boat in Gilbert's arms sharing the same picnic because you did say it was a huge one.'

'Who said you'd been invited to share the boat?' Arlette teased.

'Well, at the beginning of my dream moment you'd invited us!'

Arlette laughed then winced. She held her back with one hand.

'Are you all right?' asked Francine.

'I'm fine. Just another twinge. I don't think sitting on this cart and being jiggled around is helping my backache.'

'Look, we're here now. Let me help you down and you can have a stretch.'

Arlette stopped the cart next to the ornate cemetery gates and was helped down by Francine. She tied Mimi's reins onto a swirl of metal on one gate and patted her horse's thick neck. In the arch that had been carved in the cemetery's wall, Arlette noticed that someone had placed a bunch of purple lilacs beneath the rusting, orange figure of Christ. With His head bowed, He appeared to be admiring the profusion of blossoms at His feet.

Once inside they made their way to Fleur's plot and Francine's grandparents' graves. They left bluebells and wild flowers on each headstone.

'Mother would have become a grandmother soon,' said Arlette.

She felt her best friend link her arm through hers in silence. A minute later, Arlette leant backwards, her hands pressing against her lower back. 'I don't think I can manage a walk around the village this evening.'

'Of course. You can drop me off home so you can go back and get some rest.'

Arlette shook her head. 'No, I'd like to talk but I need to sit down. We'll take the cart around the village and then perhaps I can stop for a cold drink when I take you back.'

They returned to the cemetery gates.

'Let me take the reins while you try and relax. Here, sit on my shawl.'

Mimi trotted past Saint-Pierre's.

'Just look at Mimi strutting along,' said Francine, giggling. 'It's as if she knows she's the only horse that's been left with her owner.'

Arlette smiled through a frown. Her backache was growing worse. Perhaps it would be a good idea to head back to her friend's house for a cool drink now and maybe mention her backache to Francine's mother. Monique could suggest something to ease the pain, being the village's unofficial nurse and midwife.

Francine pulled sharply at the reins, causing Mimi to rear up and stamp her hooves on the cobbles. The momentum caused Arlette to lurch forwards and grab hold of a wooden bar on the trap.

'What's the matter?' she asked.

Francine didn't answer. She just stared ahead into Montverre's main square. Arlette pulled a face and followed her friend's gaze. The square was devoid of any villagers but nothing else appeared out of place. Then she caught sight of strange shapes. They were partly hidden from her view by a branch of a linden tree. Something was swaying to and fro. Arlette leant forwards trying to focus on the suspended objects and began to climb down from the cart for a closer look.

'Don't,' Francine called sharply.

'What is it?' asked Arlette. She walked past Mimi and towards the trees.

'Arlette! Come back. Stop!'

The silence and emptiness of the village was unusual in the early evening. A dreadful curiosity deafened her to Francine's desperate calls. Far across the river on the opposite side of the valley a dog howled, its call haunting in the stillness. Faint whisperings from the linden trees' canopies hushed in the air. Arlette stepped onto a raised area close to the memorial to the Great War. She sensed the eyes of the villagers were watching her from behind curtains, through half closed shutters and from the safety of attic windows. She moved around the bronze sculpture. She saw. The shock of it made her call out.

Three bodies hung side by side from the tree. Their limp grey corpses were surrounded by a flurry of flies. Brown sacking covered their heads and necks. The hands of two bodies occasionally touched as they swayed side by side. Two of them wore only trousers, their bare torsos cut and bloodied, revealing the abuse they'd received before they'd died. The third was a woman. She wore a dress that had ridden up to her knees. Her toes were muddied and bruised. Her feet pointed towards the ground like a ballerina dancing *en pointe*. Pinned to the woman's dress was a sign.

Collaborators of the Resistance.

Arlette gagged. She turned and staggered back to the cart. Francine had already climbed down and rushed towards her.

'You didn't listen,' said Francine. 'Why did you go?'

'I didn't know. I didn't understand. Aaah!' Arlette bent double in agony. She held her stomach.

'Is it the baby?'

Arlette clenched her teeth in pain 'No. I don't know. It's too early.'

Chapter Twenty-Nine

'Let me help you into the back of the trap,' said Francine. 'You'll be more comfortable if you lie on the empty hessian sacks.'

Arlette bent forwards clutching her stomach. 'I can't.'

'But you can't stay here and give birth. Please try to climb in.'

Arlette was helped to gingerly lift one knee onto the back of the cart. She groaned. Another pain ripped through her abdomen.

'I can't. I can't. Please go and fetch your mother,' she pleaded.

'But she's not at home.'

Arlette felt a wave of panic surge through her body. 'What?'

'She left this morning.'

'Where to?'

'She's staying with her sister in Boisseuil.'

Arlette's voice broke. 'She can't be. I need her.'

'I know. I'm sorry. She'd never have gone if you were due. But you've only carried your baby for seven and a half months.'

Arlette began to cry. Her strength evaporated. The one woman who she was relying on to deliver her baby safely was away. Added to that, the horror of finding the murdered Resistance fighters was a nightmare too far. She crumpled onto the cold cobbles and sobbed uncontrollably. She cried for the lives that had been so cruelly ended, for her missing father and brother, for her mother whom she needed more than ever right now, and for her love who was locked away in a dark room for fear of being taken from her.

Arlette sensed Francine fussing around her. Her friend was trying to comfort her but all Arlette wanted was her own mother. No one else would do. She imagined her mother must have felt just like this before labouring with her third baby. A baby that had never been born. A baby that had died cocooned inside her womb at the same time as she had taken her last breath.

Arlette's weeping continued. She leant forwards on the dirty ground while hopelessly banging her fists on the smooth stones. Her body rocked to and fro in despair. She felt as if she was losing her senses. Then she heard another voice and felt pressure beneath her arms. She experienced a sensation of rising and moving but with her hair covering her face, stuck with tears and mucous, she couldn't see where she was going. After a few minutes she was led through a doorway. Was she in a house? The sound was cushioned and there was soft matting beneath her tread. Within seconds she felt the comfort of a mattress beneath her body and was soothed by a warm cloth wiping her face.

'There now,' said a gentle voice. 'Sitting in the square is no place to bring a beautiful baby into the world.'

With her face clean and her hair pushed away from her face, Arlette began to feel calmer. Her sobbing had stopped and become juddering breaths. Her eyes gradually focused on the face leaning over her as she listened to the gentle voice assuring her that all would be well. She could see dark eyes on a woman's face and feel hands pacifying her anguish by stroking her hair.

No, it couldn't be her mother, could it? Her mother was dead.

'Hello, my lovely. Who would have thought we'd meet again in such circumstances?'

'Camille? I thought for a moment that you were my ...'

Another pain scorched her stomach. She gripped the shoulders of her late mother's best friend. She could smell a mixture of rose water and carbolic soap on Camille's skin. She hyperventilated against Camille's neck, images of her mother's scarf punctuating her muddled thoughts. When the pain subsided, she released her grip and sank back against the pillows.

'I still have your scarf safe,' said Arlette. 'Father told me that mother bought it for you when you left for Paris.'

Camille smiled. 'Silly thing! It's yours now, but it's touching to know that Henri remembered.'

'He's been sent away,' said Arlette, her eyes welling with tears again.

'Shhh!' Camille stroked her arm. 'I know. I heard in the post office that he'd been sent to Germany to work. Now, don't you worry. Grandfather Henri will be back soon to meet his first grandchild.'

This remark made Arlette smile. She wiped a tear away with the back of her hand and looked around the room. 'Where's Francine?'

'She's taken the cart to fetch your grandmother. I've nursed my elderly mother but have never delivered a baby before, so I may need a little instruction.'

Arlette raised her head off the pillow. 'It's too early.'

'I don't think your baby understands that. He wants to meet you.'

'Will he be sick?'

'Maybe a little small. If he's sick, we'll do all we can to look after him.'

Arlette laid her head back on the pillow. It occurred to her that she was lying in a bed that was downstairs. 'How's your mother?'

'She died in January. Pneumonia.'

'I'm so sorry.'

'It's what she wanted. She prayed to be released from her pain and to join my father in heaven. God answered her prayers.'

Arlette laid her hand on Camille's. 'How are you feeling? You look much better than when I last saw you in the market over a year ago.'

'I feel much better too and I do believe I've put on a little weight with all the potatoes I've been eating. I'll soon look like a bulbous *pomme de terre* if I eat many more of them!'

Arlette gave a small laugh before looking seriously at Camille. 'It's wonderful to see you again. I was thinking about mother when I was in the square just now. Do you think the same might happen to me and my baby?'

'Certainly not,' said Camille. 'Poor Fleur had complications, but you're strong.'

Arlette paused. 'Have you been in the square today?'

Camille set her mouth in a straight line and shook her head. 'The Aumonds were executed last evening. A neighbour told me what was happening because I heard a commotion outside and opened the front door. Are the poor souls still there?'

Arlette nodded.

'Murderers,' said Camille. 'There's no other word for it. We can only pray that justice will be served in the months and years to come.'

'I think it's a bad omen. I saw them and then my first pain came. It's nearly two months too soon.' Arlette felt her stomach tighten. Another pain gripped her body, more severe this time. She panicked and looked wide-eyed at Camille for assurance.

'It was just coincidence, that's all. Try to remain calm and concentrate on breathing evenly,' said Camille. 'That's it. In and out. Good girl. Wonderful.'

When the pain had faded, Camille stood up from the edge of the bed. 'I'm going to heat you some vegetable broth I made yesterday. You need to keep your strength up. It's not called labour for no reason, you know?'

Arlette watched Camille leave the room, then her eyes scanned its interior. Faded floral wallpaper, formal nineteenth-century furniture, a threadbare rug and gloomy décor made the room appear subdued. Another wave of pain took her mind off the colourless space. She gripped the bedcovers and groaned through clenched teeth. It felt as if her insides were being pulled and squeezed whenever her stomach tightened. She let go of the eiderdown with one hand and felt her hard stomach. As the contraction intensified, she took a deep breath and called out for Camille.

Several hours later, Arlette lay panting in bed without any sign of Francine or Grandma Blaise. Camille was helping her to sip a glass of water having wiped her brow.

'Something's wrong. I know it. I told you the hangings were a bad omen.'

'I want no more of this nonsense,' said Camille. She plumped the pillows. 'Your little baby needs positive thoughts.'

Arlette looked up. 'That's what Saul says.'

'Saul? I wondered who the baby's father was. Where's he from?'

Arlette hesitated. If she couldn't trust Camille, then there was no one who would keep her secret. 'He's a doctor. He's training to be a doctor. In Lyon.'

Camille had moved to the curtains and was peering through them as she spoke. 'How wonderful! Where did you meet him?'

'It's complicated. He's Jewish.'

She saw Camille freeze for a second then turn slowly. 'Please tell me that he has escaped south or is in hiding somewhere else.'

'He's in hiding.'

Camille let out a long sigh and crossed the room back to the bedside. 'Thank goodness. I thought you were going to tell me that he was still in Montverre. If he was linked to your family it would be extremely dangerous for you all.'

Arlette looked at her without answering and bit her bottom lip causing the smile to fade from Camille's face.

'He's at the farmhouse, isn't he?'

Arlette nodded.

'Dear Lord! Where exactly?'

'Father and Gilbert built a secret room at the back of the barn. It was originally for hiding food but when the Germans came to Montverre, we hid Saul in there.'

'He's been there all this time?'

Arlette pulled a face. 'But he's safe. Unless you knew the room was there it would be almost impossible to find.'

'And Henri was in agreement with this perilous idea?'

Before Arlette could answer someone tapped on the window, startling them both.

'It must be Grandma Blaise,' said Arlette.

'I'll let her in.'

Arlette tensed as another pain tightened her stomach. She closed her eyes and held her breath, certain that she needed to visit the outside washroom. Someone squeezed her hand. She clenched her teeth and groaned through the agony. When the pain receded, she opened her eyes expecting to see her grandmother. She gasped. Saul was kneeling beside her.

'What are you doing here? I don't understand. It's too dangerous.'

'Shhh,' he soothed. 'Your grandmother has had a little accident. She's fine but twisted her ankle when she fell. I've been beside myself with worry about you, but we had to wait until dark before I could chance leaving the farm.'

Francine stepped from the shadows to stand beside Saul. 'I didn't know what to do so I asked Saul. I'm sorry.'

'There's nothing to be sorry about,' said Saul.

'It's past curfew. How did you get a noisy trap past the manor?' asked Arlette.

'I walked here with Francine. As you say, we couldn't risk the trap.'

'You walked! I've put you in so much danger.'

'We took care and walked across the fields instead of taking the road into Montverre.' He kissed Arlette, stood up and turned to Camille.

'Thank you for looking after her.'

'It's the least I can do. I'm an old family friend. How else can I help?'

'Is there somewhere I can wash my hands? I need to do an examination to see how her labour's progressing.'

'I'll show you.'

Arlette was still stunned by Saul's presence. He returned with clean hands and his sleeves rolled to his elbows. His hair was dishevelled. His clothes were as creased as cabbage leaves and his cheekbones prominent on his handsome face. She lay back as instructed and closed her eyes. Saul's hands pressed and squeezed her stomach.

'Have the baby's waters been expelled yet?'

Arlette shook her head. 'Why're you frowning?'

'Our baby is lying in a transverse position. I need to try and turn him.'

'What does that mean?' asked Arlette.

'He's lying sideways but don't worry, everything will be fine.'

Saul turned towards Camille and gave her a look that left her in no doubt but to follow him out of the room. Once in the small kitchen she turned to face him.

'It's not all right, is it?' Camille whispered.

Saul vigorously rubbed his face with his palms as if to clear his head. His face was red and creased with worry. 'The baby can't be delivered in the position it's in. It's a shame it's May or I could have used ice.'

'Ice?'

'If you rub it near the baby's head, it sometimes persuades the baby to move of its own accord away from the cold. I need you to keep Arlette calm while I try a few things.'

Camille nodded.

Back in the room Saul knelt beside Arlette, took her hand and waited for another contraction to fade. When her face relaxed against the pillow he carefully explained what he needed her to do. 'You have to listen to me, darling. Our baby can't come out in the position he's lying in. We have to persuade him to move by himself. I need you to kneel on the bed with your head lower than your hips.'

'Will that make him move?'

'Hopefully.'

'I'm scared.'

Saul smiled. 'Don't be. I'm here. Didn't we work well as a team to save the breech calf? Well, we're going to work as a team again and deliver our baby. Come on then.'

Saul and Francine helped Arlette to turn over and kneel on the mattress. She rested her head on the counterpane. After ten minutes and three painful contractions, Arlette was helped to lie on her back again. Saul felt her stomach for any change.

'I think he's moved a little but not enough. I'll have to try and turn him myself.'

Arlette began to cry. 'He's going to die, isn't he? It's too early for him to come and now he's stuck.'

Saul shook her gently but firmly. 'Stop this silly talk. He's small but that's a blessing in this situation because it'll be easier to move him. There's room in your womb because he's coming early, so it's much safer than if I was trying to change the position of a bigger baby. It's going to be a little uncomfortable but we need to do this. Do you understand?'

Arlette nodded.

Chapter Thirty

Arlette clenched her teeth. The pain was excruciating. Saul leant over her, applying firm pressure to her stomach. She growled through the pain, her eyes squeezed shut.

'He's moving,' said Saul.

Arlette felt his hands push and twist. Ripples of agony forced another deep groan from her throat.

'That's it,' said Saul. 'The baby's turned the right way now.'

Arlette panted with relief. She felt Saul push her hair back from her face and wipe her forehead with a cloth. It felt cool and relaxing.

'Clever girl. You did a great job.'

Arlette bit her bottom lip. Another tightening gripped her body. She reached out for Saul's hand and clutched it to her cheek. Her body seemed to be in control, not her. She felt impelled to inhale deeply and push with every ounce of energy she had left. Another guttural moan filled the room.

'Do you have any old sheets for when the waters break?' Saul asked Camille.

She nodded. 'I'll fetch some.'

'And scissors and string.'

'Yes.'

He turned to Francine. 'I need to examine Arlette again. Can you hold her hand?'

'Of course,' said Francine. She squatted next to her best friend and cradled her hand.

An hour passed.

Saul was kneeling on the mattress at the bottom of the bed. 'I need a warm towel here,' he urged.

Arlette screamed.

'He's coming,' said Saul. 'A towel, quickly.' He beckoned with his hand.

Francine removed a warming stone from a towel. She hurried across the room and passed him the heated fabric.

Arlette looked up at Francine and saw her best friend's eyes widen.

'I can see the baby's head,' said Francine.

Arlette panicked. 'Is he all right?'

Francine nodded, her hands held to her mouth in wonder.

Arlette stretched out her arm towards her best friend. 'Hold my hand. I'm scared.'

Francine knelt down beside her.

'Another pain's coming,' cried Arlette. She squeezed Francine's hand.

'Put all your effort into pushing, my love,' said Saul. 'Try not to use your strength on crying out. Push!'

'Push,' said Francine.

Arlette squealed.

'His head's out. His head's out,' repeated Saul. 'Have you got those scissors?'

Camille stepped forwards and waited close to Saul.

'He's got black hair,' said Saul.

'Did you hear?' said Francine, leaning closer to Arlette. 'Your baby has hair.'

'Another long but more gentle push, Arlette. You can do it,' said Saul.

Arlette squeezed her eyes tightly and took a deep breath. She could feel her stomach clench and a pain grip her body. She groaned and pushed. 'Oh!' She felt her baby slip from her body.

Francine began to cry. 'It's wonderful. You've done it.'

Arlette wiped tears from her cheeks. 'The baby? Is he breathing?'

The baby cried and she laughed with relief. She turned to Francine who had tears streaming down her face. 'I did it.'

'You did. You clever thing.'

Arlette looked up to see Saul carrying a bundle towards her. He was smiling with glistening eyes and placed their baby in her arms. He kissed her forehead and whispered, 'We have a daughter.'

Saul had to leave shortly after the birth to ensure he made his way back before dawn. Francine had left with him because she knew the lay of the land: its ditches, fences and impenetrable gorse bushes. They had lain motionless in a muddy ditch after headlights of a car had appeared on the road adjacent to the field they'd been struggling through. They didn't dare move for half an hour. It wasn't before the first purple shades of dawn were streaking across the horizon that Saul slid open the partition and crawled through into the relative safety of the secret room.

Francine had collected Arlette and her baby in the trap the following day. Now, in the quiet of her own bedroom, Arlette watched her daughter. Estelle Fleur was sleeping in a padded drawer beside her bed. The drawer had been lifted onto two dining chairs to prevent her baby from lying in a draught. Only a tuft of dark hair and one tiny hand was visible. Arlette gently moved the blanket a few inches. Estelle was sleeping, her cheeks a bloom of pink, her fingers curled into loose fists and her rosebud lips pursed into a kiss.

Grandma Blaise knocked on the bedroom door and poked her disembodied head around it. She smiled from beneath her cotton cap. 'Do you want anything, my dear?'

Arlette thought for a moment. Everything. Nothing. 'No, thank you.' She wiped away a tear from her cheek.

'Now what's all this for?' said Grandma Blaise, hobbling on her swollen foot into the room. She fussed around the bed, tucking in sheet corners and stroking blankets flat with the palm of her hand before pushing the shutters open. 'Whatever are there tears for on such a wondrous day?'

Arlette shook her head. 'How can it be wondrous? A mile away a whole family are dead for helping someone like Gilbert. How could I have brought a baby into such a world?'

Grandma Blaise sat on the edge of the bed between her granddaughter and Estelle. She took Arlette's hand in hers and rubbed it. 'We have to stay positive in whatever situation we're faced with, my dear. With your father working in Germany for the foreseeable future, we three girls must stick together and make the best of things.' She smiled. 'Bad things happen to good people every day and although we all feel the anguish and fear, we must stay strong and move forwards. One day this war will be over and your little family will be free to live openly. Sadly for the present we must lift our chins and soldier on. Now,' she said, patting Arlette's hand, 'you've been discharged from service across at the manor for the time being, so you'll have time to recover and adjust. It's not easy, but we've been blessed with this little angel and there's a handsome young man in the barn anxiously waiting to see his daughter.'

The following week after plenty of sleep, the world didn't seem like such a black place to Arlette. Saul's adoration of his daughter had brightened her mood. He became transfixed whenever Estelle's dark eyes flickered open and stared back like black olives into her new unfocused surroundings. He would grin inanely whenever their daughter's tiny hand grasped one of his fingers.

However, one dark obstacle remained. Kommandant Steiner. His long trench coat would billow like crow's wings each time he entered the farmyard. He had visited three times in the first week of Estelle's life, on each occasion bringing unwanted gifts for her. On his first visit he had tentatively stepped inside and laid a celluloid pink baby's rattle on the kitchen table. The second time he visited, Arlette had just returned from the outside washroom and was horrified to find him bent over the drawer in which Estelle lay sleeping in the kitchen. On that occasion he had left a lemon dress. It was far too large and would have been more suitable for a two-year-old child.

Arlette had been sitting in the garden singing *Au clair de la lune* to her daughter when the Kommandant made his third visit. The shadows in the farmyard were growing longer while she waited for the sun to set. She only ever took Estelle to see her father in the barn under the safety of darkness.

'What a charming sight,' said the Kommandant. He strode into the yard.

Arlette stopped singing and bristled.

'Please, do continue.'

'I'd rather not in company. I was singing to my daughter.'

The German stood a few feet away from the bench on which Arlette sat.

'May I?' He gestured to the space beside her.

'I was just going inside to put her to bed.'

'Just a few more minutes won't cause any harm.' He sat down beside her without permission.

This evening he wasn't wearing his coat; in fact, even his top shirt button was undone. He sat forwards leaning his forearms on his knees and stared into the distant hills.

'It is beautiful here. We have similar hills and valleys in Germany. It can make a soldier quite homesick.'

Arlette didn't reply. Her body was taut. She subconsciously leaned away from him. Estelle began to wriggle, sensing her mother's tense embrace.

The German leant back against the vertical wooden struts of the bench and looked at Arlette. 'How are you feeling?'

'Well, thank you.'

He nodded thoughtfully. 'I've been meaning to apologise.'

Arlette kept her eyes on Estelle. 'What for?' She knew exactly what for, but wasn't going to let him off so easily. She would make him spell it out.

'Some months back. In my office. It was wrong.'

'Yes.'

'I was jealous. You must know I have feelings for you.'

Arlette closed her eyes, willing him to go away and leave them. His French was spoken with a German accent that sounded like each syllable had been ground into shards of glass.

'I couldn't bear the thought that ... that a man might have ...'

She snapped her head sideways and finally looked at him. 'So you thought you'd take advantage of me too.'

She saw a muscle in his jaw tighten.

'It was wrong. I wish to make it up to you.'

She shook her head. 'There's nothing I need.'

'You need a father for your child.'

Arlette's jaw fell open. 'What?'

'A father figure.' His thin lips were set in a straight line causing them to almost disappear.

'Are you suggesting ...' She couldn't bring herself to speak the rest of the sentence.

'I am here for you and your little girl. You don't need to make up stories about being in love with someone else. I don't admire you any less because you've been taken advantage of and found yourself with a child out of wedlock. Many will condemn you, but I want you to know that I don't.'

'I think it's better if you leave, Herr Steiner. I need to put my daughter to bed.'

He closed his eyes and inhaled a deep breath through his nostrils. His shoulders rose and his chest expanded. 'I understand. I am a German and we're in your country. But I will show you my intentions are for your welfare.' He bent his arm and felt in his jacket pocket. He retrieved a silver-wrapped chocolate bar. 'More chocolate. This time for a new mother.'

Arlette didn't move when he held it out towards her. He waited a second then laid it on the bench beside her. He stood up, clicked his heels together and nodded his head curtly. She watched him walk out of the yard.

When he was out of sight, Arlette stood up and settled Estelle so that her baby's head was resting on her shoulder. With one hand under Estelle's nappy of torn sheets, she picked up the chocolate bar and walked to the front border of the garden that edged the lane. Reaching her arm back as far as she could, she hurled the chocolate bar across the road. She watched as it fell deep inside a hawthorn bush.

Chapter Thirty-One

Summer passed leaving parched and puckered bronze leaves to cartwheel across the farmyard. Saul remained hidden in the secret room. Arlette visited with Estelle as often as she dared, but now that Estelle had grown stronger and more vocal, distracting her from squeals of happiness or wails of impatience was becoming more difficult. How could she explain to a five-month-old baby that she had to keep quiet?

Arlette held Estelle in her arms and looked across the valley towards the river. It looked like a wrinkled canvas in the autumnal breeze, reflecting the colour of the sky in its surface. She could smell a hint of winter in the air. Arlette blew a raspberry into her daughter's neck, delighting in making Estelle laugh. Two white teeth, like grains of rice, sat in the baby's lower gums. They turned when Grandma Blaise waddled into the front garden and watched the old lady hang nappy-sized squares of old sheets on the line. It was a daily chore.

'They shouldn't take long to dry in this breeze,' said Arlette.

'I dare say I'll be folding them away in only a couple of hours.'

Arlette walked towards her. 'Thank you, Grandma. I don't know what we'd do without you.'

'It's good for an old lady to feel useful. Besides, I enjoy it. Don't I, little lady?' Grandma Blaise tickled beneath Estelle's chin, making her squirm. 'I'll tell you what I don't enjoy though. That German. Why does that man come round here so often? It's strange the amount of attention he pays to you and the baby.'

Arlette hugged Estelle closer. The Kommandant had continued to call two or three times a week throughout the summer. She never made him feel welcome and refused to converse with him, apart from rudimentary responses to questions. 'He likes me. I don't know why. My rudeness doesn't seem to deter him.'

'In all my years I've never understood men. But if there's one thing I've learnt about them, it's that they like to hunt. Whether it's the thrill of fish lurking beneath the water, a wild boar hiding in the undergrowth or an unwilling woman, they feel compelled to chase.'

'He's wasting his time.'

'I've no doubt, but I don't like it. Especially with your father away.'

Arlette looked up at the clouds; white on blue, like an artist's sky. The Kommandant's visits were a continual cause of anxiety for her. Although his occasional gifts of food were accepted for her family's sake, she knew that each visit was dangerous for Saul. She also knew what she had to do to stop these intrusions. She would have to return to work back at the manor.

Grandma Blaise lowered her voice to a whisper. 'And what about Saul?' She motioned to the barn with her head. 'It gives me sleepless nights to think that he might be discovered on one of the Kommandant's visits.'

'I've been thinking about it too. The only way to stop him visiting is if I go back to work.'

Grandma Blaise paused, her arms raised, her hands resting on the washing line. She lowered them and stroked Estelle's cheeks. 'For Saul's sake, for all of our sakes, I think it would be for the best.'

'I'll speak to the Kommandant next time he visits,' said Arlette. She started to turn but her grandmother stopped her with the touch of her hand.

'He hasn't … he hasn't been ungallant, has he?'
Arlette frowned.

'He doesn't expect … he hasn't suggested …' stammered Grandma Blaise.

'No. I think he misses his own family. That's all.'

Grandma Blaise turned back to the line and smoothed the pegged nappies with sharp swipes of her hand. 'I hope so. I have a bad feeling about him.'

Arlette carried Estelle back inside and sat at the kitchen table. She held her daughter on her knees, facing her. Estelle's hair was as fine as a dandelion seed head and she wore a cream cotton dress and was wrapped in a shawl that had been recently bought with coupons.

'How can I tell your great grandmother that he wants to look after us?' whispered Arlette. 'A father figure! He's a silly man, isn't he? You already have the best daddy in the world. Tell me what to do, little one? If I tell him to leave us alone, it will put all your family in danger. But if I say nothing, am I encouraging him?'

Estelle gave her lopsided smile. Arlette closed her eyes and held her daughter even closer. 'I love you so much.' She began to slowly rock backwards and forwards, humming once again the tune of *Au clair de la lune*.

While she hummed, she looked around the kitchen. Baby clothes and blankets were folded on the mahogany table, a spinning top lay on the floor and a collection of crib toys and baby rattles sat on the armchair. A jar of lavender filled the room with fragrance. Potatoes and carrots picked from their own garden were scattered next to the sink, ready for peeling. Saul was missing all this. The small things that all add up to make a family home.

Later that evening, when dusk silhouetted the shapes in the farmyard, Arlette crept outside the kitchen door. She looked towards the entrance of the farm where Grandma Blaise's outline could be seen checking the road. When her grandmother lifted her arm, Arlette hurried across to the barn and slipped inside. She lit the lamp she had been carrying and made her way to the back of the barn, stopping at the secret room's partition.

'It's only me,' said Arlette.

'Wait a moment. I need to block the hole in the wall.'

She heard Saul shuffling back towards the entrance. 'All right.'

She slid the partition open and handed him the lamp. Next she opened her coat and untied Estelle who had been strapped to her chest by a length of material. She crouched and handed her daughter through the opening, before crawling through herself.

Saul greeted her with a kiss and wrapped an arm around her shoulders. In his other, he cradled his daughter who blinked in the dim lamplight.

'This is the highlight of my day,' said Saul. 'Holding my two girls in my arms.'

'Ours too,' Arlette said, with a smile.

'Come and sit down so I can see you both.'

Arlette sat down next to Saul on the straw mattress. The lamp shed a warm glow around the room, casting shadows of their movement. A chair and small table had been carried in earlier in the year to make eating and reading more comfortable. A cracked mirror hung beneath the opening in the wall that Saul had made, so he could shave by meagre daylight. The hole was now stuffed with straw to block light escaping. Several books, a change of clothing, a jug of water and several chunks of stale bread sat in a wooden crate in one corner of the room. A bucket with a lid for bodily necessities stood in the furthest corner.

Saul grinned. 'I think she's grown in two days. Hello, beautiful,' he said to his daughter. 'Have you been good for Mummy?'

Estelle smiled and reached for her father's hair. She grasped a handful and attempted to pull it to her mouth.

'Ouch!' joked Saul. He turned to Arlette. 'How are you, my love?'

Arlette shooed several moths away that were flitting around her head. 'Fine.'

'Has *he* been to the farm today?'

'Yes.'

'What did he want?'

'I was telling Grandma that he's probably homesick.'

'Well, I wish he'd stop getting his fill of family life from here.'

'I have a plan to stop him.'

Saul looked up from Estelle. 'What plan?'

'I'm going back to work at the manor.'

'Has he asked you to?'

'No, but I think it will stop him from coming to the farm. It will be safer for you.'

'If I'm quiet, I'm safe here.'

'It's not just you, though. He touches Estelle and Grandma is jittery. I hate him visiting.'

Arlette watched as Saul laid Estelle on the straw. He turned to Arlette and pulled her against his body. She wrapped her arms around his neck, inhaling the scent of his skin. His smell made her ache with longing.

'Stay strong,' he whispered.

She felt his warm breath on her neck. Her skin tingled. 'I will. For you and Estelle.'

'Don't bring any more books or food from the manor. Don't give him a reason to pay you any more attention.'

'I won't.'

'Have you heard any further information about the war?'

'Francine's mother still listens to the wireless in the square. The latest news is that Hamburg has been badly bombed by the Allies. Apparently the city is all but destroyed.'

'Let's hope Hitler was visiting at the time.' Saul pulled back and gazed at Arlette. 'You grow more beautiful.'

Arlette smiled and lowered her head. He lifted her chin with his fingertips and pressed his lips against hers. She moved her body against his and returned his kiss, an involuntary sound escaping her throat as he slid his tongue between her lips.

Estelle began to whimper and Arlette reluctantly pulled away from his embrace.

'We can't risk her crying out here. She may be heard from the road if soldiers are passing.'

Saul turned and picked up his daughter and the baby's mouth found his knuckles. She began to suck his skin.

'She's hungry,' said Arlette. 'We'd better go.'

'Can't you stay and feed her here? You've only been ten minutes.'

Arlette paused, then nodded. 'Of course.' She undid the buttons of her dress and slipped the straps of her undergarments from her shoulders. She felt Saul's eyes on her body as the sheer material slipped down to reveal her swollen breasts. She looked up and met Saul's eyes. She longed to be intimate with him and the desire in his eyes told her that he felt the same. He blinked, kissed Estelle and passed the baby to Arlette.

Chapter Thirty-Two

Arlette spoke with Herr Steiner about returning to work when he next visited the farm. He had seemed pleased with her decision and informed her that her timing was perfect. An important meeting was to take place the following Monday. An SS delegation was arriving from Berlin so it would be helpful if she could be available to be on hand for running errands.

At eight the following Monday morning, Arlette stepped through the front door to the manor and made her way to the kitchen. The Kommandant was busying himself with last minute preparations before the official visitors arrived. Usually so composed, he appeared preoccupied. He paused and blinked quizzically. A second later, he nodded and continued to pace the rooms and mutter under his breath. Arlette felt relieved. If he was busy, she would be left in peace.

By mid-morning, Arlette had made breakfast, cleared away, cleaned the bathrooms and was now sweeping the flight of stairs. She had started at the top of the curved staircase and was working her way down. Nazi flags were hung at intervals along the camber of the banister, adding colour to an otherwise dull décor. When she was nearing the bottom step, there was a knock on the front door. She continued to use the hand brush to sweep debris into a dustpan, but no one arrived to open the door. Whoever was there rapped again, this time faster and more impatiently. Arlette set her dustpan and brush down and walked downstairs into the vast hallway. She approached the front door and looked around once more. The hall was empty. She opened the door.

Six uniformed men stood before her, two of them heavily decorated with insignias and badges. Initially the first man seemed surprised to see her, but then straightened his shoulders.

'We're here to see Kommandant Hans Steiner,' he said.

Arlette pulled the door wide open, the sound of birdsong entering the hall at the same time as the men. She shut it again, still searching for someone to show the delegation to the Kommandant's office. The men looked at her expectantly. She had no choice.

'Please, come this way.'

They followed her, their boots clicking noisily on the parquet flooring. On reaching the library, she knocked and listened.

'*Herein!*'

She stepped inside. 'The delegation from Berlin have arrived, Herr Kommandant.'

He straightened his jacket and ran his palms across his cropped hair. 'Send them through and then bring us some coffee, please.'

They all walked past her and the last man closed the door. She breathed deeply, closed her eyes and rested her head against the door surround. She hadn't anticipated being asked to serve them refreshments. What would Gilbert, or any of the members of the Resistance for that matter, think of her for serving refreshments to Nazis?

'Are you well, miss?'

Arlette jumped and spun round to find a portly soldier standing in front of her. She stood up straight and said, 'Quite well, thank you,' before hurrying to the kitchen. She was far from feeling well. Her head throbbed, her full breasts were aching and she knew her daughter would soon need feeding.

Returning with a tray of seven cups of coffee, a sugar

bowl and a jug of milk, Arlette balanced the tray in an open palm and knocked. She was instructed to enter. Inside, four members of the SS were sitting around the desk with Kommandant Steiner. The other two men were writing in notebooks close by. They continued to converse but because they were speaking in German, Arlette couldn't understand what was being said.

'Thank you, Arlette. That will be all for the moment,' said the Kommandant.

An hour later, Arlette was walking back towards the kitchen when the door to the library opened. Her fingers were threaded through the handles of several mugs she had collected while cleaning the bedrooms. The delegation walked into the corridor and unwittingly blocked her way. Pressing her back against the wooden panelling on the wall, Arlette hugged the cups to her body. One by one, the Gestapo soldiers walked past her. She didn't raise her eyes. She watched the soldiers' shiny boots as they passed, her nostrils inhaling a mixture of tobacco, coffee and pine scent. The echo of their retreating footsteps grew quieter before she hurried into the kitchen. She sighed with relief and unwound her fingers from the cups' handles. Her thumb became stuck in one of them and the residual cold coffee spilled down her pinafore. Another set of footsteps echoed on the tiled floor. She looked up. It was the Kommandant.

'I have to leave with my visitors for Limoges. I will be gone for the afternoon,' he said.

She saw his eyes register the wet stain on her thigh. She pulled her thumb from the cup's handle. 'My thumb was caught ...'

He looked distracted. Maybe the meeting hadn't gone very well. He turned without another word and followed the delegation down the corridor and across the hallway.

A few minutes later, Arlette had washed the cups and was drying them when a bright light outside the kitchen window caught her eye. She leaned closer to the glass and saw that the sun was glinting off car windows. The delegation's vehicles were driving down Montverre Hill. She recognised the third car as the Kommandant's. Thank goodness they had left. Her relief was palpable.

Arlette took this opportunity to leave the manor and hurry home to feed her daughter. Her breasts had become so heavy with milk that her back was aching. She found her grandmother pacing in the shade of the mulberry tree while jiggling Estelle up and down.

'Thank goodness,' sighed Grandma Blaise. 'My arms are fit to drop off!'

'I'm sorry. I couldn't leave until the visitors had gone.'

'No matter. You're here now.'

Having fed Estelle, eaten a bowl of soup and changed her damp dress, Arlette returned to the manor. All was quiet. The building was silent and the large day room was empty. Usually she could tell if members of the High Command were in. She would hear the low hum of distant conversation or the creak of floorboards from movement upstairs. The library hadn't been cleaned due to the meeting, so Arlette decided to tackle that next. If the Kommandant returned from Limoges earlier than expected, she'd have no need to go back inside his office that afternoon – unless summoned.

Stepping inside the library, she breathed in the familiar musty sweet smell of old books. She had missed flicking through their pages whenever an opportunity had arisen. Stale cigarette smoke lingered in the air and clung to the curtains and the furniture's fabric. The Kommandant's desk was piled high with files, paperwork and books, but otherwise she saw nothing of interest in the room. The library appeared tidy except for coffee cups that were strewn where they'd last been put down. There was also a full ashtray on the desk that she would empty.

Curiosity led her closer to the paperwork. What had this important meeting been about? She scanned the papers on the desk but the Kommandant's notes were scribbled in German. *Mein Kampf* remained on his desk alongside a French dictionary. She collected the coffee cups and stacked them on a tray. One was missing. She looked around the room, scanning the tables, shelves and mantlepiece. There was no sign of the cup on any of the surfaces. She moved towards an upholstered armchair where one of the soldiers had been sitting and taking notes. She spotted the cup pushed beneath it. Bending to collect it, she caught sight of a folded sheet of paper that the cup was sitting on. Arlette looked around the room before kneeling on the rug and pulling the paper towards her. She stood up and walked towards the window where the light would be better to read by.

She was surprised to see that the bullet points on the page were written in French.

* *Heinrich Himmler has ordered that gypsies and part-gypsies are to be put on the same level as Jews and placed in concentration camps.*
* *Mass deportation of French Jews in Paris. Jews shipped by railroad freight cars to labour camps.*
* *Liquidation of ghetto has taken place.*
* *The evacuation and extermination of the Jewish race must never be spoken of in public.*

Arlette's eyes snagged on one word. Her gaze couldn't move from thirteen black letters. *Extermination.* Not the murder of numerous prisoners, but the killing of the entire Jewish race. It was impossible to absorb. Horrifying to imagine. Her mouth was open in disbelief. All those innocents. Saul must never be found. She'd die before giving away his whereabouts. Her legs lost all their strength and she sank into the chair.

Chapter Thirty-Three

December brought with it a bitter easterly wind, but inside the kitchen it was silent, warm and drowsy. It was Sunday, Arlette's day off from the manor. Despite being midday, the grey skies caused a gloom to descend upon Montverre so Arlette was letting out a seam in one of Estelle's dresses by candlelight. The shuddering light flickered against the walls.

Arlette jumped as the door flew open. She looked up and slowly lowered her sewing. Kommandant Steiner's silhouette filled the door frame. His forehead was corrugated with lines. She'd never seen him look so angry.

'Where is he?' he demanded.

'Who?'

He stepped inside. An icy chill followed him in before he slammed the door shut. The German closed his eyes and inhaled silently. His chest expanded and his shoulders rose. 'I am a busy man, Mademoiselle Blaise.'

He hadn't called her by her formal name for many months.

'I do not intend to play games,' he continued. 'I am looking for the Jew.' He removed his black leather gloves and wrung them impatiently between his hands.

Arlette could feel damp patches forming beneath her arms. Fear sent adrenalin coursing through her body and she could feel the slamming beat of blood in her head. 'If you mean the farmhand, he left last year.'

The Kommandant's boots clicked across the stone floor. Each hurried step took him closer to Arlette. His bare hand grasped her around her neck. He pushed her backwards. Her back hit the wall, knocking the breath from her lungs like a sigh. Breathing rapidly through her open mouth, she felt her eyes bulge as he pressed her throat. With difficulty, Arlette turned her head to one side and away from his hot breath. It was pungent from a recent *café noirissme*. She squeezed her eyes shut hoping darkness would help diminish her fear.

'You've taken me for a bloody fool. I've been informed that it was a Jew who fucked you. It's his bastard child, isn't it?' His mouth twisted as he spat words out. 'To think that I felt tender towards you. You make my skin crawl to touch you.' His German accent sounded harsh and full of granite consonants. 'No more lies.' It was almost a whisper. He stroked the side of her jaw with his forefinger. 'Tell me where he is, Jew-whore.'

Questions were clawing at her thoughts. Who had betrayed Saul? Was it someone they knew? He didn't know about the secret room, she reasoned through her panic. He was testing her. 'I've told you,' said Arlette, still not looking at him. 'He left.'

Silence.

The Kommandant didn't move for a few seconds. He dropped his hands to his side and took a step backwards. Arlette held her neck with the palm of one hand. She dared to glance at him. His lips were set in a straight tight line, his nose wrinkled in distaste. A V-shaped frown sat between his eyebrows.

'Why do you persist with lies?'

'I'm not lying, he—'

'Enough!'

His spittle hit her face, making her blink. Arlette saw his lips slope downwards in the shape of a sickle blade. He pointed a finger an inch from her eyes. She hoped he couldn't see her trembling. She must keep him calm. Estelle would wake up if he shouted.

'You disappoint me.' He lowered his hand but his eyes remained focused on her. 'You don't seem to recognise how much you owe me. I could have had you arrested many times. And your father too.' He shook his head slowly. 'Where is the Jew?'

Arlette remained silent.

'You're making this very difficult for me because I've received information that he's hiding here. I know you are lying to me. If you don't tell me, I will take this farm apart stone by stone.'

Arlette blinked and swallowed loudly, a reflex action she couldn't control. He must be bluffing about dismantling the farmhouse, and surely the secret room wouldn't be found now that the new wall had weathered over time? She remembered the notes she found in his office after the meeting with the SS. The Jewish race was to be exterminated. 'He left a long time ago. Someone's lying to you.'

The Kommandant turned and sat down at the table. His hands covered his mouth as if praying. His seemingly calm exterior felt more chilling than his raised voice. 'I believe that the liar is you, Mademoiselle Blaise. A member of the Resistance was captured yesterday. He was arrested trying to commit an act of sabotage in the vicinity. Let's just say that with a little persuasion, he talked. Don't look so worried. It wasn't your brother this time, but we will find him too.'

Arlette felt sick. How did he know Gilbert was a *maquisard*?

'It took some time for him to talk, but a whip usually loosens the tongue. He gave us a lot of information before he was shot.'

Arlette closed her eyes.

'Don't look so distressed, Mademoiselle Blaise. We were compassionate. His body resembled raw meat after two hours. We took away his pain. Before he died he named several *maquisards* who worked alongside him. Your brother's name was mentioned.'

Arlette could feel her heartbeat thumping against her ribs. She glanced at him.

The Kommandant continued, his demeanour seemingly calm. 'This man told us something very interesting. It seems that your brother isn't happy that his sister is hiding her Jewish lover and the father of her child here at the farm.' He stood up and hurled the dining chair across the room. It crashed against the fireplace, snapping a leg. He took several strides towards her.

Arlette lowered her chin against her neck, hunched her shoulders and squeezed her eyes shut. She knew that he was capable of striking her, but she could endure anything as long as Estelle and Saul were safe. She prepared herself for the pain and waited for the blow. His hot breath touched her skin when he spoke against her face.

'I show you civility and you repay me with disdain. I know you are hiding this Jew. Don't think me a fool, because I am telling you now, I will not be leaving this farm without that scum.'

Arlette didn't reply. He could beat her as long as her family was safe.

'And so you see, my next action is your own fault. I don't want to do it.' He spoke quietly while looking down at his fists. 'You have forced my hand.'

Arlette's shaking intensified. She stood up straight, determined not to flinch before he struck her. She would not cower or run. She would face this for the two people who meant the world to her. Closing her eyes, Arlette prepared herself for a sharp pain, but all that touched her bare arms was a gentle waft of air from his billowing coat. He swept past her into the sitting room.

At first she was confused. Then the dreadful realisation hit. 'No!' she screamed. Arlette ran after him. She caught up with him at the bottom of the stairs. She grabbed at his coat. The coarse material slipped through her fingers when he took the stairs two at a time. She followed. She tripped in her haste then clambered on all fours.

'No! Not my baby!'

At the top of the staircase he marched into Estelle's room. His footsteps thudded on the floorboards. His greatcoat leant over the baby's crib like a black shadow. Mucous and tears streamed down Arlette's face. She clawed at his impenetrable coat, its metal badges and buttons bruising her fingers. He knocked her to the ground when he turned and walked back out of the room. She scrambled to her feet. The crib was empty. Obscenely empty. Hurling herself towards the staircase she stumbled down. A clog fell off so she kicked the other from her foot. She ran through the empty living room and kitchen and staggered outside. Arlette was shivering violently and the snow stung her bare feet.

At that moment Grandma Blaise and Francine walked into the yard carrying kindling. They stopped, fear etched on their faces. They were looking towards the front corner of the farmhouse. Klara was barking wildly, the hackles on her back standing erect. Arlette turned to see what they were looking at.

The Kommandant was holding a gun in one hand. Estelle was in the other, poised over a barrel of rainwater. Jigsaw pieces of ice were floating on its surface. A scream rang out and Arlette's throat ached. She could see Estelle wriggling in his outstretched arm. One of her daughter's arms escaped from the blanket and pink fingers splayed, searching for her mother's touch. Grandma Blaise gave a guttural groan.

'My baby, my baby,' mumbled Arlette. She wiped mucous from her nose with the back of her hand. She began to stumble towards them, each step moving closer to her daughter. A sharp stone punctured the ball of her freezing foot. Just a few more steps. Her footprints were tinged red in the snow.

Kommandant Steiner raised the gun to prevent Arlette from coming any closer. In his other arm, he held Estelle high like she was a trophy. 'Not one more step or I will drop the baby. Where is the Jew?'

Arlette stopped abruptly. She held up her hands in surrender. She had to assure him she would move no closer. Someone was crying. A bird chirruped in a skeletal tree. Arlette knelt down in the snow. She clasped her hands together. 'Please, I beg you. Give me my baby.'

'Where is the Jew?' The Kommandant lowered Estelle so that she was only a few inches above the icy water. The baby began to cry.

Arlette leaned forwards on her hands and knees, one arm extended pleadingly towards the Kommandant. She didn't care how she grovelled. Only Estelle mattered at this moment. 'My baby,' she sobbed.

The Kommandant appeared unnaturally calm. His coat occasionally caught a sudden gust and wafted behind him. He lowered Estelle. The blanket and the back of the baby's head dipped into the water. Ripples patterned the water's surface and chunks of ice began to slowly spin. Estelle was startled. She stopped crying and splayed out her arms and legs in shock. Klara barked manically and ran in circles around the barrel. The Kommandant kicked her. Klara yelped and Estelle screamed.

'The Jew?' shouted the Kommandant.

'No!' screamed Arlette. Her arms extended towards her baby. She grazed her knees as she stumbled to standing.

She had screamed 'no' instinctively because every sinew in her body cried out against her baby being dropped into the barrel. She hadn't meant it to be a refusal to tell where Saul was. Estelle was plunged into the barrel and swallowed by black water. The baby's screaming stopped but Arlette's began. She was clawing at the Kommandant's face and scratching at the arm that held Estelle submerged. She screamed as if possessed.

There was a sudden commotion and scuffling behind her but Arlette didn't care and didn't look. At that moment, Kommandant let go of Estelle and walked away from the barrel. Without hesitation, Arlette plunged her arms into the icy water. She searched frantically for her daughter. Her fingers searching, she screamed her daughter's name. She grasped at clothing and the baby's blanket. She pulled them upwards towards her.

Estelle floated to the surface. Her shapeless body morphed into lumps and bulges. The dress was swollen with trapped air. Francine ran to her side and the two of them pulled the baby's limp body from the water. Arlette held her daughter to her body and ran towards the house. Francine supported her stumbling steps. Grandma Blaise joined them inside and tried to take Estelle from her granddaughter's arms, but Arlette screamed and fought.

'Arlette!' shouted her grandmother. 'We need to try and save the baby. Quickly. We don't have time for histrionics.'

Arlette blinked in recognition, releasing her daughter. She watched her grandmother take Estelle and lay her on the kitchen table. The child's skin was white, her lips and eyelids grey. She looked like a porcelain doll. Arlette shivered. She watched Grandma Blaise lean over her granddaughter, breathing air into her lungs. She felt Francine's arm wrap around her shoulder, her friend's sobbing breaking the silence. Arlette watched while trembling.

'Don't just stand there!' shouted Grandma Blaise, over her shoulder. 'Stoke the fire and find some dry clothing for Estelle. Go and get changed, Arlette. You can't feed the baby if you're wet and cold. Hurry.'

Through tears and pain Arlette hurried upstairs. She shivered violently as she stripped naked and pulled on one of her mother's slips, a thick dress and a shawl. Within seconds she was back downstairs. Francine was warming a blanket against the open fire. Grandma Blaise's shoulders were rising and falling with each breath she gave to Estelle. The kitchen was silent apart from her grandmother's inhalations. Arlette continued to shake, her muscles in spasm and her feet sore and bleeding. 'Please God, please God,' she whimpered.

Estelle coughed. Arlette's laugh was fractured with disbelief.

'Francine, fetch a chair for Arlette and take it to the fire,' ordered Grandma Blaise.

Francine did as she was asked.

'Now wrap your daughter in her warm blanket and put her to the breast. She needs some warm milk inside her.'

In a daze, Arlette sat on the chair and opened the shawl in which her now naked daughter was wrapped. Her own fingers struggled with the buttons of her dress so Francine undid them and helped Estelle to her breast. Arlette squeezed a little milk onto Estelle's lips encouraging her to feed. Her daughter wouldn't suckle but at least she was breathing. Arlette sat cradling her, rocking to and fro for twenty minutes by the warmth of the fire's embers. Then she looked up and blinked. 'Saul. Where's Saul?'

Chapter Thirty-Four

Grandma Blaise pulled a chair next to her granddaughter and held Arlette's hand.

'You need to concentrate on yourself and your daughter now.'

'What do you mean?'

'Saul has surrendered.'

Arlette stared open-mouthed at her grandmother. 'It's not true. Tell me it's not true.' She looked at Francine. Her friend slowly nodded.

'He protected his family,' said Grandma Blaise.

'He must have heard the commotion and come out of the secret room,' said Francine. 'What else could he do? He couldn't watch his daughter drown.'

Arlette stood up and handed Estelle to her grandmother. 'I'm going to the manor. I'm going to speak to the Kommandant. He'll listen. I'll make him.'

'Sit down!' shouted Grandma Blaise.

Arlette's eyes widened. She was shocked by her grandmother's severe tone. 'I need to find Saul.'

Grandma Blaise stood up. 'Don't be ridiculous. What a stupid idea. Just listen to yourself. The manor is full of the Gestapo High Command and you want to run and ask them for your Jewish lover back? I've never heard you speak such dangerous nonsense. You're not thinking properly.' She handed Estelle back. 'You're a mother and you need to put your child first. Your father and Gilbert would agree. You've no idea how fortunate you are that this German is fond of you.'

'I hate him. How can it be a good thing? He's vile.'

'You're fortunate because you haven't been arrested for

hiding a Jew. Fortunate because Francine and I haven't been arrested either. Yet. Who knows if soldiers are on their way to us now? We can only pray that Herr Steiner doesn't arrange for a firing squad for us. We must count our blessings that he didn't march us all at gunpoint across to the manor. And that includes Estelle.'

Arlette began to cry. She sank back into the chair. 'He'll be sent to a labour camp. He'll die. I love him.'

She began to rock to and fro in despair.

Several days had passed since Saul's surrender. Arlette had been inconsolable and Francine had been told to return home and not to visit. It was too dangerous at present. Each day Arlette and her grandmother had moved like sleepwalkers around the farmhouse, speaking little and dreading the sound of footsteps in the yard. As yet, Kommandant Steiner hadn't returned and Arlette had refused to go back to cook and clean at the manor, despite her grandmother's protestations about keeping the German appeased. The old lady still didn't dare to believe that there wouldn't be some kind of reprisal.

It was late afternoon when Grandma Blaise drove the trap to Saint-Pierre's. She said she needed to pray in God's house for their safety and she promised to light a candle for Saul's well being. Arlette was in her bedroom folding clean linen when Estelle began to cough. She lifted her daughter out of her padded drawer, concern creasing her brow because her little girl hadn't been well since she had been plunged into the freezing water. She had suckled poorly and her chest rattled with each breath. Arlette sat down and patted her daughter's back as long dribbles fell from her baby's mouth. Estelle was then sick and a curdled puddle of milk emptied from her belly onto her mother's knee. It smelt sour. Arlette bent forwards and kissed her daughter's head. 'My poor darling. Lie down on your side while Mama changes her clothes.'

Arlette opened the bedroom window to let some fresh air in. She looked out beyond the gates, past the bleak branches of the orchard, the manor's tired exterior and across the misty valley. It had begun to drizzle with tiny silver drops of rain patterning the glass. She heard the light notes of the chapel in Montverre village chime the hour and hoped that her grandmother had made it to evening prayers before the rain had started. She focused on the river, now grey in the late afternoon light, and wondered where Saul was. Her body ached when she thought of him, as if a fist clutching a handful of longing had thumped her in the stomach. She could still imagine his face, but already the memory of his voice and touch was diminishing. It was Estelle who was saving her from madness.

Arlette unbuttoned her milk-stained dress, remembering how Saul's long slim fingers had undone her buttons beside the river on the evening that Estelle had been conceived. And now, fourteen months later, he was gone and their daughter was sick. She laid her shawl on the bed and slid her dress over her shoulders and let it fall to the floor. Naked apart from her underwear, she picked it up and dropped it into a wicker laundry basket in the corner of the room. She heard movement in the living room downstairs and was secretly pleased that her grandmother had changed her mind about going. She felt anxious alone with Estelle, but now she would sit in front of the fire and watch her grandmother knit. She could hear her walking up the stone staircase.

'Did you change your mind, Grandma?'

Arlette crossed to the wardrobe and froze. The pungent aroma of tobacco wafted into the bedroom. Her fingers gripped the brass handles of the wooden doors. A shadow fell across the doorway. Kommandant Steiner. He noticed her lack of clothing and smiled. She tried to cover herself with her arms and turn her body towards the wardrobe.

He smelt of alcohol. Arlette stepped towards the bed and reached for her shawl, holding it close to her body. Despite her hatred for this man, she knew that she must afford him some civility. Her grandmother had made her understand how dangerous he was. He could have them shot with the snap of his tobacco-stained fingers.

'What are you doing here?' she asked.

'You haven't been at work.'

'My daughter is sick.'

'Why can't the old woman look after the child?'

'Perhaps next week.'

His smile disappeared. 'Tomorrow.'

His eyes were glazed. His speech was slurred. He was drunk. Arlette squeezed the shawl even tighter between her fingers.

The Kommandant's forced smile retuned. 'Surely the child will feel better tomorrow?'

'She'd be a lot better if you hadn't tried to drown her.' Arlette bit her lip. She mustn't anger him.

'Now, now.' He sounded as if he were chastising a small child. He took two unsteady steps inside her bedroom. 'We both know you brought that about yourself. You had ample opportunity to obey my orders but your stubbornness led to consequences we'd all rather not have happened. And please, call me Hans.'

She took a step backwards. 'Please will you wait downstairs until I'm dressed? The smoke won't help her chest.'

She saw the German's gaze move from her bare shoulders to her legs, and shivered.

'Arlette—'

Her name sounded like an obscenity spoken with his accent. 'My name is Mademoiselle Blaise.'

'Arlette, you don't seem to acknowledge how much I have protected you. You owe me.' He sucked on his cigarette, holding it between his thumb and forefinger, squinting when the silver smoke reached his eyes.

Arlette swallowed audibly. 'Please can we discuss this downstairs? My grandmother's outside with the dog and you being here in my room is inappropriate.'

He raised his voice and struck his boot with the crop, startling her. *Thwak!* 'Lies! I saw your grandmother close to Montverre's church as I walked here and I tied your dog to the doorway of the barn.' He closed his eyes for a few seconds, inhaled deeply then spoke more quietly. 'Let's try and remain on friendly terms, shall we? I could make life very difficult for you if I wished. You've broken many rules. *So* many rules.' He took a step towards her and tapped his riding crop on the bedpost. 'One. Your family built a room to hide provisions.' He hit the bedpost a second time. 'Two. You hid a Jew. And three,' he said, pointing the crop a few inches from her face, 'you lied about both these violations. I don't think you realise the seriousness of your situation.'

Arlette didn't reply and hoped he couldn't hear the violent thudding of her heart in her chest. She felt dizzy with fear.

'All I'm asking for is a little kindness on your part,' he continued. 'Is that too much to ask for someone who has saved your life? Your family's lives?'

Arlette could feel her body shaking but met his eye with defiance. 'I believe I've always been civil to you, Herr Steiner.'

'Civil?' He grimaced as if he'd just tasted something

sour. 'You could be civil to a stranger in the street. It means nothing. I'm asking for a little kindness in exchange for your life. After all, what would happen to your child if you and your grandmother were arrested? Or shot?' The stirrup on his boot clanked as he took the final step that separated them. 'What would happen to a defenceless child then?' He cocked his head to one side in question. 'However, as I'm the only person who knows where I found the Jew, I can be persuaded to look the other way. That is, if you show me how grateful you are that I've spared your life.'

He stroked her arm. She froze with repulsion. An insect-crawl of understanding caused her to shiver. He was looking for sex in exchange for her life. Arlette instinctively glanced at Estelle. Her baby's lips moved as if she was suckling in her sleep. She was aware that Kommandant Steiner was following her gaze towards the drawer. His breath smelt of brandy and she could see two healing scabs on his chin where he had cut himself while shaving. She had to remain calm. Sickening images of his last rough attempt to kiss her sprang to mind, but now that she was a mother, she knew that she would endure any appalling situation in order to protect her daughter.

She tried one last time to distract him and pretend that she didn't know what he was alluding to. 'You're right, Herr Steiner ... Hans. I've made mistakes. I've been worried about my father and grandmother and you have been very understanding. Please forgive me if my manners towards you have suffered. If you would kindly wait downstairs while I make myself decent, I'll be pleased to offer you some refreshment and we can talk.'

'A man needs more than one type of refreshment, Arlette. I haven't seen my wife for two years.' He pulled a face. 'Hildi is a good woman, but plain. A simple woman.

I was young and foolish when we married. She arouses no passions.'

He belched quietly into his fist. The odour from a digesting meal seeped through his fingers. He raised the riding crop and once again lifted it towards her head. Arlette blinked then silently berated herself for showing weakness. He slid the crop against her neck and using it, pulled a lock of her dark hair so that it fell forwards. He stroked her cheek with it. The smooth leather felt like a serpent against her skin. She stepped backwards once more, her bare shoulders coming into contact with the wall. She had retreated as far as she could.

Estelle began to cough, drawing Kommandant Steiner's eyes towards the baby for a third time. Arlette needed to get him away from her daughter.

'Not in here. Come through to the spare room next door. The baby may settle if we leave her in peace.'

The German's eyes glinted predatorily. She forced herself to take his hand and lead him out of the room and away from her daughter. The ever-present smell of alcohol was on his breath. The stairs looked so close; so inviting. If it weren't for Estelle she would make a run for it. She took him into the next bedroom. Her father's armchair was by the window where he used to look across the valley, cigarette in hand, by the open window. The shutters were partly closed, leaving the room dim and cold. He closed the bedroom door and threw his cigarette on the wooden floor, twisting his boot into it. Next he pulled the knitted shawl from her shoulders and leered at her young breasts swollen with milk beneath her bra.

'Won't you be late for manoeuvres?' asked Arlette. She was trying to delay the inevitable. 'We could always arrange to meet tomorrow if you think you'll be missed.'

His hands went to his waist and he began to unbuckle

his belt. 'I won't be missed. I have toothache and requested leave this afternoon to visit a dentist in Limoges. I travelled with another officer who had business there, but the damned dentist was Jewish and has been forbidden from practising due to the new rules.' He laughed at the irony. 'So I spent the afternoon in a bar and brandy has been my painkiller.'

The Kommandant unclipped his revolver and threw it on the bed. His belt followed. 'I came back on a filthy tram, walked up the hill from the village and thought I'd pay a visit to my beautiful Arlette. She owes me, I said to myself.' He unbuttoned his breeches. 'No one passed me on the way so don't worry that we'll be disturbed.' His trousers fell to his calves, revealing his legs, white against the dark material of his uniform.

Arlette's mouth twisted with loathing. He looked ridiculous standing there, unable to pull his trousers off because he'd forgotten to remove his high-buckled boots.

He started to chuckle to himself. 'You see what you do? You drive a man insane with desire.' He sat on the bed and raised one boot to remove it. In a split second, Arlette realised that he couldn't run. Not only was he drunk but his legs were bound together by his breeches and restricted movement. Taking this chance of escape, she ran towards the door. Her fingers fumbled with the handle. She wrenched it open but he was quick. Startlingly quick. Perhaps, despite his stupor, he'd been half expecting her to run. Before she'd even reached her own room to fetch Estelle, he'd caught hold of her long hair and jerked her backwards. She fell against his body. His breeches were still in a pathetic pile around his knees. She could feel the cold metal of his jacket buttons pressing against her skin. He pulled her head back by her hair.

Arlette fought with all her might. This seemed to excite

him further. His tongue probed her lips and teeth. He tore off her bra, crushing a breast with his rough hand. His foul breath was in her face. His teeth knocked against her top lip, filling her mouth with the metallic taste of blood.

The Kommandant paused for a second. His breath was rapid with desire. He gripped her upper arms and pushed her back against the landing wall, banging her head.

'*Saumensch*!' he spat. 'France rolled over without much of a fight and now you will do the same. Do as I say or your father will be arrested immediately, and don't think of reporting this because no one will believe the word of a Jew-whore against a senior member of the Reich.'

He took a step backwards to gaze at his prize before claiming it. For a second, he froze, as if suspended. His eyes fixed on Arlette's. Then they bulged in horror when he realised the solid ground had disappeared from beneath one of his boots. His breeches, still gathered around the top of his boots, prevented any chance of saving himself. He started to claw at empty space. He grasped at the walls on either side of the staircase. Before he fell, he stretched his hands towards her.

Arlette didn't move. She made no attempt to catch him. They stared at each other. She saw resignation in his eyes. Before he fell, he knew she wouldn't save him.

Arlette watched motionless, frozen with fear. He fell backwards and landed on his back halfway down the staircase. The force of the impact knocked the air from his lungs with a groan. Momentum swung his legs over his head. He continued to fall, finally cracking his head on the stone floor.

Silence.

The chaos had stopped. Nothing moved except her heaving chest as her lungs gasped for air. For several minutes she couldn't move or take her eyes from the motionless figure lying at the bottom of the stairs. Herr Steiner was lying on his side with his head turned at an odd angle. His face was pressed against the floor. His head appeared to be growing, expanding until his outline became grotesque. Shaking uncontrollably, she edged forwards. She covered her lips for fear of being sick. Step by slow step she descended the stairs. Still the outline of his head appeared to swell. She stood three steps from his body, the strange vision becoming clear. In the dim light she saw that a dark pool of blood was expanding beneath the Kommandant's head. It spread outwards, dark purple in the shadows, until it began to slowly sink into the stone floor. Arlette knew that this was far from the end. This was just the beginning of something far more terrifying. A Kommandant of the Third Reich had died in her house. She had to act. For the safety of her family, she had to move. Every second was as precious as they were. She had to hide the body.

Chapter Thirty-Five

Arlette couldn't move Kommandant Steiner by herself but she knew that he would eventually be missed at the manor later that evening when his prolonged absence would be noticed. Questions would be asked. Klara had been untied from the barn and watched while her mistress strode back and forth in tortured despair until Grandma Blaise returned from Saint-Pierre's. Arlette listened for the sound of Mimi's hooves. She wouldn't be long now. It was nearly curfew.

A few minutes later, she lit the lamp on hearing the trap and stepped outside into the yard. Her fear of attracting the attention of a passing German patrol had prevented her from doing so until now.

'Woah, girl,' said Grandma Blaise.

Mimi shook her thick neck and whinnied as she came to a standstill.

'Thank you for coming out with the lamp, my dear. I'm sure I can smell snow in the air. It's definitely cold enough for it.'

Arlette held up the lamp so her grandmother could climb down safely.

'Grandma ...'

'What's the matter? Have you been crying?'

'Grandma, something terrible has happened.'

'You're shaking. Is Estelle all right?'

Arlette began to cry. 'He came and tried to ... he tried to ...'

'Come inside.' Grandma Blaise held Arlette's elbow and guided her granddaughter across the yard. They stepped inside the kitchen. Shutting the door, the old lady took the lamp from Arlette's trembling hands. 'What's happened? Who's been here?'

'Oh, Grandma, he's dead. I don't know what to do. They're going to hang me in the square.'

Grandma Blaise set the lamp to one side and grasped Arlette firmly by her upper arms. She urged her to calm down. 'Now explain slowly what has happened.'

Despite hyperventilating, Arlette managed to tell her what had happened. 'But he fell, Grandma. I swear I didn't push him.'

'By the sound of things I shouldn't think anyone would blame you if you had. Stay here for a moment. I'll take the lamp and check if he's just unconscious.' After a few minutes the old lady returned. 'He's dead. We don't have long. By the morning there'll be a search party looking for him.'

'He's too heavy. What shall we do?'

'I want you to take the lamp and carefully dig up the winter kale.'

'What?'

'Do as I say. Protect the roots and don't damage the leaves because we're going to replant them.'

'I don't understand.'

'Just do as I say and do it quickly.'

Outside, the strengthening wind bit her skin. She grasped the winter kale by its stalks and pulled both the leaves and root balls from the vegetable plot. The absurdity of the present moment struck Arlette as she stacked bunches of kale in the darkness. The weak glow of the lamp seemed to transform their curly green leaves into hideous black blossoms.

Arlette continued to dig. Nausea overwhelmed her, making her throat sting with stomach acid. She heaved into the soil, spitting bitter bile into a hole where she'd dug up the vegetables. They would kill her. They wouldn't believe her story. What would happen to Estelle? She wiped hot tears from her cold cheeks with the back of her hand. The earth smelt sweet and acrid, like a forgotten jar of perfume. Grey flakes floated around the lamp. It had started to snow.

Klara wagged her tail and sniffed around the fresh holes before squatting to leave her scent. Arlette shooed her away and when she'd dug up the kale, stood up and went to find her grandmother. Inside the kitchen, she found her unravelling a large skein of string.

'I've done it. What are you doing?' asked Arlette.

'By using this thick twine and Mimi's strength, we'll be able to move the body.'

Arlette recognised the ball of string as the one that had brought the breech calf into the world when she'd first met Saul. Now, instead of helping bring life into the world, it was helping to drag a dead body. She followed her grandmother through the sitting room and into the hall where Kommandant Steiner lay in a fetid state, dark blood coagulating around a head wound. A shadow of liquid circled his underwear where his bladder had emptied after he'd fallen. His trousers still lay crumpled around his knees revealing his pale twisted thighs.

'We must be quick. His body hasn't stiffened yet but it won't be long. Here, your fingers are younger than mine. Tie this around his ankles.'

Arlette looked horrified and didn't move.

'Come along. He can't hurt you now. Think of Estelle.'

Arlette took the twine and edged closer to the Kommandant's body. Her fingers shook. She tied it around his ankles and secured it with a knot.

'Tie it tightly,' said Grandma Blaise.

Arlette stood up. 'I've done it.'

'Right, now listen. I'm going to fetch Mimi and bring her round to the front door so she can drag the body to the vegetable garden. I want you to take a shovel from the front of the barn and dig a hole where the kale was growing. A big hole. Do you understand?'

Arlette nodded.

'Take the lamp with you because I need to move the body in darkness. Be as quick and quiet as you can.'

Arlette hurried back outside. Snowflakes melted on her face. She retrieved a shovel and returned to the vegetable garden. She began to dig, thankful that the well-tended soil wasn't too hard to cut into with the blade of the spade. Klara began to dig too, nose down and paws scraping soil behind her. The irony of the situation didn't escape her. She remembered that the Kommandant had sanctioned the return of their horse at her own request. Due to that decision, they now had a way of disposing of his body.

After ten minutes of digging and with sweat sticking her undergarments to her clammy back, Arlette heard a noise. She stopped shovelling and listened. There was a hushing sound. Something was scraping. She strained her ears in the darkness to hear above the gusting wind. Klara growled deep inside her throat. The noise grew louder. Then Mimi's outline lumbered around the corner of the house. Her hooves were clomping on the gravel as she dragged the Kommandant's body behind her.

She heard her grandmother order the horse to stop. Grandma Blaise appeared beside her and they both continued to dig. After twenty minutes, they stopped.

'We're going to have to drag him ourselves now. You can do this, Arlette. Think of Saul and Estelle. We need to do this to survive. Are you listening to me?'

'Yes.'

'Good girl. Come and help me then.'

They walked around Mimi's huge frame and looked down at the Kommandant's body lying outstretched on the ground. His legs were raised because the twine tied to his ankles had been attached to a strap across the mare's flanks. His arms had splayed out behind his body, raised above his head as if in surrender.

'I'll cut the string,' said Grandma Blaise, 'and you lead Mimi out of the way.'

The body was released and the mare was led inside the barn. They began to drag the German's dead weight towards the vegetable plot. Arlette grasped at his shirt. It ripped under the pressure.

'His arm. Grab his arm,' said the old lady. 'I'll grab the other one.'

Arlette shuddered and reached for the Kommandant's wrist. It felt like cold wax but she grasped it and pulled. He didn't move until her grandmother told her to pull at the same time as she did.

'One, two, pull. One, two, pull.'

Slowly the body inched closer to the hole but Klara began to yap loudly. She growled and barked, snapping at the body's clothing. She snarled, pulling at the material with her teeth.

'She'll disturb everyone in the manor. Put her in the kitchen,' said Grandma Blaise.

With Klara inside the farmhouse and her barking muffled by the thick walls, they continued to drag the corpse until they reached the vegetable garden. They leant the Kommandant against the low wall. The wind abated for a few seconds and a low groan emanated from his body.

Arlette let out a shriek and took several steps back. 'He's alive. My God. He's alive.'

Grandma Blaise put her finger to her lips. 'Shhhh! He's not. Calm down. He's not. We've just dislodged some air in his body. It's normal for dead bodies to make sounds when they're disturbed.'

'Are you sure? Are you sure? I don't like it.'

'Arlette! Calm down.' Grandma Blaise was beside her now. 'Stop making a noise. Do you want an entire manor of Germans to come and find out what all the noise is about? He's dead. He can't hurt you any more, but those men over there certainly can, so come along.'

Breathing through her open mouth, Arlette helped her grandmother drag the body over the low wall of the vegetable garden and lay it beside the hole.

'We haven't made it long enough,' said Arlette.

'It'll do. It's deep,' answered her grandmother. 'We'll have to fold the body into it.'

Together they pushed his upper body into the void head first, leaving his legs lying flat on the soil. By pulling and pushing in turn, they folded his legs into the hole and stood up gasping for breath. Snowflakes danced and swirled on top of his crumpled uniform.

'We can't stop yet,' said Grandma Blaise. 'We've got to fill it in now.'

'The gun!'

'What gun?'

'He took off his gun and belt off upstairs.'

'Fetch them. Be quick.'

Arlette ran inside and through the kitchen. She skirted the congealed pool of blood and hurried upstairs. Once she'd picked up his belongings she sidled downstairs, carefully cradling the cold heavy gun in her palms. She feared that a sudden movement might make it fire. Back outside, she threw them in to the hole and the women began to dig the soil back over the body. When half the soil had been evenly spread over his body they replanted the kale on top of the makeshift grave.

'What shall we do with the soil that's left over?' asked Arlette. 'We need to move it.'

'It needs distributing. Spread it everywhere. Like this.'

Grandma Blaise dug a spade into the remaining earth and walked to the back of the vegetable plot. She scattered it evenly. Arlette joined her until the pile eventually disappeared. Standing back, she held the lamp at shoulder height to view where they'd been. Small drifts of snow were already banking against one side of the kale stems, slowly hiding any evidence of disturbed earth.

'We have some cleaning to do now and we need to get our story straight. Neither of us have seen the Kommandant in several days, do you understand?' said Grandma Blaise.

Chapter Thirty-Six

For a week following the Kommandant's disappearance, it continued to snow while soldiers searched every house in Montverre. Soldiers were brutal in their interrogation of households and everywhere from attics, outhouses, cellars and garages to dog kennels and rabbit hutches were searched. Every home in the village was left in disarray, the wreckage of many pieces of furniture now only worth burning in the hearth for half an hour of heat. Valuables were discovered missing after the inspections, but not one person dared to report the stolen items.

The hunt for information into the German's absence included the farmhouse. Another painstaking search took place, this time by a dozen grim-faced soldiers who cared little for the neat home they damaged and disrupted. Arlette and Grandma Blaise held each other in fear as they watched from the kitchen window while several soldiers strode around the yard and garden, sometimes walking less than a couple of metres from where the Kommandant was buried. They could hear clattering and shouting from the barn, but after half an hour and no traces of the Kommandant to be found, the troops left.

Later that week rumours grew like bindweed that Kommandant Steiner had absconded while visiting the dentist in Limoges, because Germany was losing its stronghold in Europe. Local gossip said he was a coward who had escaped before he'd been arrested for war crimes. Posters had been hung in the village offering extra coupons for any news of Kommandant Hans Steiner's whereabouts, but after a couple of rainstorms the posters ripped and hung like catkins. They weren't replaced.

* * *

A fortnight after the Kommandant's accident, Arlette was woken at five in the morning by Klara snuffling on the other side of her bedroom door. She'd ordered her dog back to the kitchen before lying back down again, her mind immediately returning to the thoughts which haunted her waking hours: the vegetable garden. Snow had fallen thickly the night they'd buried the German, its white shroud covering the land and hiding every trace of disturbed soil and scraped gravel. Grandma Blaise said that up in heaven Fleur had protected them and made it so.

Arlette pushed these intrusive thoughts from her mind. Estelle had slept soundly and she couldn't hear her daughter's crackling chest or wheezing breath. Please God, let it be a sign that she was recovering. Klara had come back upstairs and could be heard whining intermittently outside the bedroom door. Several minutes passed. A chill of doubt began to prickle at Arlette's arms. It prevented her from falling asleep again. She sat up and slid her legs out of bed. Shivering in the darkness, she fumbled to light a stub of a candle on the bedside table. It flickered into a yellow flame. Shadows shuddered and danced on the walls of the bedroom. Arlette looked into Estelle's makeshift crib.

Her screams brought Grandma Blaise scurrying into her bedroom. She was tying a robe around her waist as she bustled around the bed. The old woman looked into the padded drawer where the baby lay. She lifted Estelle in her shawl and laid her on the bed. Estelle's ashen features resembled a mannequin's.

'Breathe for her, Grandma. Like before. Breathe for her.' Arlette gripped her own hair close to her scalp and squeezed her fists. She clenched and pulled at her hair in panic. 'Grandma!' She looked pleadingly into the old lady's eyes. Tears were rolling down her grandmother's cheeks when she gave an almost imperceptible shake of her head.

'No! No!' wailed Arlette.

'My dearest child, it's too late.'

'No, it's not. You're wrong.' Arlette was rocking on the bed hysterically. 'I'll do it. It's not too late.' She pulled Estelle's lifeless body towards her and laid her palms on either side of her daughter's cheeks. Before attempting to breathe into her mouth, Arlette's hands shot back against her own body. She looked at her grandmother, open-mouthed. Grandma Blaise closed her eyes slowly and nodded in affirmation. Estelle's skin felt like ice.

Arlette gave a guttural wail like that of a wounded animal. Grandma Blaise pulled her into her arms and they cried until daylight began to seep in through the gap in the shutters.

Estelle's weakened body had succumbed to pneumonia and she died during that particularly bitter night. Death had barged in through the farmhouse door and taken up immediate residency without explanation or warning. Arlette's visceral response was to retreat into a sepia-coloured hibernation in order to protect herself from losing her mind with grief. She lost her appetite, both refusing the offer of meagre rations or platitudes from her grandmother. She sat and stared at the flames in the hearth, her mind disturbed by images of her daughter. She existed in a kind of limbo, at night reaching out into the darkness to the vacant space where Estelle's drawer once sat. She cursed the transience of life; one moment cradling her baby in her arms and the next, Estelle's short story was over.

Thoughts of the Kommandant's body, Saul's absent emaciated frame and her father's face interspersed her grieving. Her Brittany spaniel's presence became a balm for Arlette's grief-induced malady. Klara's warm soft body and unconditional love gave her some solace. Her dog was a lifeline as delicate as a silken thread, but a lifeline nonetheless. She would look back on this month in happier times to come, as time spent in the pits of hell.

Chapter Thirty-Seven

A positive effect that had come about from the Kommandant's death, in addition to the relief that he was gone, was the return of Arlette's father. Without official monthly directives coming from the manor, Henri was free to return home to his daughter and mother. Despite grief weighing heavy on the women's moods, his unexpected reappearance had been embraced with joy. Neither woman mentioned Kommandant Steiner.

The chill of winter dissipated and spring's warmth and scents awakened the countryside. In between practical considerations and relief at her father's return, Arlette's state of mind still led to long bouts of silence and inactivity. Her voice was hesitant and dull and her thoughts slow and confused. Rays of sunshine shone through the latticework of branches and the aroma of blossoms filled the air like sweet cologne, but she was immune to the beauty surrounding her. The emergence of buds and new life in the fields felt like a slap having lost Estelle. It seemed abhorrent that life continued. Why hadn't the world stopped spinning at the moment her baby had died? She'd mechanically recommenced the domestic chores required and managed to eat a little more of their unappetising rations, but life seemed like an endless hill of traps and pitfalls where the summit was never reached.

One morning in April, Arlette sat beside her father on the wall of the well threading daisies and making a flower chain, the repetitive movements of her fingers preventing her from biting her nails any shorter. Every now and then a petal resembling a tiny drop of candle wax would fall onto her smock.

'Remember the dragon that lived down the well when you and Gilbert were children?' asked Henri.

Arlette nodded.

'You pushed past your fear and began to use the well again. Try to see your sadness as the dragon. It's preventing you from moving forwards. It's standing in your way and you need to fight it.'

'But how do you fight against what's already happened? Estelle's dead.'

'But never here,' he said, touching his chest. 'Your mother is still here after all these years. Sometimes when you feel like you're falling, you just have to surrender to the inevitable and see where you land. You can grasp life and pray for Saul's return or you can wither like an untendered vine. I can't tell you how it's breaking my heart to see you like this.'

'I feel as if I'm leaving Estelle behind with each step I take forwards.'

'No one's suggesting you forget. You'll remember her for the rest of your life. She's engraved on your heart. Letting go takes time, a bit like wrapping a gift with delicate sheets of paper, folding the layers over your grief. You can still feel the gift but it's cushioned and less evident.'

'Do you believe Saul will come home?'

'I believe he will fight to survive because returning to you will give him strength. And you must do the same for him.'

'How will I tell him his daughter's gone?'

'You'll find the words, *ma pêche*.'

Arlette leant against her father and he stretched his arm around her shoulder.

'Your grandmother is talking about returning to Oradour,' he said.

Still leaning against him, Arlette threaded a thin hairy daisy stem through another. 'Why doesn't she want to stay with us?'

'She loves us but she's a strong woman who cherishes her independence. She's lived in Oradour all her life and it's where her friends are. With the Allies making progress and the Germans losing ground, there are hopes the war won't last much longer. I suppose it's her way of getting back to normal.'

'The world carries on regardless, doesn't it? The trees are thickening with leaves, the birds are singing and Grandma's making plans to go home.'

'Of course. But that's a good thing, *ma pêche*.'

'I suppose.'

'Nature knows nothing of our heartache.'

'No.'

Arlette felt her father's warm hand hold hers. 'Don't feel you're going through this alone. Just remember that everyone runs away from something in the quiet hours of the night.'

Arlette nodded.

'I need to talk to you about something,' said Henri.

Arlette closed her eyes, knowing where the conversation was leading but aware that she couldn't explain to him why she wouldn't acquiesce to his idea.

'Estelle,' he said, softly.

'She's safe.'

'I know, but it's not right—'

'What isn't right is that she's dead,' she interrupted.

'That's true, but she needs to be laid to rest.'

Grandma Blaise came out of the kitchen and stood beside her son and granddaughter.

'She is at rest. She's safe where she is and no one can hurt her now,' repeated Arlette.

'Let me talk to her, son,' said Grandma Blaise. She smiled at Henri, her lips closed and the smile not spreading to her eyes.

Her father sighed and walked towards Klara who was chewing a stick close to the front gate. His head was bowed.

'Before you ask again, I'm not burying Estelle in that poisoned soil,' said Arlette.

'We don't need to bury her anywhere near ...' She looked over her shoulder to make sure that Henri was out of earshot. '... him. We'll lay her to rest with your mother in Saint-Pierre's cemetery. There's a wonderful view of the valley there.'

Arlette stood up, the daisy chain falling to the floor. 'I'm her mother. I know what's best. When it rains, Herr Steiner's poison will seep through the soil. It'll roll down the hill, find its way into the cemetery and rot everything it touches.'

'Shhh, my dear, please. Your father will hear. Besides, all that's left of the German will be bones now. Your thoughts are muddled with grief.'

Arlette covered her ears. 'I don't want to talk about it.'

Grandma Blaise gently pulled her hands down and held them between her fingers.

'This pain you're feeling will fade in time to be replaced by a wistful ache.'

'That's impossible.'

'What about your father? He not only lost the love of his life but also the baby your mother was carrying.'

Arlette felt hot tears sting her eyes. 'I know I'm being horrid, Grandma, but I'm so angry. I miss her lips spreading into a smile when she looks at me. I miss her downy hair. I never had the chance to tie it into a ribbon. I miss her, Grandma. I want her back.'

Tears that had been balancing precariously on Arlette's lower lashes now spilled down her cheeks. Her body shook with sobs and Grandma Blaise pulled her against her bosom. Arlette's agonised cries reverberated around Montverre's hilltop. It took ten minutes for her sobbing to subside, but when she gently pulled away from her grandmother's embrace she felt calmer. She believed that she would never be free from the pain of loss but she felt as if she'd been released from the madness of grief.

'Will you come with me to speak with Father Jules?' asked Arlette.

The following week, a small group of people assembled outside Saint-Pierre's, their heads bowed in hushed conversation. The sky was a canvas of blue and white smudges. It had rained overnight and the smell of damp earth and pleasantly pungent flowering raspberries hung in the air.

Beneath the lichen-encrusted lychgate, Bruno and Thierry were talking to Father Jules, the village priest, occasionally nodding their heads in solemn agreement at something the priest had said. Monique stood quietly next to Francine. Several villagers, who were also friends of the family, stood beside the rusting statue of Christ, their voices hushed and heads bowed in respect.

Arlette walked out of the incense-perfumed nave and into the warmth of the morning, her floral dress billowing in the breeze and with her grandmother at her side. She squinted in the sunlight and paused, waiting for her father. He followed seconds later, carrying a tiny coffin held close to his body. Conversation stopped when they joined the group. The gathering fell into step and walked towards the cemetery. Once they had reached the grave of Fleur Blaise, everyone encircled the area of freshly dug earth.

Father Jules held out his arms with his palms upturned. He addressed everyone.

'Thank you all for joining us today. We're here to remember Estelle Fleur Blaise and to celebrate her life. Thank you also for the touching readings and poems you shared during the service. Estelle's story may have been short, but it is a chapter filled with love and laughter. Her brief life was just as precious and meaningful as any other in the eyes of the Lord. We're living through terrible times and I'm sure none of us here can begin to comprehend how someone could cause such pain to an innocent life. Estelle was dearly loved and her memory will live on through that love. Memory is love's last light. While ever someone remembers her, she will remain with us.'

Father Jules joined his hands together. 'But now as Arlette and Saul's daughter is laid to rest beside her grandmother, please join me in reciting the Lord's prayer.

'Our Father ...'

As the murmur of the Lord's Prayer filled the graveyard, Estelle's white coffin was lowered into the earth and ropes were pulled from the depths of the opening. A sob escaped Arlette's mouth as she kissed her mother's embroidered scarf and let it fall. She watched it float down inside the hole and come to rest on the small box. Each person sprinkled earth and petals on to its lid and closed their eyes in private thought. As tears blurred her vision, she felt her grandmother's arm encircle her shoulders and pull her close. Then her father's fingers tightened around hers while two men began to shovel earth back into the void, the percussive sound of earth on wood puncturing the silence.

Chapter Thirty-Eight

Grandma Blaise stayed at the farm for another five weeks but when June bloomed, she decided to make plans for her return to Oradour-sur-Glane. The previous Tuesday, Francine's mother had arrived at the Blaises' farm, red-faced and eager. She had been listening in secrecy to old Monsieur Péricaud's wireless and couldn't wait to share, the news of the Allied invasion. Monique had relayed the headlines that together with parachute and glider landings, massive air attacks and naval bombardments, the Allies had arrived. They'd waded ashore onto five beaches in Normandy.

'Will the war end soon?' Arlette asked.

'It sounds like it's the beginning of the end,' said Henri.

Now that Henri was back home and news was spreading through France that the Germans were retreating, Grandma Blaise had chosen this weekend to return home. She felt safe due to the recent good news and decided that they should all try to get their lives back to some semblance of normality. Seeds of hope were sprinkled all over Montverre and although local atrocities would never be forgotten, several villagers were occasionally seen smiling with renewed hope. For Arlette however, a happy future seemed to be as impossible as grasping a fistful of the River Glane. Estelle's death, Saul's absence and the secreted body rotting in the vegetable garden turned inexorably over in her mind.

It was the morning of June 10th 1944. The day had dawned overcast with a pale light filtering through the farmhouse's shutters. A thick layer of pewter clouds had been holding back the summer sun, but now the day was hot with the countryside bathed in sunshine. Arlette was in her grandmother's bedroom helping her to pack for her journey back home. Scents of lavender, jasmine and celandine wafted in through the open windows.

'I think that's everything, mother,' said Henri. 'I'll carry your bags downstairs.'

Outside, Henri loaded bags and boxes onto the back of the cart. He hugged his mother. 'I'll visit in a fortnight so if you've forgotten anything, I'll bring it then.'

'It's so good to know that you're home and looking so well, son. Take care of this little one for me,' she said, tapping Arlette on the arm.

He helped his mother into her seat at the front of the cart, assuring her that his daughter would be his priority.

'I'll see you this evening, Father,' called Arlette.

'Safe journey. If you're delayed on the road, stay with your grandmother tonight. I don't want you travelling back in the dark.'

Turning to look back one last time, Arlette saw her father lift his battered hat in salute.

'Bye.'

She shook the reins and encouraged Mimi to set off at a trot. The verges of the lane were a sea of coloured blooms, while overhead, leafy boughs hung low enough to touch on occasions. The distant landscape appeared to levitate in the heat haze.

'Here's your bonnet, my dear,' said Grandma Blaise. She passed Arlette a ragged hat with loose pieces of straw escaping from its rim. 'We don't want you fainting in the heat.'

Arlette placed it on her head, catching sight of the manor, golden in the sunlight. The trap passed the perimeter of the wood. Images of Kommandant Steiner lying at the bottom of the stairs in a pool of blood turned over in her mind like a dirty franc coin, obliterating the beautiful countryside. She cracked the reins a little harder than necessary against Mimi's flanks. She was glad he was gone. Estelle would still be here if it weren't for him.

Arlette felt her grandmother's hand pat her knee and turned to look at the old woman who had been such strength to her over the past two years. She always seemed to sense when Arlette was reliving the horror and sinking back into her living nightmare.

'Time will help to numb sorrow and dampen anger, my dear,' said Grandma Blaise.

'I'm going to miss you so much, Grandma.' Arlette wiped away an errant tear.

'And I'll miss you too, but I don't live too far away. You can come and stay whenever you like but I think now's the time that we should all begin to let the Germans know that the life we lived before they invaded hasn't disappeared. They may have destroyed large parts of our country but hold your head up high and show them that they haven't diminished our spirit. You have grown from a little girl into a brave young woman during these war years. When all the prisoners are finally released, I shall pray every day that Saul is among the living and will find his way back home to you.'

It was early afternoon when Arlette shuffled in her seat to ease her discomfort. It had been a long journey to Oradour-sur-Glane and the midday sun had bitten their exposed skin until it turned pink. They entered the village and relief swept over her. It was Saturday and many people from outlying villages were swelling the population having travelled for hair appointments, to visit the chemist or to buy provisions for the coming week.

Arlette clicked her teeth to encourage her tired mare to continue past the tram station and post office.

'Come on, Mimi. We're nearly there, girl.'

They continued down the main street until they came to a grassy area at the heart of the village. This was known locally as the *Champ de Foire*, or fairground. Skirting the fairground several neighbours and friends of Grandma Blaise recognised her sitting like royalty on the cart. Elderly men raised their caps and women called out her name to which her grandmother would reply with a cheerful, *bonjour*.

'It's just as I left it,' the old lady said with a sigh.

Arlette could see the joy of returning home sparkle in her grandmother's eyes and it gladdened her heart. Maybe one day if Saul came back, she too would find some sort of happiness again.

Large jigsaw shapes of blue sky pushed their way between white clouds. Arlette looked around the small town, taking in the convivial atmosphere. She directed Mimi round a corner. A line of men waited patiently outside the tobacconist's shop, queuing for their weekly ration. Children played hopscotch in squares scraped in a patch of gravel. People congregated in cafés, drinking weak war coffee and the streets clicked to the sound of wooden clogs.

'Mathilde! You're back. Mathilde!'

Arlette looked across the tramline that was shimmering in the sunlight. An elderly woman was carrying swathes of flowers that partly hid her face. It had been a long time since she'd heard her grandmother's Christian name.

Grandma Blaise clapped her hands together, a smile lighting her face. 'Oh, please stop the cart, my dear. It's my good friend, Jeanne.'

The woman crossed the road, readjusted her bouquet

and stretched one arm up to Grandma Blaise. The two old ladies clasped each other's hands.

'How are you and your family?' asked Grandma Blaise. 'Everywhere looks so peaceful compared to Limoges and Montverre. It's so good to be home.'

'We're all well,' said Jeanne. 'The good Lord continues to bless us all with a comfortable seclusion from the war. If it weren't for the rationing of some items and the enlisting of our young men, we'd hardly know the Germans had invaded. And now it sounds as if France may soon be liberated.'

'It's wonderful news, isn't it? That's why I feel that now is the time to come home.'

'How has your stay been with young Henri?' asked Jeanne.

Arlette thought it was amusing to think of her father as young.

'He's well,' said Grandma Blaise. 'He was forced to work in Germany for a while, but thank the Lord he's back home safely. Perhaps we should have all moved here to the peace of Oradour instead.'

'It's good to see you back. I'll call round to see you this evening but I must rush to the church and arrange these flowers now.'

'Is someone getting married?'

'No. Tomorrow some of the children are taking their First Holy Communion.'

'How lovely. I look forward to seeing you later and we'll catch up properly.'

Jeanne nodded her head at both of them and hurried on her way. Arlette clicked her tongue at Mimi and her horse trotted forwards. Five minutes later, she tethered her mare to the railings in the shade outside Grandma Blaise's home. To the sound of groans and spluttering, she helped her grandmother down from the cart's wooden seat.

'Oh dear,' the old lady said with a chuckle, 'I think my old bones have set like stone during that long journey.'

'Steady,' said Arlette, holding her arm. She guided her grandmother towards her front door. 'Hold on to the railings on the steps. You seem a little wobbly still. I'll fetch your bags in after I've given Mimi some food and water.'

Arlette heaved several bags up the stone steps and through the front door into the cool interior of the hall. She noticed that her grandmother had found a surge of renewed energy. She had already tied her favourite flowered apron around her waist and was throwing open the windows and shutters to allow the summer breeze to flow through the house. Arlette watched the old lady pat her Singer sewing machine and walk into the kitchen. She smiled to herself. Her grandmother was excited to be home again. She followed her into the kitchen and sat the bags on the dusty tiled floor. The small room smelt saccharine and fusty.

'My goodness, it needs a good clean in here,' said Grandma Blaise. 'Just look at those.'

Arlette noticed that the kitchen windows were filthy, preventing much of the daylight from penetrating the grime. She touched one of the many blackened strings of cobwebs that hung from the ceiling in tendrils, each swaying as their movement stirred the air. Dust particles danced like plankton having been disturbed by the uninvited draught that had followed them in through the house.

'It won't take long to clean it,' said Arlette. 'Afterwards we could wander across the fairground and see what provisions we can pick up.'

'Yes, my dear, that's a good idea. I need to get my joints working again after sitting on the trap for so long.'

'Oh look!'

They watched a yellow butterfly flit around the kitchen having flown in through an open window. It settled on the top of a framed photograph of Fleur, decorating it like a child's lemon bow.

Grandma Blaise picked up a cloth and wafted it towards the window. 'Shoo! Off you go out into the sunshine.'

Arlette stood raising her hands, moving them from side to side to stop the butterfly from flying deeper into the house and becoming trapped. The women laughed as they jiggled this way and that, encouraging it towards the freedom of the open window. But despite their comical efforts its delicate wings fluttered even higher towards the ceiling, where it settled.

Grandma Blaise sighed. 'It has a whole garden of flowers out there and it chooses my dark kitchen to rest.' She looked at Arlette. 'Whatever's the matter?'

Arlette stood with her hand over her mouth and spoke through her fingers. 'I laughed. Estelle is dead and I laughed.'

'You're allowed to laugh, my lovely.'

'But how could I have forgotten her at that moment and laughed?'

'Do you think she would have wanted the legacy of her short life to be a future of misery for you? She would have wanted you to celebrate her life and to be happy. Besides, who's to say that this little butterfly isn't Estelle come to pay a visit?'

Arlette gave a weak smile. 'I like that thought.'

'Let's go and buy a cold drink on the café's terrace now. We can do a little cleaning afterwards.'

They left the bags on the floor and walked down the hall. When Arlette opened the front door, German soldiers were swarming the road, barking commands. Looking left and right along the road, the two women watched open-mouthed as residents were being forced to leave their homes and ordered to assemble in the main square.

'Where in heaven's name did they come from?' asked Grandma Blaise.

'I don't know. Do you think they're checking everyone's papers like they did in Montverre? Have you got yours?'

The old lady patted her handbag. 'Yes, but why don't they check them from door to door? What's the point of making everyone leave their homes?'

A soldier walked towards them waving his gun impatiently in the direction of the village fairground.

'Out now! Go to the square. Move!'

Chapter Thirty-Nine

Waiting in the centre of the village, Arlette saw townspeople converge from all directions at gunpoint. She was standing on the fairground, a gently sloping hill of grass from where she watched while the elderly were hauled from their homes and clients were pushed out of the hairdressers' with wet hair. The baker joined them, still covered in flour. Teachers led children by the hand and diners streamed out of restaurants. The carpenter was forced to leave his work, as were the cobbler, the village cartwright, the blacksmith, the butcher and the confectioner. The Hotel Avril and Hotel Milord's guests were being ushered from the buildings by Nazis shouting orders. Arlette then noticed a large car drive into the village and stop on a grass verge.

'That's the doctor's car,' said Grandma Blaise.

Arlette could see the doctor's perplexed face turn towards the large gathering on the fairground. Immediately a soldier was sent in his direction and ordered him out of his vehicle. Within minutes the doctor was standing beside his numerous patients.

Someone mumbled behind Arlette. 'Perhaps they're searching the houses for contraband.'

A voice answered, 'Then why are they gathering the field workers up and scouring the nearby fields? Look. They've even got Monsieur Blanc who was fishing in the river.'

Arlette followed the direction of the woman's finger and saw a group of farmers being ordered from the back of a truck and pushed towards the assembled villagers. Behind them were several fishermen wearing waders and carrying their rods. She felt her grandmother's grip tighten. A high-ranking German soldier walked to the front of the villagers and silence ensued. Everyone strained to hear what he had to say. He stood upright, distant and correct, before speaking.

'I can't hear,' whispered Grandma Blaise.

'He said that arms destined for the Resistance had been reported to be hidden here. They're going to search every house, establishment and barn.'

'That's a relief. With so many soldiers they should make short work of the search. Can you believe I'm still wearing my apron? Do you think they'd mind if I sat on the grass?'

Although there wasn't any panic among the gathering, Arlette could feel a mounting anxiety. The air was heavy with anticipation and a low murmuring of conversation spread between the villagers. How long would they be delayed? She didn't need this hold up if she was going to make it back home today. Perhaps she would be staying overnight after all.

Lines of people continued to scurry along the main road towards them. Mademoiselle Petit, a schoolteacher, ushered a group of children in front of her and joined the congregation of villagers. The click-clacking of their small wooden clogs was silenced by the grass.

'It's Saturday. Why are the children at school today?' asked Arlette.

The schoolteacher sounded impatient. 'They're attending an immunisation programme and all this nonsense is very disruptive.' She shook her head with irritation and turned to count her pupils.

Arlette looked into the sky hoping to see white clouds that might give them respite from the relentless intensity of the sun's rays. The sky was cloudless, but a single buzzard soared in a wide circular pattern, its wings outstretched and static.

Grandma Blaise held her lower back and spoke to Berthe, an acquaintance who had worked in the hairdressers' for more than twenty years. 'Goodness, I do ache.'

'Hopefully they won't be too much longer,' said Berthe. 'I'm dying of thirst.'

'I hope they're being careful with my ornaments.'

'Look, Grandma.' Arlette pointed to a lorry convoy that had parked in the lower part of Oradour. Soldiers wearing flecked waterproof clothing in yellow and green swarmed out of the back of the trucks and through the streets.

'Why are there so many?' asked Grandma Blaise. She slipped her arm through her granddaughter's. 'The village is already swarming with them.'

Arlette shook her head. She didn't have an answer.

Everyone was watching and waiting in a dignified silence. Soldiers continued to empty surrounding houses and shops of their occupants. They were being herded in groups towards the green. The crowd was now so large that it was spreading out towards a covered well. A woman stumbled towards them with her hair in curlers. A half-dressed child was held in his mother's arms. Still with his jaw covered in shaving foam, a man had been ordered out of the barber's. Worried mothers clutched the tiny fingers of their children or pushed prams towards the assembly point, its numbers growing by the minute. Next the grocer and another teacher arrived, accompanied by a larger group of children. The priest arrived, followed by a man carrying an elderly woman on his back.

The throng began to move. Arlette looked around in confusion. 'What's happening?'

A voice in the crowd answered. 'They're separating the women and children from the menfolk.'

'Why?'

The question went unanswered. Arlette took hold of her grandmother's hand and moved closer to the front of the crowd.

From where they were now standing, Arlette could see and hear the SS officer more clearly. He was a solid man whose uniform was decorated with emblems and badges. The letters SS were zigzagged like two lightning strikes on his collar. He demanded that the elders of the village reveal the hiding place of the ammunition. Arlette heard the mayor respond by denying any knowledge of the presence of arms. The officer turned to another German soldier and spoke out of earshot. Arlette guessed he was translating.

'The mayor's just offered to be held hostage with his sons so the elderly and children can get out of the sun,' said Arlette.

'How brave,' said Grandma Blaise.

Arlette felt a trickle of sweat run down her spine. The sun was sweltering. Her mouth was dry and she was worried for her grandmother. Why had they decided to come here today? If only they had made the journey the following day.

She immediately became more alert. Commands were being shouted to the gathered men. They were ordered to walk away from the fairground en masse. At gunpoint.

'Where are they taking them?' asked Berthe. 'My son is with them.'

'We don't know.' Arlette shrugged. 'Try not to worry. They won't hurt them because they haven't done anything wrong.' She realised how naïve she sounded. Hadn't little Maurice only been trying to keep warm? Hadn't the Jewish people only been trying to work hard and settle into a community?

Arlette watched several men turn to look back at the women. She recognised them: the ticket seller at

246

the tram station from when she used to travel to sell her silk cocoons, the owner of her favourite café, her grandmother's elderly neighbour, Jean-Philippe. The men's eyes searched for glimpses of their wives and children. They were led away, their faces drawn with fear. They looked confused, many trying to dodge the pushing and shoving of Germans fists. Next the SS officer turned his attention to the remaining women and children.

'What's he saying?' asked Grandma Blaise. 'I do wish he would speak up.'

'We've got to go to the church,' said Arlette. 'Maybe they realise that we need to sit down in some shade.' She patted her grandmother's hand for reassurance and helped her along the main street towards the village's place of worship at the southern end of town. In front of the church grew a tall tree in full leaf. They walked beneath its dappled shade. Several women sighed audibly at the momentary respite from the sun's rays. German soldiers shepherded the women and children towards Oradour's church entrance.

German voices grew more frenzied. Women and children were hurried along and pushed inside. An old lady fell at the doorway. Arlette recognised her as her grandmother's friend, Jeanne. She didn't mention it to her grandmother who was looking anxious enough. There was momentary turmoil when the women behind helped her to stand. People behind were bumping into each other. Arlette stumbled but she steadied herself and her eyes began to adjust to the dim light inside the church. Looking down, she saw flowers being trampled underfoot. They looked like the same flowers that Jeanne had been carrying. She reached for a pew for balance, smelling the familiar aroma of incense and candle smoke. It comforted her a little. She grasped Grandma Blaise's hand as they were pushed to the back of the church. In seconds they were next to the altar.

Arlette didn't let go of her grandmother's hand despite the bumping and jostling from others. They were ordered deeper inside. The cool interior was a welcome relief from the fierce heat outside and many women and children settled themselves on the wooden benches. She helped her grandmother to sit on a stool beside the altar but as more women were herded inside, the crowd pushed Arlette a short way from the old lady. Helpless to stop the momentum, she was thrust to the opposite side of the altar.

A cough. A baby's whimper. A child's voice calling for *maman*. But still the women remained calm, their ears straining for any communication or sign of what was going to happen next.

Then it came.

Distant machine gun fire could be heard through the open church door. It continued for a long minute until it slowed. Then just occasional short bursts.

'What are they firing at?' someone whispered.

'Perhaps they're destroying something.'

'The men ... you don't think ...'

The woman didn't finish her sentence and no one answered. Arlette sought out her grandmother's face. They exchanged reassuring tight smiles until a commotion at the entrance of the church made everyone turn and look. Two German soldiers were carrying a large chest into the building. They struggled under its weight.

'Perhaps they've brought us water,' someone suggested.

A soldier attached a thin rope to the chest and laid it on the ground. He walked backwards out of the door. An orange glow could be seen in his hand. He bent to the ground. The doors were slammed shut.

'He lit a fuse!' screamed a young mother. She turned and lifted her baby over the heads of others. She begged someone to take her baby from her and further away from the danger.

The previous calm was replaced by terror. Children screamed. Women pushed. The mass of bodies moved as one towards the back of the church. Arlette lost sight of her grandmother. Arms and legs floundered around her. The commotion caused her to fall beneath the altar, banging her head on the stone floor. Then … a deafening explosion. Women and children fell to the floor around her. Debris fell like a plague of rubble and glass. Arlette curled herself into a ball beneath the shelter of the altar. Her mind silently screamed for her grandmother. Blood mingled with dust and Arlette pulled herself to standing by clutching at the altar's stone sides. Through the smoke and flames she saw dead bodies. Severed limbs littered the floor. People were on fire. This was madness. This was impossible.

'Grandma!' Arlette screamed. 'Grandma!'

Bloodied women scrambled over bodies towards the door. Wailing and screaming echoed around the interior. Her own cries added to the chaos. The main door was flung open and soldiers entered. They strafed their machine guns around the interior, back and forth. More bodies fell.

Arlette scrambled over corpses to get further away from the gunfire. Shards of glass and shrapnel were embedded in their bodies. Blood stained their clothing and many had been hit by falling masonry. A child lay as if asleep on the stone floor, the horrific position of her limbs betraying the fact that she would never wake.

Arlette struggled to the stool where Grandma Blaise had been seated. It was empty. Staccato popping made her crouch even lower while gunshot punctuated the air.

Flames were taking hold of the pews. The smell of burnt flesh assaulted her nostrils as she tried to raise limp limbs. Maybe someone had fallen on top of her grandmother. The heat of the fire was pinching her skin and stinging her lungs. The smoke stung her eyes and throat. A rivulet of sweat ran into her eyes from her scalp but on wiping it away she saw that it was bright red. Soon the benches were crackling and spitting with fire. It was becoming difficult to see at all.

Then she saw it. A brightly-coloured flowery apron. It was close to the floor where the smoke was thin. Her grandmother was sitting with her back to the wall in a side chapel. She was bent forward with laboured breathing.

'Grandma, Grandma, I'm here.'

The old lady's face was bloodied and blackened. She cradled her left arm and looked at her granddaughter. 'The devil has visited Oradour today,' she croaked.

'Oh, Grandma.'

'*Ave Maria, pleine de grâce ...*'

'Grandma, we can pray later. We need to move back.'

'Back home?'

'No. Yes. If we can.'

'Are we trapped?'

Arlette sat down beside her and hugged her fragile body. 'Yes, Grandma.'

They looked up towards the open door of the church. Through the swirling dust and smoke, German soldiers were waiting with raised guns ready to shoot anyone trying to escape. The women and children who were still alive wailed and moaned in pain. A few could be seen crawling over dead bodies looking for loved ones or a place to hide. Arlette could see that the fire was spreading rapidly and soon they would all suffocate or burn. Several soldiers stepped inside the entrance and unhooked something from their belts. They pulled at the objects and threw them around the church. Running back outside, the Germans slammed the door shut once again. Instinct told Arlette to bury her head under her arms. Explosions erupted around her.

A vision of Saul's face appeared in her mind's eye as clearly as if it had been preserved in resin. Surely she and her grandmother couldn't just sit here and wait until the fire fused their bodies together in a final embrace. She needed to see Saul again. She needed to tell him of their daughter's death. And she must stay alive for her father. He would be a shell of a man if he also lost his mother and daughter.

The heat from the fire was now so intense she had to gasp for breath. The air was thick with smoke and it was impossible to stand up. She knew she only had seconds to think of a way to escape. The lack of air was making it difficult to focus. Seeing that the window behind the altar had been blown out, she was spurred into one last attempt to save their lives.

'Grandma, we've got to move behind the altar. We need to try and escape out of the windows.' She shook the old lady. 'Maybe the soldiers aren't around the back. Wake up.' Arlette knelt in front of her and shook her shoulders. Grandma Blaise groaned in pain. She half opened her eyes.

'Please, my arm. Don't touch my arm.' The old lady's voice was slurred.

'But, Grandma, we have a chance. We only have seconds left before it's too late.'

'I can't, my dear. I can't move. Let me sleep.'

'No. I won't. Wake up. I'll help you,' said Arlette, lifting her grandmother's unbroken arm. 'Grandma, wake up. You need to help me. I can't carry you.'

Arlette coughed, her lungs so painful that she

thought they would burst in her chest. She let go of her grandmother's arm to wipe her mouth then tapped her grandmother's cheeks to rouse her. 'Grandma?'

The old lady didn't move. Her eyes were open, unseeing in death.

Gunfire rattled once more throughout the church's interior. Bullets ricocheted off walls, shattered statues and destroyed holy pictures. Some hit cowering women, children and a figure of Christ. Arlette threw herself to the ground and crawled over bodies, severed limbs and through pools of blood. The smoke had descended to a metre above the floor so she had to feel her way with her hands. By now the fire was growling and snapping like an angry beast. The heat was blistering her skin. With her arms spread wide, her hands searched for the step up to the altar. Relieved to have found it, she pushed aside some tubing. She looked again. Intestines. Then another obstacle. A smouldering pram. Arlette felt inside for signs of a baby, clenching her teeth against the pain. The skin on her hands and arms blistered as her fingers probed the mattress of the pram. It was empty. The smoke in her lungs felt like hot knives carving at her organs. She collapsed, coughing until she retched. Hot cinders fell into her eyes making tears stream down her face. Slithering on her belly towards the back wall, she edged closer to the windows. With her nails ripped and bleeding, she clawed forwards on the stone floor until she reached the wall behind the altar. The layout of the church's interior was ingrained on her memory from childhood. Arlette knew she had to climb onto stone ledges in order to reach the broken window. Smoke was being sucked out of the shattered frames. For a second, a gust cleared the air immediately in front of her. Thinking of Saul, she summoned her last vestiges of strength.

Chapter Forty

Arlette landed heavily, knocking the air from her lungs. She lay motionless, listening. Gunfire splintered the air. German voices shouted. Weak cries for help could be heard on the other side of the window from where she had jumped.

After a few minutes, when no one came towards her, she began to crawl towards dense shrubbery. She had to hide. Despite the hedge's close proximity, she made slow progress. Her eyes streamed, her throat ached and each breath caused a spasm of pain in her chest. She stopped. Footsteps. German voices. Had she been seen? She stifled a cough and pressed her face into the grass, holding her breath. The soldiers passed close by, their conversation punctuated with laughter. She didn't move for several minutes. The earth smelt of hay and musty soap. The dry grass scratched her cheeks. Any cries for help had stopped. Only the snapping and hissing of flames could be heard from inside the church.

Oh, Grandma.

It was dark when Arlette next opened her eyes. All was quiet except the occasional creak from inside the church window above her. She couldn't move but her mind was reeling with images. She imagined the noise was heated metal cooling and contracting; communion rails, candlesticks, plaques on the walls telling of Christ's journey with the cross. Charred baby carriages.

Arlette tried to lift her head but a bolt of pain seared through her temple. She groaned, then immediately bit her lip to silence herself. She tried again, just a few inches. The eyelids of her left eye were stuck together. With difficulty, she turned her head to one side. Orange embers glowed in a local café across the road. The air smelt putrid, a mixture of burnt flesh, charcoal and rubber.

Her grandmother had been right. The devil had visited Oradour today.

The following day, a ray of sunlight penetrated the leaves of the bush she was lying beneath, its brightness stabbing at her eyelids. She turned her head away from the dazzling light. Her lips were stuck together, so she parted them by pushing her tongue between them. They felt cracked and rough. With pain splintering every part of her body, she slowly unfurled herself and rolled on to her back, facing the sky. White clouds had parted to reveal a wide band of blue. She could smell a bitter sweetness in the air, a mixture of charred wood and the hanging blossoms of the flowering redcurrant she was lying beneath. She listened. There was birdsong and the hum of bees. It reminded her of home. She needed to move.

With great effort, she hauled herself to a sitting position. Her head throbbed and a moan escaped her mouth. Using what strength she had remaining, she rolled on to one side until she was on all fours. Grabbing hold of an old tree stump, she dragged herself slowly to standing. When she inhaled, it seemed as if the air had grown spikes that caught in her throat.

Through her one good eye, she scanned the road in front of the church. Nothing moved except wisps of smoke that seeped from broken buildings like dying breaths. Arlette stumbled out of the churchyard and leant against a brick wall. Standing amidst its ruins, she could see that all of Oradour had been brutalised, not just the church. She was almost incapable of absorbing the magnitude of what had happened here. Every building was a shell. She moved along the wall, her hands never leaving the rigid support of the bricks. Hand over hand she walked alongside its length, her feet scraping along the ground with each footstep. When the wall ended, she stopped and searched for her next source of support. She would have to let go and make her way to a large tree across the road. She coughed and faltered, then steadied herself and tried again, this time staggering across the road. Her arms hugged the tree's rough trunk. Leaning her head against its warm bark, she looked upwards towards telegraph poles and tram wires that hung limply. Where once rattled carriages carrying chattering townspeople to and from Limoges, the wires had been destroyed, now swinging uselessly in the breeze. Was she the only one who had survived this massacre?

Arlette followed the road, lurching from one charred building to the next. She reached out to ledges and walls in order to steady herself. Homes surrounding the village green still showed hints of their previous décor. Windows were blown out and front walls had collapsed, revealing metal skeletons of tables and chairs, blackened ornaments, distorted cooking implements, warped bicycles and melted picture frames. Many cars were still parked in roofless garages beside burnt-out houses.

Pausing at the gate of her grandmother's house, Arlette stopped. She began to tremble. The door was hanging from its hinges, the shutters were streaked with black stains and the front windows were smashed. Inside the burnt interior she could see her grandmother's Singer sewing machine sitting on the remains of a table. It was too much. She lowered her head and closed her eye while she hung onto the railings at the front of the house. Her breath came in quick shallow gasps. An image came to her. It was of her grandmother sewing while humming, the old lady's grey curls escaping from her bonnet. Arlette had no idea how she was going to tell her father that he had lost his mother.

Then something touched the back of her hand. She opened her eyes to see Mimi's reins hanging from the railings and brushing against her skin. There was no sign of her mare.

She moved on towards a barn, her heart beating fast from the effort. The Laudy barn was smouldering as Arlette passed it. Something caught her eye. She paused momentarily. Turning, she looked inside the opening of the barn. Burnt bodies were fused together and piled on top of each other. Their blackened contorted limbs resembled a macabre sculpture. Arlette's hand slapped against her mouth but she couldn't prevent bile from dribbling between her fingers.

She followed the main road, too shocked to weep. A body lay face down on some steps, congealed blood pooled beneath its head. Then another ... executed against a wall. The peppering of holes in the wall indicated where the bullets had missed. Bloodstains revealed where they had found their target.

Crouching in pain and shuffling with difficulty, she passed houses whose grey walls were burnt black from fire, their water pumps still standing in front of their ruined facades. The upper floors of houses had their roofs missing, revealing castellated walls and jagged charred beams. Tiles and bricks were exposed like weatherworn tombstones. The air seemed to weigh heavy with the horrifying randomness of suffering that had been inflicted on these streets.

The butcher's shop still had the skeletal remains of the awnings that had protected its produce from the sunshine, yet the shop's roof was missing. A bird hopped on to twisted weighing scales on the counter. Arlette moved on. Turning the next corner, she reached the village green where they had all gathered the previous day. The doctor's Peugeot was still there, its wheels in the position that he had parked it for the last time. Feeling overcome with weakness and nausea, Arlette collapsed on the grass and leant against one of its doors.

Minutes passed and the sun's rays gradually crept around the side of the car. Its heat stung Arlette's arms. She looked down at the singed sleeves of her dress and noticed her burnt forearms for the first time. They were red and black. Blisters oozed clear fluid. She was too exhausted to move on and find shade, but the sun was fierce. She rolled sideways and lay down, shuffling beneath the Peugeot's bulk to find shade. Protected from the heat, she drifted in and out of consciousness. Bizarre dreams repeatedly tormented her until her undamaged eye opened and focused on the undercarriage of the vehicle.

She was awoken by a sound. Rapid clicking.

Arlette held her breath and strained to hear. It was getting louder. Had the Germans returned? Then voices. French voices. From beneath the car, she turned her head sideways to see a limited view of the village green – a strip of grass and a section of road. The clicking noise was almost upon her when two sets of bicycle wheels came in to view. She could see the legs of the riders, their boots scuffing the dust when they stopped.

'I knew something terrible had happened when I saw smoke in the distance,' said a man's voice.

'Where is everyone?' asked another man's voice. 'Every single building has been destroyed. It looks like the end of the world.'

'You don't think ...' The first voice paused. 'You don't think they've been killed, do you?'

'Of course not. Hundreds of people live here. They've probably been evacuated. There are bound to be many injuries though so we need to inform the authorities.'

Arlette began to panic. They couldn't leave. She tried to roll over but her shoulder banged on to the metalwork beneath the car, restricting further movement. She tried to shuffle back out, but her muscles wouldn't move the weight of her body. Her arms lay at her sides and with her fingers splayed, she searched for something to make a noise with. She felt grass, soft daisies on hairy stalks, tiny balls of earth. Then a stone. She grasped it. Bending her arm at the elbow, she hit the stone repeatedly against the metal pipework of the under carriage.

'Shhh! Listen,' said one of the men.

'It's coming from that car. Is someone still inside it?'

Arlette saw the bikes being laid on the floor and four legs walk towards her. The stone had fallen out of her hand and she couldn't find it. Her hands patted the grass but the stone must have rolled out of reach. She tried to call out, but no sound came from her mouth except a quiet rasping that wouldn't be heard by others. The cyclists' boots were so close as the men inspected the interior of the car that she could see scuffs and dust on them. One had a broken and frayed lace.

'Nothing. It's empty,' said one of the men.

'Come on. We need to fetch help.'

The thought that they might leave terrified her. She stretched her arm out as far as she could towards the boots. She was inches short of reaching them. The grass scraped her burnt forearm, sending shooting pains towards her shoulders. Wriggling her shoulders first and then her hips, she edged a little nearer to the men. Her hand edged closer towards a shoe, her fingers crawling in the grass. With one painful stretch, she grasped an ankle.

Chapter Forty-One

Arlette was woken by a gentle touch to her forehead. Her eyes flickered open momentarily, but the light was too bright. The familiar squeak of her bedroom shutters brought tears of relief. She was home. Opening her eyes again, Arlette saw her father sitting on the edge of her bed. He seemed older. The mesh of lines around his eyes deeper. '*Ma pêche?*'

Arlette tried to clear her throat and speak, but her voice rasped.

'Shh! Don't talk.' He wiped her tears. 'Do you think you can sit up? You need to eat something.'

Arlette grimaced. She rolled to one side and dug her elbow into the mattress to help her move. She saw that her arms were covered in strips of ripped pillowcases. Her fingers protruded from the end of the dressing. They resembled raw sausages. Henri pushed a bolster behind her and settled her back against it.

'Grandma?' she croaked.

Henri shook his head. 'There's enough time to talk when you're feeling stronger.' He lightly touched her cheeks. 'It's a miracle you survived. I think your mother must have been watching over you.'

'I'm sorry.'

Her father stood up and wrapped his arms around her shoulders. His touch was barely discernible as he held her lightly, not wanting to cause further pain. 'There was nothing you could have done. You must never blame yourself. I've heard what they did in Oradour and can't believe you're ...' His voice broke. 'I should have taken your grandmother home. It's me who's sorry.'

She could feel his head resting against her temple. His skin smelt of carbolic soap.

He sniffed, raised his head and wiped his eyes with the back of his rough hands. 'I've warmed you some soup. Camille made it.'

Arlette looked up. 'Camille?'

Her father gave a weak smile. 'They found your identity papers and brought you home. Francine fetched Camille because I didn't know what to do when they brought you back. She came to look after you for a few days.'

Arlette frowned. 'A few days?'

'It's Tuesday,' said Henri. 'You've been back home four days. Camille had some medication that she used to nurse her mother. It helped you to sleep and eased your pain. She boiled endless pans of water for you and dripped some embrocation into them. She said the steam would help your lungs while you slept.' He paused. 'It was good to see her again. I don't know how I would have managed.'

Arlette nodded.

'Oh, and we have Mimi back. She was found in a field close to Oradour. She must have pulled free and bolted in terror.'

'Poor Mimi.'

'Don't worry. She seems settled now. Come on, I think your soup will have cooled by now.' Henri turned and lifted a bowl from the bedside table.

Arlette watched him scoop a spoonful of vegetable broth and carefully move it towards her lips. She remembered doing the same to Estelle. Pursing her lips, she sucked the liquid into her mouth.

'That's better. It makes my heart glad to see you eat something,' said Henri.

'Where's Camille?' croaked Arlette.

'She cycled home for a change of clothing and to pick up some provisions. She's coming back, don't worry.'

Arlette was surprised at how relieved she was to hear that Camille would be returning. She was a link to her mother; a source of comfort that both she and her father had yearned for. The soup eased her throat but Arlette needed to ask a question. 'How many people?'

She watched her father close his eyes. 'Eight people escaped. Four of them were working in the fields and hid in nearby woods.'

Arlette took an intake of breath. 'The rest?'

Henri shook his head.

Chapter Forty-Two

The moment Arlette's burns healed she began to clean. The kitchen's stone floor was swept, the pans gleamed, the windows shone and the oven looked like new. Although the patterns of red and pink scars on her skin were a constant reminder of that hideous day, she refused to let the haunting images infiltrate her thoughts. This worked to some degree while she was busy. The moment she stopped for more than a few minutes, the visions reappeared.

Arlette wiped her brow with her forearm and used a fingertip to push an escaped tendril of hair back behind her ear. Francine had been sitting at the kitchen table watching her friend for half an hour.

'That's enough. You're exhausted. Why don't you sit down for a minute?'

'I'm fine,' said Arlette.

'Come and have a drink and talk to me. Mother made us some strawberry tea. She soaked and sieved the fruit and leaves. It's delicious.'

'I don't want to sound unfriendly, Ci-Ci, but I don't want to talk.'

Francine sighed into her tea. 'We don't have to talk about … that.'

'Cleaning keeps my mind and my hands occupied. It helps.'

'It won't scrub away what's happened.'

Arlette stopped rubbing a copper pan and stared at her friend. 'I'm well aware of that. I've lost my baby, my grandmother and probably Saul. I haven't lost my mind.'

'Of course you haven't. I'm sorry. I didn't mean that. I'm just worried about you.'

Arlette continued to buff the saucepan. 'Don't be. I'm safe. It's Saul and Gilbert we need to think about. Maybe if you thought more about your brothers, René and Albert, you wouldn't feel the need to constantly watch me.'

Francine stood up, scraping the chair on the floor as she did so. 'You don't need to remind me that my brothers risk their lives every day fighting this awful war. You're not the only one worrying about loved ones.'

'I'm just saying I don't need anyone's sympathy.'

'It wasn't sympathy I was giving. It was company.'

Arlette didn't answer. She rubbed at a non-existent mark on the pan.

'I'll leave the jug here,' said Francine.

'Thank you.'

'I'll be going then.'

Arlette could sense Francine lingering in the doorway, but she ignored her and sat the clean pan on a shelf before lifting another one down. The next time she looked up, Francine had gone.

Henri came in through the front door. 'Hello, *ma pêche*? I've just seen Francine. She didn't look very happy.'

'She wanted to talk and I didn't.'

Henri raised his eyebrows. 'She loves you. We all do.'

Arlette shrugged and put down the saucepan. 'I know. I'm busy though.'

'How many times has she come to visit you over the past couple of months and how many times have you pushed her away?'

'I'm not pushing her away. I don't want to talk about what's happened and I know she'll ask me.'

'I think you'll be surprised just how sensitive she will be.'

Arlette pressed her palms to her temples. 'Please, Father.'

'I'm just saying, don't keep her at a distance. There's been enough hurt.'

Arlette's shoulders drooped and she sighed. 'I know I'm being mean but I can't help it. I feel so angry with everyone. At everything.'

'You've been through a terrible ordeal.'

'I can't talk about what I saw. My head aches.' She tapped the side of her head with a closed fist. 'Nothing can make the pictures in my head go away.'

'You're right. We can't make them go away. But we are here for you. We can support you in other ways. By showing love.' Henri picked up the jug of cold strawberry tea and smelt it. 'All I'm saying is that Francine is a loyal friend who brings you gifts to let you know she cares.' He raised the jug a fraction higher as if to prove the point.

'Cleaning helps me to keep occupied. I don't think as much.'

'You think you're protecting yourself by hiding behind a mop, but it's not a wooden handle that will heal your mind. It's the strength and love of family and friends.'

Arlette looked at the jug and thought of the summer flowers and pretty pebbles her friend had regularly brought to the farmhouse. 'But I'm losing everyone I love.'

'There's more than one way to lose someone you love. Some people only need to be pushed away so many times before they won't return. Don't let the evils of this war claim another friendship. Prove that you're stronger than that.'

'I don't mean to be horrid. I couldn't bear to lose Francine too. I should go after her and say sorry.'

Her father replaced the tea on the table, crossed the floor and kissed her forehead. 'You must do what you think best.'

Arlette turned and clattered across the stone floor in her clogs. Outside, the countryside was mellowing in the late September sunshine and the first yellow leaves were falling. She ran to the top of the hill expecting to see

Francine at least halfway down it, but she wasn't there. Arlette pursed her lips in thought.

Of course! She knew where her friend would be.

Arlette hurried through the orchard. Many trees had been chopped down for fuel the previous winter, their stumps now sprouting twigs with a profusion of small leaves covering them. A chill caused her to shiver when she passed the manor's entrance. No one had visited the farm to ask why she no longer worked there. Thankfully they seemed to have more important things to think about these days. She hurried alongside the manor's perimeter wall and continued until she reached the bridge. There she saw fresh footsteps in the mud before adding her own. Arlette followed the path along the riverbank until she came to the clearing beneath the slender poplars. Francine sat cradling her knees on the small river beach. She jumped when her friend approached.

Arlette sat down beside her. She offered her hand and was relieved when Francine took it. They sat side by side in silence for a few minutes.

'I'm sorry. I don't mean to be nasty, Ci-Ci. I don't want to remember what happened so it seemed easier to not talk at all. Some acts are so awful that even the memory of them causes anxiety.'

'You don't have to explain.' Francine rubbed Arlette's hand, before stopping abruptly. 'Sorry. Does it hurt?'

Arlette looked down at the red scars on her hands. 'No. Not any more.'

'I don't know what to say. I understand you don't want to talk about it, but talking about anything else will sound as if I don't care. And I do.'

'I know you do. I haven't thanked you properly for my flowers and pebbles. I've saved them all.'

'I came here. I chose the prettiest ones I could find.'

They sat in silence for several more minutes.

'Has your mother listened to Monsieur Péricaud's wireless recently?' asked Arlette.

Francine gave a weak smile. 'Yes. She comes back giddy with excitement now that the Germans are retreating. Even Papa seems less depressed. He waits for her at the door and doesn't even let her sit down before she has to give him the latest news.'

'What is the latest?'

'Mainly that Paris is liberated and Pétain has fled. They think he's gone to Switzerland. Papa actually clapped his hands and laughed when he heard that Charles de Gaulle had formed a provisional government.'

'That's wonderful news.'

There was another pause in conversation.

'There's still hope for Saul,' said Francine.

'Maybe.'

'They say that many Jewish people were rescued when those awful camps were discovered.'

Arlette nodded. She also knew that the people freed were a fraction of the number of those who would have died. 'I can't ask Father because of Grandma, but what is being said about Oradour? Just the outline, not what was found.'

Francine scooped a handful of sand and let it fall between her fingers. 'People are still in shock even though it's been over three months. Some say this generation will never get over what happened there. Bishop Rastouil organised a Mass to be held for the victims.'

'I didn't know.'

'It was only ten days after the killings and you were still quite sick. I went with Mother.'

'Have they said why the Germans did it?'

Francine shook her head. 'There's speculation that they wanted to show that they were still powerful because the

Allies had landed on the beaches of Normandy. But no one knows why they chose a quiet town that had been relatively ignored by the Germans up until then.'

'I don't know. I only know that I hate them. I was angry with Gilbert for leaving us to fight for the Resistance, but I would join him tomorrow if he visited. I would ...' She punched the sand. 'I would ...'

Arlette's eyes stung. She wiped a tear away but another fell. A gasp caught in her throat followed by a low howl that came from deep in her chest. She couldn't catch her breath. Her throat ached and her shoulders shuddered. The emotions she had kept locked away were finally released. She felt Francine's arms pull her into a hug while she sobbed loudly, deep guttural cries escaping with each breath she took.

'I'm here,' said Francine. 'Let it out. You haven't cried properly since that day.'

Arlette cried into her friend's shoulder. 'I couldn't move Grandma. I watched her die. I left her, Ci-Ci.'

'You had no choice. You did the right thing.'

Tears ran down Arlette's face onto Francine's dress. 'We chased a butterfly in her kitchen. She was so happy to be home.'

Francine rocked her friend and rubbed her back without answering.

'The Germans laughed.' Arlette pulled back and wiped her eyes and nose on her pinafore. 'Can you believe that? They killed so many and they laughed. I can understand that occasionally a mad man will commit an atrocity, but there were hundreds of Germans slaughtering families in cold blood. How could they? I keep asking myself. I don't understand.'

Arlette's body crumpled again, sobs convulsing her body. 'I saw a baby. They crucified a baby. My God, they crucified a baby.' She shook her head to dispel the image. 'There were so many bodies. Piled on top of each other. They'd tried to escape, but the fire ... I can't understand man's inhumanity to man.'

'I'm here. You're safe. It's over.'

'I feel like I'm going mad, Ci-Ci. I can't get the pictures out of my head.' She jabbed her forefinger against her head. 'That's why I keep busy. I need to concentrate on something or the visions come back.'

Francine held her hand. 'I'm so sorry you were there. I'm so sorry you saw those awful things but try to focus on the future. You're alive. It's a miracle. Remember that the majority of human beings are capable of wondrous achievements and amazing kindness. Most people possess a conscience. The majority of us have a voice inside us that tells us what's right and what's wrong. You must keep faith that overall mankind is good. Sometimes, either through weak self-preservation, fear or madness, people do things that shock us to the core by their cruelty. Oradour was one of those occasions.'

'But it seems that only the good people suffer. I miss Estelle, Saul, Grandma and Gilbert so much that it hurts here.' Arlette touched her chest. 'It physically hurts, Ci-Ci. I feel as if my heart is bruised.'

'Of course it does. But one thing that makes us human is that we have hope and faith. Believe that Saul will come home and that you will spend the rest of your lives together as I believe that Gilbert will come back to me. Focus on something positive rather than the evil of the past.'

Arlette saw Francine's fingers touch the felt rose pinned to her smock, the gift from her brother. She hugged her friend tightly. 'Thank you for everything. I wish I'd spoken with you sooner. I'm so lucky to have you for a friend.'

Chapter Forty-Three

Sitting in Camille's small kitchen, Arlette watched her pull a saucepan from the heat of the stove and prick vegetables with the tip of a knife. She could see something in Camille's face that had softened recently. Gone were the thin pinched features of a convalescent that she had first seen in Montverre square. Was it relief? Perhaps it was the knowledge that the end of the war was in sight and that she'd rediscovered old friendships. Arlette felt grateful too. Along with her father and Francine, this woman had enveloped her with the emotional and physical support of a mother over the past few months.

'It's ready,' said Camille. She'd turned and blew her long fringe away from her face. 'Can you fetch two plates from the cupboard, please?'

Arlette crossed the kitchen and brought two dinner plates back to the table. One had a brown-stained chip on its edge. The table had been covered with an old sheet and a washed jam jar of jewel-coloured nasturtiums sat at its centre.

'Did your father say how long he would be away?' asked Camille.

'Just one night. It's too far to travel to his brother's and back in one day. Thank you for letting me stay with you for the night.'

Camille rubbed Arlette's upper arm before turning to lift the vegetables for draining. 'It's a pleasure to have company. And as for Klara, you wouldn't know that she was here.'

Arlette looked down at her Brittany spaniel curled nose to tail on the rug beneath the kitchen table. A slice of early evening sunlight streaked across her fur from the open shutters.

'She's a sleepy old thing these days,' said Arlette.

Camille laughed. 'Aren't we all?'

Arlette smiled back. She was growing to love Camille.

The two women sat down, scraping their chairs closer to the table. Camille used two forks to ease meat from the cooked rabbit, placing it in small piles on their plates. Next Arlette spooned boiled potatoes and vegetables next to the meat before they both sat with their hands together. They lowered their heads.

'Thank you for this meal, Lord, and for all our blessings,' said Camille. 'Please bring Saul, Gilbert and Henri safely home so that we may all, one day, share in your bounty together. Amen.'

The clatter of cutlery was the only sound to disturb the room for a few minutes. A petal fell silently from a flower onto the tablecloth.

'This is wonderful. Where did you get the rabbit?' asked Arlette.

'The butcher says he goes shooting before opening his shop.'

'But the Germans would arrest him if they knew he had a firearm.'

'He says he walks miles into the countryside so he can't be heard. It's a risk he's willing to take to earn money and put food in his shop. Besides, the Germans are running as scared as the rabbits these days.'

Arlette chuckled then thought for a moment. 'I suppose during wartime everything we do is a risk. Like the butcher, we just have to weigh up the benefits against the consequences.'

'True. But that's not just during the war. That's called life.'

'Father took a risk last night.'

Camille rested her cutlery on her plate and frowned. 'What did he do?'

'There hadn't been any sign of movement at the manor for days,' said Arlette. 'He walked through the wood to see if any lights were on last evening, but it was dark and quiet.'

'Why would he do such a dangerous thing?'

'He wondered if they'd left any livestock behind. They were ours in the first place so it wouldn't have been stealing.'

'And were there any?'

'He came back with three chickens flapping under his arms.'

Camille clapped her hands and laughed. 'How wonderful. I'm sure he would have been very pleased with himself.'

'He was, although they didn't look very healthy and he doesn't think all three will survive. The Germans must have neglected them before leaving the manor.'

'They must have heard that they were losing the war town by town. I imagine they've all been ordered back to the larger cities. I wonder what happened to that German who went missing from the manor? Did they ever find him?'

A mouthful of meat became stuck in Arlette's throat. She began to cough. Immediately Camille's chair scraped across the floor and she hurried to her side. Arlette felt sharp slaps on her back and gasped for air. She swallowed and breathed deeply.

'Is that better?'

Arlette nodded. 'Thank you. I think I was rushing my meal.'

Camille sat down and continued with her own dinner.

'Take your time. There are even a few more boiled potatoes left. Your father has worked wonders with what few vegetables he's grown this year. There'll be plenty for when the men come home next year.'

Arlette changed the subject in case Camille mentioned the Kommandant again. 'Do you really think that Gilbert and Saul are alive? Do you think they'll both come home?'

Camille smiled a smile that didn't reflect in her eyes. 'You must have faith.'

Arlette bit her lip as she considered this. 'It's difficult for me to keep the faith when I've seen such dreadful things. Why does God let these things happen?'

'He plays no part in war. He gave man free will and many of them, with their lack of wisdom or greed, chose to use it to dominate and destroy. It's always been that way. It's sometimes easy to forget that there are so many good people in the world, too.'

Arlette realised that she had been wringing her hands beneath the table. An ache from below the surface of her scars made her flinch. She had to change the subject before the images of Oradour began to seep into her mind again. They were never far from the surface.

'Won't it be wonderful when the war is over and the Lamonds come back home? They'll replant the vines and Saul says we're going to get married and toast our future with their best wine.'

'I'll drink to that,' said Camille, lifting her glass of water.

Arlette raised her glass and chinked it against Camille's.

The following afternoon, Arlette and Camille left the townhouse and set off towards the Blaises' farm. It was a mile outside the village and would take them half an hour at a gentle pace. It had rained overnight and the village

272

looked bright, as if it had been rinsed and polished. They walked, deep in conversation, occasionally lifting their heads to admire the autumnal colours of paprika and cinnamon or to inhale the aromas of wood smoke and sweet fermenting fruit. When they reached the bottom of Montverre Hill, Klara became agitated. She began sniffing the ground, pulling on her lead and walking in circles trying to pick up a recent scent.

'What's got into her?' asked Camille.

'I've no idea. Perhaps a pheasant crossed nearby a short time ago. Klara! Stop pulling!' Klara continued to whine and pull Arlette up the hill. 'I'm coming, there's no need to pull.'

Arlette glanced up the hill. Close to the summit was an old man. He was struggling to walk, dragging one leg on the floor behind him. With each step he would lean his body to one side and use momentum to swing his bad leg forwards. She felt uneasy.

'Oh, you silly girl,' said Arlette. 'It's just a stranger.' She looked at Camille. 'As well as sleeping too much, Klara hates outsiders passing by the farm now she's getting older. She usually barks wildly. She has done since the refugees kept knocking.'

Because the old man was walking so slowly, the two women gradually caught up with him. Klara continued to pull and breathe noisily because she was pulling the lead tighter around her neck.

'Stop it, Klara! You'll strangle yourself.'

The stranger's oversized clothes hung like dust sheets from his skeletal frame. Arlette considered offering him some water before he passed by the farmhouse, but was ashamed to admit to herself that the thought of the old man's dirty and dishevelled appearance made her wary. She whispered to Camille.

'Shall we offer him some refreshment before he walks down the other side?'

Camille raised her eyebrows. 'Remember we were talking about risks? We don't know who he is.'

'He can hardly walk and there are two of us. I don't think he's a danger. He could be someone's father. If my father was injured and alone, I'd like to think that someone would take pity on him. I think I'll ask him.'

The man reached the summit of the hill while Arlette and Camille were still several yards behind him. He stopped at the farmhouse gate and looked towards the building. The women paused too. Klara was pulling strongly, causing Arlette to use all her strength to keep her dog from reaching the man. He was still seemingly unaware that they were behind him. Arlette looked at Camille, pulled a face and shrugged her shoulders. She whispered, 'I'll ask him if I can help. Can you hold this silly dog?'

She handed the lead to Camille and walked closer towards the man. His hair was lank and appeared to have been cut recently with a blunt pair of scissors. Just as she was about to speak, she noticed him lean forwards and touch the sign that was fixed to a post by the farm gate; the sign she had painted which read, House In The Clouds. His shoulders drooped and began to shudder beneath his oversized jacket. He could have been laughing had it not been for his pitiful sobs. Then he did something that made Arlette catch her breath. With a swift movement of his hand, he swept his hair from his eyes.

Chapter Forty-Four

Her voice seemed to come from elsewhere. A hidden place. A place secreted deep within her heart for fear of losing it. Part whisper, part sigh, she said his name.

'Saul?'

The man stopped shaking. He looked up towards the farmhouse.

'Saul?' she repeated.

Slowly the huge coat began to turn. She scanned the patches, the seams, the pockets and the stains for any hint that this was her beloved Saul. As the man turned, he scraped his leg behind him. She saw a bruised hand – a young hand. Buttons at the wrist of his coat. Sharp cheekbones. Then with one more drag of his leg, he turned to face her.

She hesitated. She was breathing fast. Was she wrong? There were similarities to Saul: olive-black eyes, the curve of his lips, the way he pushed his hair from his eyes. But this person was more like Saul's shadow; like seeing him through misted glass. A vague resemblance to someone she had once loved. Apprehension smothered any joy she felt. Had he been so traumatised that he didn't remember her? There was awkwardness between them. It felt as if they had forgotten how to be with one another. How to feel. As though they had to relearn the words to a poem.

Then he spoke. It was Saul's voice. Deep and calm.

'My love.'

She could see his hollow eyes glisten and he held his arms out towards her. Arlette took three steps and fell against his shoulder, her arms encircling his body and coat with ease. He was skeletal. 'It's you! It's really you. You've come back to me.'

Camille must have released Klara because the next second, her dog was leaping up against Saul and licking his hands. She nearly knocked them both sideways.

'She knew. Klara knew it was you. She was pulling us up the hill.'

Arlette reluctantly let go of Saul and looked at him. She touched his cheek. 'Come inside. Come inside and rest. You're home. You're safe now.'

Arlette eased Saul into a chair, stood back and wrung her hands together. She wasn't sure what to do next. She was shaking. Noisily swallowing a sob, she pressed her fingers against her lips, shaking her head in disbelief. Tears blurred her vision but she wiped them away, not wanting to miss another second of looking into Saul's face.

'I missed you,' said Saul.

A noise escaped Arlette's mouth. Part laugh, part cry. She lunged forwards and dropped to her knees in front of him, clinging to his waist, her head pressed against his chest. She could feel his arms encircle her shoulders and they rocked gently to and fro. He was home. Her Saul had come back.

It was many minutes before Camille spoke. Her voice came as a surprise to Arlette. She'd forgotten that Camille was there.

'I've made you both some rhubarb tea.'

Arlette pulled away from Saul, shaking her head for clarity. 'Oh. Sorry. I didn't hear you making it.'

'You needed a little time. Here. Take these,' said Camille, handing Arlette two cups. 'You've had a bit of a shock and I'm sure Saul needs some refreshment. I'll go and prepare a room upstairs. Is it all right to use your grandmother's room?'

Arlette was a little confused. 'A room? What for?'

'For Saul, of course.'

Arlette's frown faded as realisation replaced bewilderment. Her mouth fell open in understanding. Saul could stay with them in the house now. No more hiding in a damp secret room. No more pretence. Saul would live with them, at least until he was strong again.

'Yes. Grandma's room. Of course,' stammered Arlette.

Arlette watched Camille put a light to the fire that had been prepared the day before and leave the kitchen. She placed the steaming drinks on the floor then turned back towards Saul, but his eyes were already searching her own face. She leaned forwards and tenderly pressed her lips against his, inhaling the scent of his skin. Taking hold of his grazed hands, she kissed his bloodied knuckles. 'Welcome home, my love.'

'I can't tell you how …' He paused. 'How wonderful it is to be back and hold you once more. But where is she? I'm desperate to see her. She must be almost walking now. Is she asleep upstairs?'

Arlette held her breath. She had been so caught up in the wonder of his return that she'd forgotten that he didn't know. Her chin began to quiver uncontrollably. She tried to speak, but despite the tumultuous responses playing in her head, no words formed in her mouth. All she could do was to slowly shake her head. Tears balanced precariously on her lower lashes and her lips trembled.

'She's not asleep?' he asked.

Arlette's mouth made the shape of a silent word, no.

'She's not here?'

Arlette shook her head. A sob escaped. She blinked and the tears fell from her lashes. She saw Saul's hopeful expression evaporate into one of confusion. Then his mouth slightly parted when the moment of understanding dawned.

'She's gone?' he whispered.

Tears now streamed down her face. She held his face between her palms and nodded. 'I'm sorry, I'm sorry. She died. Oh God, she's gone.'

He was shaking his head, his eyes beseeching her. 'No. How? No.'

'I'm sorry, Saul. I'm sorry.' Racking sobs tore through Arlette's body. Her eyes and nose streamed until she couldn't see or breathe properly. Saul reached out and pulled her towards him. They hung onto each other, grasping handfuls of clothing, clinging tightly, crying like wounded animals. Again they rocked, more violently this time. She felt Saul's body shaking with emotion as he cried against her. Minutes ticked by. The clock on the mantle chimed the quarter hour.

Their crying eventually slowed and their breathing quietened, but they remained in a tight embrace. Arlette could hear Camille moving around upstairs readying Saul's room for him. Still kneeling on the floor, she released her hold of him and sat back on her heels. The fire Camille had lit was now crackling and filling the dim room with warmth and light. Wood-smoke perfumed the room. 'We have a lot to talk about, my love. Come and sit closer to the fire and drink your tea.'

Arlette picked up the two cups from the floor and watched this once fit man ease painfully out of the chair and hobble to another closer to the fire. She handed him a cup then dragged another chair next to his. Neither spoke. They sipped bitter rhubarb tea. Upstairs, the floorboards creaked while Camille busied herself. Klara sighed at their feet.

'When?' asked Saul.

'In February.'

Saul looked up. 'So long ago?'

Arlette nodded.

Silence. They sipped more tea.

'What happened?'

'She caught pneumonia. I found her one morning. In her bed.'

Saul leant forwards, hunched his shoulders and shook his head. He rested his forehead against the cup he was holding. 'She caught it from nearly drowning in the water barrel, didn't she?'

Neither of them had spoken their baby's name. Arlette knew that she needed to say their daughter's name. They couldn't hide from this tragedy.

'Estelle was poorly for weeks afterwards. She had a bad chest.'

Saul banged his forehead against the cup several times. A few drops spilt over the side and dribbled onto the floor. 'I wasn't quick enough.'

Arlette looked at him. 'What do you mean?'

'I didn't come out of the barn fast enough.'

She reached over and squeezed his forearm. 'No. You mustn't blame yourself. I was the one who made him angry.'

'Where is the bastard? I'll kill him with my bare hands,' he spat.

Arlette closed her eyes for a second. Now that her grandmother was dead, only she knew the secret of the Kommandant's whereabouts.

'He went missing at the beginning of the year. It's rumoured he was murdered by the Resistance. With him gone and without his orders to keep Father and me away from home, I left the manor and Father was free to return from Germany.'

'Henri's back?'

'Yes. He's visiting his brother but should be home later this evening.'

'And Gilbert?'

Arlette shrugged. 'Not yet. We haven't heard from him for several months.'

Saul reached out and took hold of her hand. 'He'll come home.' He frowned before looking more closely. 'What happened to your hand?'

Arlette watched him stroke the pink raised wheals on her skin. 'Something terrible happened. In Oradour. I was burnt. Grandma was killed.'

Another shock. Arlette could almost see Saul's frame shrink further as he closed his eyes and caught his breath. 'Grandma Blaise is dead?'

Arlette nodded and bit her lip. Klara whined in her sleep. The clock struck half past the hour.

'Grandma Blaise is dead.' It wasn't a question. It was an incredulous statement spoken quietly. 'God bless that woman.'

Arlette nodded.

'Francine?' he asked.

Arlette gave a weak smile. 'She's well. She's looked after me.'

Silence.

Saul finished his tea. 'Tell me about her.'

'Who?'

'Estelle.'

'She was poorly and didn't change in the few weeks that you'd gone.'

'Remind me. I need reminding.'

Arlette's face softened at the memory of her daughter. For eight months she'd learned how to protect the pain with a protective layer – like wrapping a precious gift in tissue paper as her father had suggested. The pain often ripped through the delicate casing, but now she could find some comfort in remembrance. 'She smiled your smile. She had your dark eyes.'

Saul closed his eyes. Arlette didn't know if it was against the pain of loss or whether he was imagining his daughter. She continued.

'Estelle was a good baby. She was small but she fed and slept well. She'd learned to sit up. She played with her toes and had four teeth, two at the bottom and two at the top. The hair behind her ears had begun to curl. I have a picture I sketched of her upstairs. I'll fetch it later.'

Camille walked back into the room. 'Everything's ready upstairs.'

Saul looked up. 'Thank you, Camille. It's good to see that you're well.'

Camille leant down and embraced Saul. 'Everyone missed you. You never left our thoughts.'

Saul didn't answer. Emotion was a powerful silencer.

'You're exhausted,' said Camille. 'I think you should lie down upstairs and sleep.'

He nodded.

'Here, we'll help you.' Camille looked at Arlette and gave a small jerk of her head.

'Yes, of course,' said Arlette, standing up.

They took hold of Saul's arms and helped him to stand. Three of them shuffled from the kitchen and through the rarely used sitting room. They paused at the bottom of the stairs, all three of them standing on the rug that hid bloodstains beneath it. Together they struggled up the narrow staircase, Saul stepping with his good foot first and then lifting his injured one. Arlette decided to ask him questions about his limp after he'd rested.

They passed Henri's bedroom and then Arlette's. The room prepared for Saul was next to the unused silk room.

The shutters had been pulled to, but a weak shaft of evening sunlight slipped through a small gap. It drew a golden line across the middle of the room.

Camille touched Arlette's hand. 'I'll leave you to settle Saul.' She left the room and closed the door behind her.

Saul waited like a child. His stooped stature broke the shaft of sunlight as he waited to be told what to do.

'Let me take your coat,' said Arlette. She stood behind him and took hold of the material around his shoulders, easing it down his arms. She silenced a gasp. He was emaciated. His shoulder bones protruded from his shirt and a line of bones ran down his back like stepping stones across a river. She mustn't show her shock. This was her beloved Saul and she would make him better. Arlette pulled back the blankets on the bed and nodded gently at him. 'Lie down. Rest.'

Saul dragged his foot towards the bed and turned. He sat on its edge before lying down sideways, groaning with effort. Arlette lifted his legs one at a time onto the mattress. He sucked in a breath in pain when she lifted his injured foot.

'Sorry, sorry.'

'It's fine.'

'Is it comfortable now?'

'Yes, thank you. Thank you so much.'

She watched him close his eyes although his forehead was still lined with corrugated frowns. After a moment she covered him with blankets and stood back. She waited until his breathing became slower and deeper, and the lines on his face softened with sleep.

Chapter Forty-Five

Arlette woke in her bed, disturbed by the baritone voice of her father, deep even in whisper. He was talking to Saul in the next room. The previous evening she had stayed with Saul for many hours before Camille had ushered her from his room and into her own bedroom at midnight. While she had been sitting with him, he had drifted in and out of sleep at irregular intervals. The clock didn't dictate his thirst, sleep or restlessness.

Arlette never questioned where Camille slept when she stayed at the farmhouse. For the past few days she had been in the house last thing at night and first thing in the morning. It was obvious that she was staying with her father each night. She smiled to herself. Her mother's friend and her father took comfort in each other's company. Yesterday Arlette had noticed her father rest his palm against Camille's back when he leant towards her and asked if she would like something to eat. She saw their secret smiles and glances, and she was glad. The farmhouse was beginning to feel like it had found its heartbeat once again. When they laughed together it sounded like a melody hanging in the air. People looked for love and kindness anywhere they could find it in desperate times.

Arlette heard someone moving downstairs in the kitchen. As yet the sun hadn't risen but she slipped her feet into her clogs and wrapped her shawl around her shoulders. She crossed to the window, opened the casements and pushed the shutters wide. The wind cuffed her face. The horizon was streaked with pale pink hues, hinting at the coming day. She breathed in the thick sweet-scented air of dawn but the chill forced her to close the windows again. She shivered and hugged her upper arms. Just to reassure herself that she hadn't been dreaming about Saul's return, Arlette left her bedroom and entered Saul's. His frail body was propped up on pillows while he spoke to her father. Both looked up as she entered.

'Good morning, *ma pêche*,' said Henri.

Saul smiled at her. He looked as pale as pastry.

'Good morning,' she said. She turned to Saul. 'How did you sleep?'

'Well, thank you.'

'Four straight hours from one until five,' said Henri. He spoke as if praising a small child.

'That's wonderful. Can I make either of you some breakfast?'

'Come and sit with Saul. Camille is making us porridge and stewing some apples to eat with it. I need to visit the washroom and then I'll help her carry four bowls upstairs. We can eat together.'

Arlette sat on the blankets by Saul's feet, the material still warm from her father's body heat. Henri kissed his daughter and left the room. She listened to his footsteps along the corridor, quietening as he went downstairs. Feeling shy once again, Arlette smiled at Saul. He held out his hand and she shuffled further up the bed and took hold of it.

'I used to dream of food,' he said. 'Roasted rabbit and hot potatoes.'

'I can see you've lost a lot of weight. We've been hungry but we could always find something. Father would fish or trap rabbits when the stores were empty.'

Saul closed his eyes for a moment and Arlette wondered for a moment if he'd fallen back to sleep. She waited and watched his face. With his eyes still closed, he said, 'I saw the moon from the windows. The glass was filthy but the white shone through. I used to imagine you looking at it at the same moment. I'd picture you holding Estelle and pointing to it. Teaching her its name.'

Arlette listened. He opened his eyes, dark as jet stones in the dim light. She said nothing, but felt an overwhelming ache in her chest because she had never pointed out the moon to Estelle.

'It helped me to think of you both while I was in that hell.'

'I can't imagine, my love. Do you know where they took you?' she asked.

'I didn't for weeks, but then I learned it was a place called Drancy.'

'Where's that?'

'Near Paris.'

'You never left France?'

Saul shook his head. 'You could say I was lucky in a way. It appeared to be a transit camp. The conditions were brutal. Little food and what we were given tasted disgusting. Filthy conditions. Overcrowding. Cruelty by the guards.' He paused. 'Cruelty you wouldn't believe.'

Arlette thought of Oradour-sur-Glane. Yes, she would believe him.

'Families were separated and after a while large groups were transported to a place called Auschwitz.'

'What was that? A prison?'

'At first the rest of us thought they were the lucky ones, but from the rumours we heard later on, a prison would have been a blessing. I met an artist called Max. He was Dutch and had been travelling through France to Switzerland when he was arrested and brought to Drancy. He spoke German and occasionally overheard the Nazis talking.'

'What did they say? No. You don't have to if ...'

His mouth twisted into a grimace and he shook his head slowly. 'The world should know what the Nazis did. They were infected with evil and even more so in the last few months when they sensed that they were losing the war. They couldn't have been human, Arlette. Humans wouldn't do the things I saw them do.'

'I'm so sorry.' Arlette wiped a tear from her cheek. 'The Kommandant arrested you and I didn't know until some time later. I didn't see what happened when he took you away. I didn't even know you'd given yourself up until Grandma Blaise told me. You could have died for us. You saved us.' She leant forwards and lay against his chest. He stroked her hair for several minutes while they embraced in silence.

'Where is she buried?' asked Saul.

Arlette paused. 'Estelle's with mother.'

Saul nodded slowly. 'That's good.'

Arlette felt her shoulders relax. How much more difficult it would have been to explain to him that Estelle was cocooned in a box in the silk room. She silently thanked her beloved grandmother who had made her understand how wrong that had been.

Dawn entered the room and colour seeped into each corner. They heard Camille's soft laughter and footsteps coming upstairs. Arlette wiped her cheeks dry and smiled when Henri and Camille opened the door and came inside carrying two trays of porridge and stewed apples. They each took a steaming bowl and sat with Saul on the bed, blowing and eating their watery porridge. The softened apples replaced the oats' blandness with a delicate sweetness.

When all the bowls were scraped clean, Saul spoke directly to Camille. 'Would you mind dressing my foot today?'

'Of course, I was going to ask if it needed some attention.'

'What happened?' asked Arlette.

'I was simply in the way of a guard one day,' said Saul. 'He shot me in the foot to teach me a lesson.'

Arlette gasped. 'My God!'

'Max gouged the bullet out with a stick. I passed out with the pain. Again I was lucky. A few weeks later the Germans disappeared and the Swiss took over the camp. The French Red Cross looked after the sick in the nearby Rothschild Hospital. I was determined they wouldn't amputate my foot and that I'd walk again.' His voice broke mid sentence and he closed his eyes. 'How could I find ... how could I find you again if I couldn't walk?'

Arlette felt his torment. She put her arms around his shoulders, understanding now why he closed his eyes so regularly. It had become his way of blocking out horrific memories from the past year. It was his way of coping with the trauma he'd experienced. He was stopping it from entering his safe place – the farmhouse.

'This Drancy place you spoke of last night,' said Henri. 'Did they take you straight there?'

'No. I was locked in a bedroom at the manor for a short while. Then I was moved to Limoges where I spent a night with many others. The next day they put us all on a train. I was locked inside Drancy until it was liberated in August.'

'August? But it's October,' said Arlette.

'I was sick. The infection in my foot was spreading through my body. They said I'd been lucky. In a few more days I wouldn't have made it.'

Arlette enclosed his fists in her palms. 'Shh. I'm here. You're safe now.' She had so many questions that were tumbling over each other to be asked, but they'd wait. They had a lifetime of talking ahead.

Chapter Forty-Six

December gusted in with bitter winds, but inside the farmhouse a fire blazed in the grate. Another fruit tree had been chopped up for fuel, but as Henri had stated, what use would plump fruit be in the summer if everyone had frozen to death the previous winter?

Christmas was going to be a frugal affair, as it had been for the past four years. A small fir tree had been cut down and decorated with a handful of old treasured baubles, fir cones and painted eggshells. It stood beside the kitchen table, far enough away from the heat of the fire but in a prominent place where everyone could see it. Hanging photographs and pictures had been garlanded with holly, its ruby berries adding spots of colour to the room in the flickering candlelight. Camille was going to be staying for Christmas so she had brought her own Christmas decorations and had arranged them around the farmhouse: strings of glass beads, delicate silver stars and a soft toy snowman that was worn in places.

Saul and Arlette were sitting in front of the open fire making paper chains from old propaganda leaflets. Logs spat orange stars into the hearth, their glow fading to black as they cooled. Camille was knitting beside two candles because paraffin for their lamps had run out a long time ago. She was trying to hide the growing garment that was to be a secret Christmas gift for someone, having unpicked an old blanket and several cardigans that had belonged to her mother. Henri was relaxing in an armchair while sipping brandy that he'd bartered for in exchange for logs and half a dozen eggs. Thanks to his care and attention, the three chickens he had re-homed from the manor were now thriving – although there would be two less after Christmas dinner.

Arlette looked up and spoke to Camille. 'Are you still free to help me make a Christmas pudding tomorrow?'

Camille readjusted her knitting to hide more of the garment. 'Of course. Have we got all the ingredients now?'

'Yes. Monique went to Limoges for brown sugar, suet and mixed spices.' Arlette tapped the side of her nose and winked. 'Apparently she knew someone, who knew somebody else, who worked in a food distribution area. Francine called by this morning with it.' She clasped her hands together. 'I'm so happy they're coming for Christmas dinner too.'

'It'll be a bittersweet day, that's for sure,' said Henri. He lifted his brandy towards the fire and peered at the golden honey tones through the glass. He swirled the liquid. 'We've lost loved ones and are still waiting for others to return. We've welcomed a new friend back home,' he said, looking at Saul, 'and rediscovered a precious friend from the past.' He winked at Camille. 'A mixed blessing.'

Arlette gazed into the fire and thought of Estelle and Grandma Blaise. War didn't care if it took the young or the old. Images of Estelle in the water barrel with her soaking, ballooning dress flashed into her mind, followed by her grandmother's favourite flowered apron. She wondered why she had remembered their clothing and not their faces and prayed that it wasn't because she was forgetting what they looked like. Saul leant across and held her hand.

'You look sad. Come back to the present.'

She smiled. He'd been back for two months and was convalescing well. He'd put on a little weight but not enough, due to the ongoing food shortages. He still limped but the colour in his cheeks and the light in his eyes had grown brighter. There were some days when the trauma of his experience in Drancy tormented his mood to such an extent that he stayed in bed, but on other days he looked forward to the future. Today was a good day.

On Christmas morning, Arlette slipped out of bed and wrapped her shawl around her shoulders. She crossed to the window where she pushed open the shutters. It had become a daily ritual to look out at the valley and river while checking on the weather. Today it was a frosty blue-sky day. A smile played on her lips as she hurried to the cupboard and took out Saul's gift. She had painted an old photograph frame and placed the sketch she'd made of Estelle inside. She had also knitted him a scarf from old scraps of wool. It had a few knots in it where she'd tied lengths of wool together, but it would keep him warm. There hadn't been any pretty paper to wrap them in, but that didn't matter. It would only have been thrown away.

Downstairs Camille was lighting candles in the living room and Henri was hunched over the grate making a fire. The living room was rarely used because the kitchen was so large and homely, but it was a Blaise family tradition that Christmas Day was spent in there.

'Happy Christmas,' said Arlette.

Camille embraced her. 'Happy Christmas.'

Henri stood up, groaning as he pulled himself upright. 'Happy Christmas, *ma pêche*. I think I could do with a gift of new bones. These ones are getting a little old.'

Arlette felt her father's strong arms enfold her. She breathed in the scent of his freshly laundered shirt.

'What have you got there?' he asked.

'Saul's gifts.'

'Is he awake yet?'

'I couldn't hear him moving in his room. I'll leave him to sleep.'

He released Arlette from his arms. 'Right, now this fire's burning, I'll clear the ashes from the oven and light that too.' He rubbed his palms together making a rasping sound. 'Roast chicken for dinner today!'

The two women smiled at each other. It was so good to see her father in such good humour. Arlette followed him through to the kitchen where she placed Saul's gifts under the tree alongside several others.

While Henri was sitting on his haunches cleaning the remnants of the oven's fire, surrounded by a halo of silver ash dust, she crossed the stone floor to the bureau. Opening the door, she took out a small posy of holly twigs full of ruby berries, trailing ivy and a small heart-shaped stone. The leaves had been dusted with Epsom salts to make them sparkle like frost, a gift for Estelle and her mother's headstone. She and Saul would walk down the hill to Saint-Pierre's after dinner.

By midday the living room was full of conversation and laughter. While Camille and Monique busied themselves in the kitchen, Henri, Bruno, Arlette, Saul and Francine played snakes and ladders at the dining table, each drinking home-made elderberry wine. Despite the log fire blazing in the grate, Saul wore his Christmas knitted scarf. Arlette's gift from Saul had been a simple carving that he had made. Two figures were holding an infant. The carving was basic but had obviously been made with love. She knew that it would be a treasured possession for the rest of her life.

The smell of roast chicken emanated from the kitchen and distracted the players. It had been a long time since they'd smelt such rich aromas and it was making mouths water and stomachs rumble.

'One, two, three ... oh no, four.' Henri slid his counter down a long snake to the sound of everyone's good-humoured teasing.

'Set the table,' interrupted Monique from the doorway.

'Well, that's a shame,' said Henri. 'I'll have to beat you all at another game this afternoon.'

'But I'm winning,' groaned Bruno.

'Come on, Papa,' said Francine. 'It's time for roast chicken.'

Bruno continued grumbling but was closing the board game and collecting the counters in haste. Arlette and Francine set the table and Saul refilled everyone's glasses. Henri threw two more logs on the fire. One by one, serving dishes were brought through to the living room. Sage and thyme filled the air with a delicious perfume and an abundance of food was placed in the centre of the table. Two roast chickens sat centre stage. Boiled potatoes, carrots, cabbage and onions steamed on separate dishes. Fleur Blaise's favourite jug was full to the brim with watery gravy.

When everyone was sitting at the table, Henri said grace.

'Thank you for our blessings, Lord. As we celebrate the day of your birth, may we cherish our loved ones and remember those who have left us to sit at your side. Thank you for the feast before us on this Christmas Day.'

Everyone bowed their heads and said, Amen.

Henri held up his hand and said in a pantomime voice. 'Oh, before we start, I thought I heard something.' He held a cupped hand to his ear in an exaggerated manner.

Arlette listened and frowned. What was her father doing? 'I can't hear—'

Henri interrupted her. 'Shhh! I think I can hear something.' His voice was almost a shout. He winked at Camille and she stifled a giggle.

There was a noise in the kitchen. Everyone turned towards the closed living room door. There was a knock and a deep voice boomed, 'Ho, ho, ho!'

'Come in,' shouted Henri.

Arlette turned to Francine with a puzzled expression.

The door opened and a scruffy *Père Noël* stood in the doorway and waved. Francine and Arlette hugged each other with delight.

'Welcome, Father Christmas,' said Francine.

'Come in and have a glass of elderberry wine to warm you up,' said Arlette, laughing. She turned to her father. 'How did you talk one of your friends into dressing up for us? Is it Thierry?'

Her father smiled enigmatically but said nothing. Arlette thought she saw him throw a knowing glance at Camille. She turned amidst the laughter and merriment and looked at the man dressed in red. He was wearing a burgundy dressing gown, black boots and belt. His hat was a red scarf and his grey-white beard looked suspiciously like dusty silk filaments that had been stuck unevenly to his face. Beneath his dressing gown hung a lopsided cushion that was trying to escape from the wrap over gown.

Then all noise faded into the background. She exchanged glances with the hidden figure. He had fern-green eyes; the same colour as hers. She looked at her father. He was watching her. There was something familiar about the man's stance. Then she noticed a tuft of deep auburn hair escaping from beneath his red scarf.

At first her voice was a whisper. 'Gilbert?'

Nothing happened. The teasing continued around her. The laughter remained noisy. She repeated her brother's name a little louder.

'Gilbert?'

Francine, who was closest to Arlette, stopped and looked at her best friend and then at the figure in red.

'*Joyeux Noël*,' said the man. It was Gilbert's voice.

Mayhem ensued. Arlette scraped her chair backwards and ran into his arms, knocking the cushion to the floor. She hugged her brother. 'You're home. I can't believe you're home.' She pulled away to look at him but the silk thread had caught in her hair, linking them together. More laughter filled the room as she pulled it free. Bruno shook his hand, followed by a tight hug from Monique. Camille kissed him on both cheeks and Saul nodded in greeting. Arlette remembered that the last time they spoke was when Gilbert had been angry that Saul was putting the family in danger. She was relieved to see Gilbert nod in return.

'You knew,' Arlette accused her father, with a playful thump to his arm. She turned towards her brother to ask him how long he'd known he was coming home, but she stopped. Her brother and Francine were embracing. Gilbert was whispering something in her ear.

Chapter Forty-Seven

The war was dragging on across Europe but the enemy had left Montverre. Everyone except the Germans realised that Germany had been defeated. By springtime, rumour had it that Hitler was in hiding and his forces were running scared. Here, on the face of things, village life was getting back to normal.

Arlette, Saul, Henri and Camille sat eating porridge at the kitchen table. They were planning the day's chores on the farm. Since Henri had decided to sell his tractor in order to raise some cash, chickens once again bustled in the farmyard and three cows, a calf and a bull grazed in the Blaises' meadow. It would take time, but with hard work from all the family, the farm would eventually grow back into a thriving business. When they could afford to, the family would buy another tractor and expand into growing crops once again. They were already reaping the benefits of buying cattle because nowadays their porridge was made with warm milk instead of water.

'Where's Gilbert?' asked Arlette.

'Where do you think?' her father replied.

Arlette laughed and helped herself to another spoonful of porridge. 'Has he gone to see Francine already? It's only half past seven.'

'He's a changed lad,' said Camille. 'Francine has become the centre of his universe. I wouldn't be surprised if there are wedding bells ringing before long.'

Arlette smiled at Camille. It was such a relief. Gone was her headstrong brother who was ready to take on the Germans single-handedly. Nowadays Gilbert appeared to appreciate the simple pleasures in his life. His eyes had been shockingly opened by man's capability of cruelty during his time fighting with the Resistance. He had spent hours regaling the family with his experiences, and although shocking to listen to, Arlette knew that he diluted their content when she and Camille were present. A simple farm life and planning a future with Francine were what mattered to him now. They had rarely been apart from the time Father Christmas had visited the farmhouse five months previously.

Monique and Bruno burst into the kitchen followed by Francine, Gilbert and a flurry of pink cherry blossom petals. Those sitting at the table stopped talking, their spoons held in midair. They looked up at the commotion.

Henri laid down his spoon. 'Whatever's the matter?'

Francine's parents were hanging on to each other's shoulders and panting, grins stretching their lips wide. 'I've been listening to Monsieur Péricaud's wireless this morning,' gasped Monique. Sweat sparkled on her forehead and décolletage.

'Did you lose a cent and find a franc on the way here?' Henri asked, grinning.

Monique wasn't going to be distracted from her news and ignored his banter.

Arlette felt her heart beat quicken. 'What did you hear?'

'Hitler's committed suicide. The coward knew he'd lost the war and killed himself.'

'No!'

'Good Lord.'

'What does that mean exactly?' asked Camille.

Bruno rubbed his hands together. 'Winston Churchill has announced Victory in Europe. The newsman said the guns had fallen silent across Europe and the Allies have accepted Germany's surrender. The war's over!'

Cheering and whooping erupted from the group at the

table. Chairs were scraped backwards and people stood up, breakfast forgotten. A carousel of noise filled the kitchen as the men hugged each other and slapped backs in acknowledgment of the news. The women wiped tears of joy from their cheeks and clung to each other with relief.

'I thought it would never happen,' Henri said with a sigh. 'Fetch the brandy, son.'

'It's not yet eight o'clock in the morning,' said Camille.

Henri kissed her full on the lips. 'We're celebrating!'

Arlette saw the kiss. It was no longer a secret that her father and her mother's friend had been a couple for months. She laid her head against Saul's shoulder, believing that if her mother could see from beyond, she would be happy with the arrangement.

'Can you smell that?' murmured Saul.

Arlette inhaled through her nose. She pulled a face. 'Smell what?'

'The Lamonds' wine,' he whispered in her ear.

She nudged him in the ribs for his silliness, then hugged him. His ribs weren't so evident these days, but his sense of humour was.

Epilogue

Montverre square was a bustle of colour, noise and movement. Spring blossoms grew in hedgerows and fledglings stretched their wings in nests hidden by thick canopies. Inside homes, pots bubbled on hobs and delicious smells wafted out through open shutters, everyone preparing a feast to celebrate the third anniversary since *le jour de la libération*.

Outside, villagers were busy tying bunting around the lower branches of fourteen mature Linden trees in the market place. Trestle tables were lined in rows alongside makeshift tables made from planks of wood and old doors that had been placed on top of boxes and milk churns. Jugs and vases sat at intervals on their surface, each frothing with summer flowers, while dining chairs were carried out of homes and placed alongside tables ready for a day of celebration and remembrance.

'I'll hold the chair still while you climb,' said Francine, her free hand caressing her swollen stomach.

Arlette laughed and stepped onto the chair. 'Of course you're not climbing in your condition.'

She reached down for the length of string, on to which were attached triangles of material. She looped the cord around a branch and tied it carefully. The length of bunting flickered in the breeze like a colourful washing line.

'That's the last one.' Arlette stepped down and stood back, admiring the decorations and absorbing the joyful atmosphere of the day.

'It looks lovely,' said Francine.

Arlette picked up several triangles of material from the ground. 'Let's have a rest for five minutes. It's so warm.'

The friends linked arms and walked towards a low stone wall where they sat down. Francine leant back, massaging her lower back with her palms.

'Backache?' asked Arlette.

'Just a little. Maman tells me it's not unusual with only five weeks until the birth.'

'Try not to do too much today. Did Gilbert say when they're all arriving?'

'It shouldn't be long. They're coming after they've finished the morning jobs on the farm. They're bringing Mimi and the trap to carry their food for the party. You should see the huge pot of chicken broth Camille has made. It's full of turnips, carrots, potatoes and onions. She had to fight Henri and Gilbert away from the oven last evening. They were teasing and threatening to eat it.'

'I sometimes miss the constant hustle and bustle of the farm,' said Arlette.

'You could always come back and live with us all. There's an empty bedroom.'

Arlette sighed. 'Grandma's bedroom.' She felt Francine place her hand on top of hers. 'I'm fine,' said Arlette. 'It's good to remember the ones we've loved and lost. What did Father Jules say at Estelle's funeral? *Memory is love's last light. While ever someone remembers them, they will remain with us.*'

'Beautiful words.' Francine paused for a few seconds. 'It *would* be lovely for us all to live together in The House In The Clouds though, wouldn't it? Although it might be a bit of a squeeze in a few weeks' time,' said Francine, pushing her round stomach out even farther.

Arlette laughed. 'Saul and I love living in Camille's old

place. We're very happy there and we visit the farm so often I feel as though we have two homes.'

'You've both made what was a dark, depressing house into a beautiful home. Saul made a huge difference by painting all the walls in fresh paint. What time does he finish work?'

'He finished at eight this morning but it's a long journey from Bergerac. He should be walking up the lane soon, so you rest while I go and meet him.'

Arlette wandered along the perimeter of the square. She breathed deeply, inhaling the warm perfumed air. How different everything was. The baker's had been re-painted, its doorway and window frame now a crisp white to highlight the fresh display of buns, pastries and loaves. A little further along, she paused at the place where she had parked her father's trap on the day she'd met Camille on market day. How sick she had looked that day, remembered Arlette. Now, she and Father were married and working alongside each other on the farm, spending each day laughing and teasing each other like love-struck teenagers.

Arlette walked on towards a corner of the market place. She paused. The shoemaker's was now a flower shop; the door against which poor Maurice had been shot was replaced with a new wooden one, varnished to a high gloss. She closed her eyes briefly, remembering the sound of gunfire.

Two young boys ran in front of her making aircraft noises and wielding model aeroplanes above their heads. Arlette smiled ruefully. They would have been babies at the beginning of the war and would have little memory, if any, of the hostilities. She turned and crossed the square to where old Monsieur Péricaud was sitting on a stool outside the front of his house, sipping from a glass of chalky-coloured *pastis* and water. Whenever he had a tipple too many, he would remind whoever was prepared to listen for the hundredth time that he had hoodwinked the enemy by continuing to listen to his banned wireless throughout the length of the occupation.

'Bonjour, Monsieur Péricaud.'

'Arlette! It's good to see you. The square is looking good.'

'It was hot work, but the decorations and the tables are ready for the village celebrations at twelve o'clock.'

Monsieur Péricaud shook his head in disbelief. 'Three years.'

Arlette waited for him to continue, but he was lost in thought.

'I hope you're hungry,' said Arlette. 'There's plenty of fish, chicken, vegetables and bread. The weather's too hot to save anything overnight so it all needs to be eaten.'

He looked up, his thoughts having returned to the present. 'As soon as midday strikes, I'll be there with my napkin knotted around my neck.' He chuckled. 'How's that young man of yours? Will he be celebrating with us?'

'Yes, Saul will be home soon. He's been working night shifts on the wards this week. This is his final year at medical school.'

'We're all proud of him. Soon we'll have our own doctor living in Montverre. By the way, if he has a moment to spare today, my left knee's been giving me some pain. Perhaps—'

'I'm sure he'll take a look if he has time, but he must get some sleep too. He has to go back to work again tonight before he has a couple of days' rest, but I'll be sure to ask him to call on you if he doesn't get to see you today.'

'Hey! I turn my back for a moment and my wife is making eyes at another man.'

Arlette turned. She smiled instinctively as Saul walked towards them, his limp almost unnoticeable in the warm weather. He pulled her close and she felt him rest his lips on the top of her head before kissing her hair.

Saul nodded towards Monsieur Péricaud. 'Good morning.'

'Three years today,' said the old man. 'Did I tell you that I snubbed those *maudit fritz* by listening to my banned wireless under their ugly noses every day?'

'You were the fount of all knowledge, back then. I heard that you had crowds squeezing into your house every day,' said Saul.

Arlette laid her head against Saul's chest, proud of the kind man her husband was. She had lost count of the times he had said this exact phrase to Monsieur Péricaud, but each time it brought about a gap-toothed grin as if it were the first time the old man had heard it.

'Be off with you,' he said, lifting his glass of *pastis*. 'Go and have some fun with the young ones. I'll see you both later.'

Arlette and Saul turned and walked back towards the square, hand in hand.

'Busy night, Doctor Epstein?' asked Arlette.

'It's always busy on the psychiatric wards. People saw so much horror that their minds can't cope with the memories.'

'I understand that. We're so lucky to have a loving family to help us through our nightmares. Many aren't blessed with family.'

Arlette felt him squeeze her hand.

'But today's not the day for such talk,' he said, 'today's for having fun and celebrating. Is everyone here?'

'Yes. Bruno, René and Albert are helping to transport a roast hog from Thierry's farm and your sister, Ruth, is with your mother at our house. Joshua's in the wash tub because he's been playing in the garden and got into a bit of a mess.'

'It's so good to see them again. I think this annual celebration in Montverre will become a regular get-together with the family.'

'Who knows, they may decide to move here from Paris one day.'

'I don't know. Ruth says she's getting to know a writer who lives in Saint-Germain. I'm pleased for her. She's been a widow for four years now and needs to find love again. She's only twenty-eight.'

'She seems happy. She's been so strong.' Arlette turned to look into his eyes. 'Now, are you going to get some sleep first?'

'I will this afternoon but I want to celebrate with everyone. Where's Matthieu?'

At that moment Monique walked out of the butcher's, a basket of warm pies in the crook of one arm and a small boy nestled against her ample bosom in the other. At almost two, the little boy had a mop of black hair, plump cheeks and eyes as dark as peppercorns, just like his father's.

The child held out his arms to Saul.

'Hello, Matthieu. Daddy missed you.'

Saint-Pierre's bell tolled twelve, the sound of its chimes now dimmed by conversation and laughter. This annual festival had become a release of fear and pain. The air smelled delicious, a mixture of garlic, fried onions, herbs and woodsmoke. Montverre square became a place of unrestrained joy. Music filled the air, small groups sang loudly as the community celebrated being alive. The Lamonds had returned from Scotland to the manor and the first post-war batch of their wine had been donated to the party and was being drunk in copious amounts, the fermented grapes leading to impassioned emotions being released through laughter and tears. Montverre was celebrating the end of suffering and hardship and the gift of freedom and peace.

A family of three sat quietly in one corner, a sleeping child draped across his mother's arms. The young man and woman kissed each other tenderly on the lips. He smiled before opening a bottle of wine and almost reverentially poured them both a glass, the pale gold liquid glinting in the sunlight. The beautiful young woman wiped away a tear but she was smiling as she kissed her son's black hair. Surrounded by family, loved ones, friends and neighbours, they raised their glasses to each other and after waiting six long years, drank from a bottle of the Lamonds' finest wine.

Thank you!

Dear readers,

I'd like to say a huge thank you for reading *Arlette's Story*. I loved creating Arlette and Saul's love story and over time I grew to see most of my characters as friends. I hope you did too.

If you loved *Arlette's Story* and have a minute to spare, I would really appreciate a short review on the page or site where you bought the book. Your help in spreading the word is greatly appreciated. Reviews from readers like you are invaluable and make a huge difference in raising a book's profile and helping new readers find similar stories, but they also hearten the author during the times they doubt their own ability.

Thank you
Love Angela xx

About the Author

Angela Barton was born in London and grew up in Nottingham. She is married with three grown up children and two spoilt spaniels she calls her 'hairy daughters.' Passionate about writing both contemporary and historical fiction, Angela has won and also been shortlisted for several writing competitions. She reads avidly, makes book-related jewellery and loves a nice cup of tea. Having recently planted a field of lavender with her husband in south-west France, she is looking forward to spending more time writing in Charente and watching their lavender grow. Angela is a member of the Romantic Novelists' Association and Nottingham Writers' Studio.

For more on Angela visit:
www.angelabarton.net
www.twitter.com/angebarton
www.facebook.com/angela.bartonauthor

More from Angela Barton

ANGELA BARTON

Magnolia House

When you open up your home and your heart …

Rowan Forrester has it all – the happy marriage, the adorable dog, the good friends, the promising business and even the dream home after she and her husband Tom win a stunning but slightly dilapidated Georgian townhouse in London at auction.

But in the blink of an eye, Rowan's picture-perfect life comes crashing down around her and she is faced with the prospect of having to start again.

To make ends meet she begins a search for housemates, and in doing so opens the door to new friends and new beginnings. But could she be opening the door to new heartbreak too?

Available as an eBook on all platforms and in audio. Visit www.choc-lit.com for details.

More from Ruby Fiction

Why not try something else from our selection:

The Purrfect Pet Sitter
Carol Thomas

**Introducing Lisa Blake,
the purrfect pet sitter!**

When Lisa Blake's life in
London falls apart, she returns
to her hometown rebranding
herself as 'the purrfect
petsitter' – which may or may
not be false advertising as she
has a rather unfortunate habit
of (temporarily) losing dogs!

But being back where she grew up, Lisa can't escape her
past. There's her estranged best friend Flick who she bumps
into in an embarrassing encounter in a local supermarket.
And her first love, Nathan Baker, who, considering their
history, is sure to be even more surprised by her drunken
Facebook friend request than Lisa is.

As she becomes involved in the lives of her old friends Lisa
must confront the hurt she has caused, discover the truth
about her mysterious leather-clad admirer, and learn how to
move forward when the things she wants most are affected
by the decisions of her past.

Available as an eBook on all platforms.
Visit www.rubyfiction.com for details.

The Best Boomerville Hotel

Caroline James

Let the shenanigans begin at the Best Boomerville Hote ...

Jo Docherty and Hattie Contaldo have a vision – a holiday retreat in the heart of the Lake District exclusively for guests of 'a certain age' wishing to stimulate both mind and body with new creative experiences. One hotel refurbishment later and the Best Boomerville Hotel is open for business!

Perhaps not surprisingly Boomerville attracts more than its fair share of eccentric clientele: there's fun-loving Sir Henry Mulberry and his brother Hugo; Lucinda Brown, an impoverished artist with more ego than talent; Andy Mack, a charming Porsche-driving James Bond lookalike, as well as Kate Simmons, a woman who made her fortune from an internet dating agency but still hasn't found 'the One' herself.

With such an array of colourful individuals there's bound to be laughs aplenty, but could there be tears and heartbreak too and will the residents get more than they bargained for at Boomerville?

Available in paperback from all good bookshops and online stores. Also available as an eBook on all platforms and in audio. Visit www.rubyfiction.com for details.

Introducing Ruby Fiction

Ruby Fiction is in imprint of Choc Lit Publishing.
We're an independent publisher creating
a delicious selection of fiction.

See our selection here:
www.rubyfiction.com

Ruby Fiction brings you stories that inspire emotions.

We'd love to hear how you enjoyed *Arlette's Story*.
Please visit www.rubyfiction.com and give your feedback
or leave a review where you purchased this novel.

Ruby novels are selected by genuine readers like yourself.
We only publish stories our Tasting Panel want to see in
print. Our reviews and awards speak for themselves.

Could you be a Star Selector and join our Tasting Panel?
Would you like to play a role in choosing which novels
we decide to publish? Do you enjoy reading women's
fiction? Then you could be perfect for our Tasting Panel.

Visit here for more details ...
www.choc-lit.com/join-the-choc-lit-tasting-panel

Keep in touch:
Sign up for our monthly newsletter Spread for all the latest
news and offers: www.spread.choc-lit.com. Follow us on
Twitter: @RubyFiction and Facebook: RubyFiction.

Stories that inspire emotions!